PRAISE FOR *FAE*

"A delightfully refreshing collection that offers a totally different take on your usual fairy stories! I should have known that editor Parrish (who also edits the cutting edge horror zine, *Niteblade*) would want to offer something quite unique. I found it difficult to stop reading as one story ended and another began—all fantastic work by gifted writers. Not for the faint of heart, by any means."
— Multiple Bram Stoker® winner, Marge Simon

"Seventeen tales . . . range in feel from horror to upbeat tales about homes where things go right, and are set everywhere from the modern day to mythical fantasy pasts. The best of these stories evoke things from real life—loves and values—and show characters making hard choices that reveal who they are and what they're made of. Anyone with an abiding love of Faerie and the Folk who dwell there will find stories to enjoy in *FAE*."
— Tangent

"Nibble on this deliciously wondrous collection of stories of fae one at a time or binge on its delights on one night, you'll love the faerie feast this collection provides. Love, loss, horror, healing, humor, tragedy-- it's all here, where stories of magical beings and the humans they encounter will enthrall and enlighten the reader about both the mundane and the otherworldly. I devoured it."
— Kate Wolford, editor of *Beyond the Glass Slipper*, editor and publisher of *Enchanted Conversation: A Fairy Tale Magazine.*

Fae

An Anthology of Fairies

Edited by
RHONDA PARRISH

World Weaver Press

FAE

Copyright © 2014 Rhonda Parrish

Published by World Weaver Press
Alpena, Michigan
www.WorldWeaverPress.com

Cover designed by World Weaver Press

First Edition: July 2014

ISBN: 0692207910
ISBN-13: 978-0692207918

Also available as an ebook.

CONTENTS

FAE

INTRODUCTION

Sara Cleto and Brittany Warman

In the dark woods, in the hidden hollows and crevices overlooked by human eyes, in the enchanted spaces between worlds, there are the fae. Magic incarnate, they haunt us in our stories, in our imaginations, perhaps even in our backyards. They are as much a part of the fabric of this universe as we are, and they are tired of being pushed aside and misremembered. This collection seeks to reestablish our conception of the fae as they truly are: powerful and playful, utterly alien yet uncannily familiar.

The choice to name this anthology *Fae* reveals much about its intentions. The word "fae" itself operates in two distinct ways. Firstly, "fae" embraces the supernatural possibilities beyond the stereotypical "fairy," as there are traditionally many different kinds of fairies, several of whom do not conform to the popular portrayal—delicate, gossamer winged, harmless. Secondly, the use of "fae" signals a deliberate rejection of the Victorian appropriation of these supernatural creatures that transformed them into diminutive beings meant to entertain—and not to threaten—children. These tales instead refer back to older, more potent portrayals common in folklore—fairies that are powerful and frightening, fairies that are "Janus-faced, ambiguous" with "lovely face[s], [faces] of promise" and "hideous face[s], [faces] of fear" (Purkiss 4). The word "fae" is a way of reclaiming the darker, more complex heritage of fairylore that spans continents and centuries in a vast web of narrative traditions, wary awe, and endless possibility.

Reflecting that complex heritage, the tales included here embrace the spectrum of what a fairy story can be—bookended with more classical, familiar stories set in recognizable "fairy tale" worlds, the collection also introduces many very different settings—futuristic, urban, domestic, medieval, and others. Yet the same themes repeat—the strength and capriciousness of nature, the conception and acceptance of Otherness, the tension between fae compassion and fae malice, sacrifice, and the inversion of power to name only a few.

Though the fae themselves remain elusive throughout these tales, their motives and realms ultimately untellable, their stories can reveal much about the human interior. Our own alienation from the environment we have largely abandoned in our quest for modernity and our yearning to connect with those around us is mirrored in fae narratives.

Come, gaze into this magic, shattered glass—seventeen stories, seventeen glances—and seek the fae as they once were, and as they still are. And don't be surprised if you catch your own reflection unawares.

Further Reading:

Briggs, Katharine. *An Encyclopedia of Fairies: Hobgoblins, Brownies, Bogies, & Other Supernatural Creatures.* New York: Pantheon, 1978. Print.

Briggs, Katharine. *The Fairies in Tradition and Literature.* 2nd Ed. New York: Routledge, 2002. Print.

Narváez, Peter, ed. *The Good People: New Fairylore Essays.* Lexington: The University Press of Kentucky, 1991. Print.

Purkiss, Diane. *At the Bottom of the Garden: A Dark History of Fairies, Hobgoblins, and Other Troublesome Things.* New York: New York University Press, 2003. Print.

Silver, Carole G. *Strange and Secret Peoples: Fairies and Victorian Consciousness.* Oxford: Oxford University Press, 1998. Print.

ROSIE RED JACKET

Christine Morgan

"Boys are the horridest," someone said. "Aren't they just?"

Georgina, on the stone bench by the garden hedge, started so that she almost dropped her book. She caught it against her lap and looked around.

Here was the yard, grassy lawns and flower-beds and tree-shaded paths sloping up toward Drewbury Hall, where her uncle's family lived. Where she, too, now lived, because she had no place else to go. The brick walls climbed green with ivy, the roof-slates were grey, and curtains stirred in open windows as the maids aired out the rooms.

The only person she saw was Partridge, the driver, out by the carriage-house. He crouched in front of the big brass-grilled snout of Uncle's gleaming auto-motor, polishing the luminaries with a soft rag. It couldn't have been him that she heard, because he was too far away, whistling as he worked.

And the voice had sounded much more like that of a child, a girl her own age.

Which would have been nice, but the only other girl for miles about was the coalman's daughter in the village. Mrs. Curtis, the housekeeper, insisted it simply wouldn't do for Miss Georgina to associate with the coal-scuttle girl. Such things weren't proper, and therefore, weren't done.

She was about to decide she'd imagined it when the someone spoke again.

"Don't you wish that they'd all get the speckles and die?"

The garden hedge rustled, shedding leaves, as the someone pushed through. Georgina saw with amazement that it *was* a girl, a girl her own age. Not the coalman's daughter, either, though her clothes weren't much better. Her paisley-print dress was faded, patched and shabby. Her feet were dirty, bare of both stockings and shoes. Her jacket, though, was fine and fancy, bright red with shiny buttons all in a row.

Georgina gaped. It was unladylike; Mrs. Curtis would have given her a stern look. But she gaped nonetheless. "Where did you come from?" she asked in a gasp.

"From here and there and everywhere," the girl said. "This side, that side, the up-side and down-side, the other side." She tossed her head and laughed. Her hair bounced. A few stray leaves were caught in it.

She had the most incredible hair, Georgina noted with envy. A moppet-mop, her mama might have called it. Curls all over, loose and springy, the effortless kind that did not need to be wrapped and pinned, and slept on so that it was like rocks in the pillow. Quite different from Georgina's own hair, thin and fine, straight as ironed flax.

Such a color it was, too, that hair! As red as her jacket, brilliant scarlet. While Georgina's was the kind of dullish-blonde Mrs. Curtis called 'wash-water.'

"I'm Georgina," she said, remembering her manners. "Georgina Drew. Who are you?"

"Rosie."

"Rosie who?"

"Rosie Red-Jacket." The girl laughed again. Rosy, as well, were her cheeks, and her pert-smiling lips, and the scatter of freckles across the bridge of her nose. Her eyes were as shiny as her jacket-buttons. "Were those your brothers that went riding velocipedalers off down the lane?"

"My cousins." Georgina closed her book and set it aside on the bench. A sort of anxious hope swelled in her heart at the prospect of a playmate.

Mrs. Curtis, she suspected, would not approve of some barefoot moppet-mop stranger in a shabby dress, no matter how splendid her jacket, but, for the moment, Georgina didn't care. It was hard to sit and read day after day, quiet as could be, a well-behaved young lady, when her cousins got to romp, and ride, and have fun with their friends in the village.

"Your cousins," Rosie said, in a musing sort of way, as if thinking this over. "So, the man with the funny moustache is not your papa?"

"My uncle. My papa was a soldier."

"What about your mama?"

"She pined away after Papa died," Georgina said.

Often, this was met with clucks and sympathy. But Rosie shrugged, said an unconcerned, "Oh," and added, "so, they sent you to live with your uncle and auntie?"

"Well, not so much my auntie." It verged on gossip, though it was hardly a secret that Caroline Drew cavalierly left her husband, home and boys to fend for themselves on a regular basis while she pursued a career as a famous opera singer. "My auntie's in New York right now, I think."

"Oh," said Rosie again, still unconcerned. She picked a daisy, examined it, and began plucking off the white petals one by one.

"What about your parents?" asked Georgina.

"*My* mama is a lady-in-waiting to the Faerie Queen, and my papa is a handsome courtier with silver buckles on his boots."

Georgina giggled despite herself. "No, really."

Rosie pursed her red lips, poked her red tongue between them, and made a noise that would have scandalized Mrs. Curtis. "Yes, really!"

"The Faerie Queen?" When the very book on the bench had for its cover a fanciful color-picture of pixies dancing in a ring to the music of a fieldmouse orchestra, and *In the Court of the Faerie Queen and Other Tales* in gilt-stamped lettering.

"The Queen, the Queen, the Queen of Between, the Queen of Underhill and Overmeade, east of the Sun and west of the Moon and north of the Stars and south of the Skies."

"You're a fairy, then?"

"Maybe." Rosie skipped around the slender trunk of a green willow tree, then cocked her head and grinned. "Or maybe I'm the devil's imp, a wicked, evil sprite!"

"Don't," said Georgina, uneasily, but still giggling.

"Oh, fine, all right." She flopped into the grass, elbows propped and chin on her hands, dirty heels kicking up. "What do you *do* all day? You looked bored half to a frazzle, sitting here with your dumb old book."

"It isn't dumb."

"I'll bet you a butterfly that those cousins of yours, *they* aren't sitting with books, bored to frazzles. I'll bet *they're* out having a grand time. Getting into plenty of mischief. Having plenty of fun."

"Well, but they're boys."

"Horrid, hateful boys who *abandon* you. And why?"

"Because I'm a girl."

"Doesn't that make you cross?"

"They're hardly going to have tea parties with me."

"Tea parties." Rosie made the rude noise again, flipped onto her back, rolled her head, and looked at Georgina upside-down. "Phooey and piffle and tra-la-la to tea parties. Why not play with them? Do what they do?"

"Because, I told you, I'm a *girl!* They wouldn't have me tagging along, even if I wanted to! And Mrs. Curtis—"

"Phooey and piffle and tra-la-la to Mrs. Curtis, too, the pinch-faced wretch!"

Alarmed, Georgina cast another quick glance around, sure that she'd find the housekeeper's grim figure looming out of the garden. But she only saw Partridge, leaning on a fence post, chatting to a laundry maid with a basket on her hip.

"What you should do," Rosie went on, "is go find them, your cousins and their friends."

"They won't—"

"Not like you are, no. Put on my jacket. It's magic. It'll disguise you as a boy so that they can't even recognize you." She sprang up, removed the bright red jacket with the shiny buttons, and held it out to Georgina.

"Magic, is it? Then how come it didn't disguise *you* as a boy?"

"Because I didn't say the magic words, silly."

"And even if I did go find them, what if Mrs. Curtis comes looking for me? She told me not to leave the garden."

"I'll sit here with your book and she'll think I'm you."

"You don't look anything like me."

"I'll use magic! Now, put on the jacket, do up the buttons, and say *snips, snails, puppy-dogs' tails.*"

"This is a peculiar game," Georgina said, but she put on the jacket and did up the buttons. It was a perfect fit. "*Snips, snails, puppy-dogs' tails.*"

A dizzy swirl rushed over her and suddenly . . .

"I'm . . . I'm a boy!"

Her dress and stockings had become a shirt, socks, and knee-britches. Her shoes were boys' shoes. Her hair, instead of falling fine and straight past her shoulders, had gone short and messy. The ribbon that had held it back was now a jaunty tweed cap.

"I'm a boy," she said again, hearing how even her voice was different. She stared at Rosie, whose grin was wider than ever. "It really *is* magic!"

"I told you!" Wider than ever, yes, that grin of hers was. And not a little bit scary. The shine in her eyes made them look like lantern-panes. "Now, go find your cousins and their friends. Play with them as long as you like. Then just come back here, say *sugar, spice, everything nice*, and you'll be a girl again."

Georgina laughed loud with delight and turned toward the gate.

"One more thing," Rosie added. "There's a packet in the jacket pocket—packet-jacket-pocket!—with hard candies inside. Lemon drops and cherry, in twists of waxed paper. Have as many as you want."

"I don't care for cherry candies, thank you," Georgina said, remembering her manners again. "They taste like medicine-syrup."

"Then give those ones to your cousins, and you can have the lemons. But don't say thank-yous that way and be all polite and ladylike. You're a boy now!"

And so she was! As a boy, why, she could run down the lane, she could whistle and whoop as loud as she wanted! Nobody tutted. Some even smiled, or called out a cheerful, "Halloo there, laddie!" as she dashed through the village.

She soon spied her cousins' velocipedalers tipped in a heap down on the riverbank under the trolley bridge. The cousins themselves— Robert, Tom, Edgar and Petey—were with a few other boys. Friends of theirs from school, she supposed.

How they shouted! How they laughed! How they rough-housed and wrestled, and splashed in the shallows, and ran races, and held mock sword-fights with sticks!

Then Edgar caught sight of the bright red jacket. He elbowed Robert. He pointed. Ruddy, muddy faces turned. They looked at her. For a moment, Georgina stood scared half to pieces.

"Oy!" cried Robert, raising a hand. "Want to play?"

"Yes, pl—" She coughed. "Yes!"

A spate of introductions followed. She almost slipped on hers, but stopped herself in time and told them that her name was George.

"We have a cousin named George-*eeeeee*-na!" Petey said in a sing-song way. "She's a g*iiiiii*rl. Tom thinks she's pr*iiiiii*tty!"

"Shut it!" Tom gave him a swat. The others laughed.

"*Is* she?" Georgina asked.

"No!" Tom had gone purple. "She's a right bland pudding!"

"Forget her," said Robert. "Come on, George. Let's play!"

"Let's!"

Such an afternoon it was! They hunted tadpoles, skipped stones, sailed twig-boats, climbed trees, and hit conkers. Two of the boys had pop-guns. Edgar had brought his yo-yo, and another had a paper kite. When they tired of that fun, those who didn't have velocipedalers balanced on the handlebars of those who did—terrifying, but exhilarating!—and they rode back into the village with clangy-bells jangling.

Georgina offered out the packet of hard candies. Instead of politely accepting a single one, her companions of course grabbed by the fistful. Waxed-paper wrappers flew like confetti. They stuffed their mouths until their cheeks bulged like chipmunks, the cherry ones turning their tongues a vivid red. It gave them great amusement when they made faces at one another.

In a brick alley, they shot marbles and aggies, pitched penny-coins, and a boy named Jack chalked bad words on the wall. They kicked a canvas ball around the market-square, trying to score it off the big bronze numerals of the steam-clock.

A better time, Georgina hadn't had since the day the wireless came with the news about Papa's regiment. On that day, the life and heart had run right out of Mama like water from a cracked jug.

The steam-clock tolled the hour of five. The smaller boys, Petey among them, began to fuss and complain. They were tired, they said. Tired and hot, half-sweated from top to toes.

"Quit your whining," Robert told them when he'd had more than his fill. "We'll head for home in a while."

"I want a cold drink," Petey said. "And my dinner."

What he *needed* was a bath and a nap. But that, Georgina didn't say. She realized she'd best hurry quick if she was to return to Drewbury Hall before her cousins. She couldn't go with them, couldn't let herself be found out.

"I'd best go," she said. "Chores."

"Chores!" They all groaned.

Jack added, "Bother chores!" and spat into the gutter. Robert gave him an envious, admiring look. Georgina wondered what Uncle would say if he knew the kind of company his sons were keeping.

They said their goodbyes, agreeing it had been jolly grand all around and they'd have to do the same again soon. Maybe they'd go down to the trolley yard to throw rocks at rats, or see if they could get their hands on some snap-bangs and spark-fizzers, or even cherry-bombs.

Tired and hot and half-sweated from top to toes herself—it was vigorous work, boy-playing was!—Georgina could not afford to dawdle. She went at a run, then a trot, then a brisk walk, keeping a ready look to throw over her shoulder if she heard the clangy-bells of the velocipedalers approaching up the lane.

She cut through the woods and came out by the garden hedge, pushing through its scratchy branches. The stone bench, where Rosie had said she would wait, stood there empty but for the book of fairy-tales.

"Rosie?"

There was no answer.

Rosie wouldn't have just gone away, would she have done? Even if she'd gotten bored to a frazzle with what she'd called a dumb old book. Had Mrs. Curtis come along and caught her, the housekeeper not fooled by whatever magic Rosie had used? If Rosie even had waited? Or had Mrs. Curtis come along and saw no one here at all? Just the book on the bench, which she'd scold Georgina for leaving behind?

But if that were the case, surely Mrs. Curtis wouldn't have left the book behind either. No, not her . . . she would have marched it right in to Uncle's study to show him what a forgetful and neglectful silly creature his niece was. An expensive book such as this, there just asking to be dew-soaked and ruined!

"*And* she went wandering off," she imagined the housekeeper saying. "When I *told* her to stay in the garden. This kind of disobedience simply cannot be permitted, Mr. Drew. I know you mean well by the child, but perhaps a girls' school would be a better place for her after all."

"Rosie?" Georgina tried again.

Yet still, there was no answer. Dusk's cool shadows had begun to stretch long across the yard. In Drewbury Hall's downstairs windows, the light of gas lamps glowed. The shapes of servants moved to and fro in the dining room, setting the table.

"*Sugar, spice, everything nice,*" Georgina said.

In a wink, she was a girl again. A tired, hot, half-sweated from top to toe girl, but a girl nonetheless. Her fine straight hair fell long down her shoulders, the cap turned back into a ribbon, the shirt and knee-britches and boy-shoes and socks became her own familiar clothes.

She undid the shiny buttons, took off the red jacket, and then did not quite know what she should do with it. Certainly, she couldn't very well take it to her room, where her cousins might see and recognize it as belonging to their new chum, George.

With Rosie continuing nowhere to be seen, she settled for folding it carefully and placing it upon the bench. Then she picked up the book of fairy-tales and walked up to the house.

Braced as she'd been to be scolded, to land in trouble for leaving the book lying about in the garden and be called upon to answer for her absence, she raised her head and went inside.

"Oh," said Mrs. Curtis upon seeing her, as if she'd entirely forgotten Georgina altogether. "Yes. You. There you are. Dinner at seven sharp."

It was, in a strange way, almost disappointing. She washed and dressed, brushed her hair, and arrived at the dining room promptly upon Cook striking the bell. Tidy, proper, and ladylike, she sat without squirming or fidgeting. A good little girl. Seen but not heard.

Uncle and his guests came in. They'd been out shooting clay pigeons, testing his new wind-up launcher, and it had put them in lively high spirits. None of them paid the first bit of attention to Georgina.

The boys were late to their chairs, clothes hastily changed, having splashed their faces but with dirt behind their ears and their hair needing combed. Petey continued to fuss and complain, whining when reminded to sit up straight. Tom and Edgar only picked at their food, declaring that nothing tasted any good. Robert had sunk into a surly mood, which wasn't mollified even when his father said he could go out shooting with the adults tomorrow.

But nobody went shooting the next day. By morning, all four of her cousins lingered in bed, feeling poorly. Their throats hurt, they said. The sides of their necks were swollen and sore. Their faces were flushed. They were itchy and hot.

Mrs. Curtis consulted her mercury-stick and pronounced them feverish. Partridge was sent to fetch the doctor. It was some while before they returned. Uncle paced the whole time, wondering aloud if he should try to get a wireless to his wife in New York, or if he should wait. She would not want to be dragged from the stage and limelights without good reason.

The doctor came in with his black bag and examined the boys. He had them each in turn open their mouths, stick out his tongue and say, "Aahhh."

Their tongues were still as vividly red as if they'd been eating cherry candies. Georgina hid a giggle, but then she saw the doctor's grim look. He had Mrs. Curtis lift their night-shirts. A rash of tiny red bumps spotted all up and down their backs.

"It's the scarlet fever," the doctor said. "I've seen several other cases of it already today; that's why I couldn't be here directly as you called. Half the children in the village seem to be coming down sick."

"Scarlet fever, dear God," said Uncle, and rushed to dispatch that wireless.

His guests took their leave with rather unseemly haste, despite the doctor's attempts to reassure them that the disease was most dangerous to young children, and that many fine scientists were making excellent progress in the development of serums to reduce the mortality rate. Mrs. Curtis put the servants to frantic work changing linens and cleaning everything the boys might have touched.

Georgina, sent to the garden and told not to get in the way, went down toward the hedge. She saw at once that what she was looking for wasn't there. The jacket, with its row of shiny buttons, was not where she'd left it, neatly folded upon the stone bench.

Something else *was* there, though. Something pale, something crumpled and dew-damp. She picked it up and smoothed it flat.

It was a bag. A small packet of white paper, the kind that hard candies would go in. Lemon drops, and cherry. The very one that had been in the pocket of Rosie's red jacket.

The other girl's words echoed through Georgina's mind.

"Boys are the horridest, aren't they just?" Rosie had said.

Her words, and her grin . . . the grin that had been not a little scary . . .

"Don't you wish that they'd all get the speckles and die?"

~*~

Editor's Note: Christine's cover letter described this tale as being a "steampunk-lite historical piece" which, since I'd asked for steampunk stories in every submissions call and update I did for *Fae*, meant I was intrigued before I even began to read. More importantly though, as I read this story the critical part of my brain turned off and I was carried away with it. The first line is fantastic, defining Rosie super clearly in just a few words, but the last line . . . the last line is what made this story for me.

~*~

The Queen of Lakes

L.S. Johnson

When my brother and I were small enough to share a bedroom without embarrassment, our mother used to read to us at night. She had an old book of stories that her mother had given her, before they left Scotland. All the stories were tales of princes and knights facing great perils. Even when she began with a swineherd, or a lowly apprentice, Tim and I knew at once that the boy was secretly of nobler blood, perhaps even royal blood. The heroes of Mother's stories always fought alone, no matter the odds. They slew each-uisges and great sea monsters, outwitted kelpies and trowes; they stayed deaf to the calls of selkies and banshees. And at the end, they triumphantly claimed their spoils: rooms full of treasure, kingdoms to rule, the most beautiful maidens for their brides.

Afterwards, when Mother's voice had faded with the candlelight, when her lips had brushed our foreheads and her cracked, callused hands had smoothed down our blankets, I would fall asleep and enter a bright world full of heat and color and blood. Sweltering in my armor, the gory head of a creature skewered on my sword, the roar of a thousand voices all cheering *me*. And then to the tower, kicking open the door and climbing the cool stone stairs, until I come at last to the enchanted chamber, where my princess silently awaits her king.

King Rose.

I didn't understand, you see. That only men could quest, and fight, and triumph.

~*~

Every day Mother wakes me to a world grey with exhaustion. I braid my hair in the dark, listening to Father snoring. A bit of bread and some cold tea and I am out the door and into a silvery dawn. I imagine I am rising in time with the sun, both of us jostled out of our beds, trudging towards our circumstances. We sit all day, the sun and I, my back aching and my eyes straining to see the thread against the cloth.

If the sun would not rise, I would not have to go, but I do not know how to make it my conspirator. Who tells the sun what to do?

With each step the sky lightens, trees forming out of the gloom. Amidst their skeletal forms I can make out patches of early snow, tinting pink. My breath makes a raspy sound, like I am old before my time. I am old before my time. There is the forest and the road weaving through and my plodding feet lumpish in my woolen stockings and clogs. If I close my eyes I can see exactly how I look: small and dumpling-plump in my layers, my scarf low over my head to cover my ears, only my chapped face visible.

My nose is running.

When the road begins to curve, the start of a wide, blind arc leading over a rise, I do not dare quicken my pace. But my breath quickens, it starts coming in short loud pants.

At the crest of the rise I can see it, its surface scummed with algae and ice. The lake is wide and deep, even in winter you cannot see the far bank. It seems to run to the very horizon; it seems without end. When I was small people fished here, Father included, and things were better then. In those days I had hoped to finish school, perhaps even go to the city like Tim did, to train as a teacher. Miss Rose.

But there was a girl, of marrying age, and then a boy, and then another girl. All found dead on the banks of the lake. When the first girl was found everyone thought it the work of an animal; but the lake began to smell, and the fish became thin and small, *not even worth cleaning* Mother said.

There were three long days between the boy disappearing and his remains being found. Abigail Fitzwilliam said she saw his body all torn to pieces, though I knew she was just repeating something she overheard, she could never bear to see even a drop of blood. That night Mother and Father stayed up late, whispering, and though I could not make out all the words I remember hearing Mother say *it's almost like that daft story of Gran's, about that man-horse creature. The each-uisge.*

And Father said something sharp and growling, his tone so enraged it made me shudder to hear it, and the next day the story book was gone.

When the second girl disappeared, when Mr. Duggan came to tell us, I remember: Mother crying, and then looking at me hard, as if I had something to do with it. Later Abigail told me the girl had been *loose*, which made me envision a doll with its joints all broken, its limbs flailing wildly. No wonder she had come apart in pieces.

Three deaths in all. For weeks after Father would go out at night with other men, carrying torches and rifles and axes, and Bart Masterson with his blunderbuss. Even when it was all right to walk past the lake again, things were never the same. There were no more fish in the water, no more birds in the trees. Slowly the soil began to grow dry and crumbling, as if some poison were leaching out from the lake itself. From my window I could watch the grey color overtake the rich brown, a few feet each year, the crops rising green on the one side, stunted and withering on the other, until we had only a cartful of surplus to bring to market.

Each summer there was a strange odor, like that of a dead animal.

And still the sun just sat in the sky, and Tim went to university with all our monies for his fees, and I was taken out of school and told I had to sew for Mrs. Duggan. Every day now for months, and it seemed that it might be this way for the rest of my life, either piecework or marriage to Bart Masterson's oldest boy Sam, doing for him and lying beneath his oafish smirk.

Every day, up before dawn. Every day, the needle or Sam Masterson. Until last month, when the each-uisge came back.

~*~

The moment the path starts to dip, the world goes silent. The very wind ceases to blow; not a leaf stirs, not an animal can be seen, not even an insect. There is only the rasp of my breath, the blood thudding in my ears.

It is forty-two steps from the silence to the far end of the curve. Forty-two steps where the only sound in the world is myself.

Myself and the each-uisge, I mean.

"Where did you go?" I ask. For he is beside me, though I did not hear him approach. I never hear him.

"Here and there," he gurgles. His voice is low and wet, as if his mouth were full of jelly. "Across great lakes and little rivers, so many lovely sights. Though not a one as lovely as you, Rose."

He teases my braid, making it sticky and knotted, and I slap his hand away. Thanks to his fondling I've been scolded by Mrs. Duggan more than once now, for looking slovenly. He strokes the bare strip of my throat instead, smearing my skin as he hooks a gluey finger beneath my scarf, trying to tug it away from my neck.

His fingers are so very cold.

The first time he touched me I was so frightened I nearly stopped walking, but I did not stop, I have never stopped.

I do not know what will happen if I stop.

"Shall I tell you all the places I have been, Rose?" His breath smells of moss. "Would you like that? To hear about the world? Would that please you?"

His hands drop to my chest, rubbing my breasts through the thick wool of my coat. Moisture begins to seep into the fabric; still he slides his hands in slow circles. No boy has ever touched me like this. The sensation makes strange muscles flex between my legs, like I'm peeing.

My feet have not stopped moving: twenty-three, twenty-four, twenty-five steps.

"You know it would," I whisper.

He raises his hands and lays them over my eyes. His palms gum my lids shut; his long torso presses against my backside. We are still walking, but we are somewhere else now: we are in a world vibrant with color, warm and rich, filled with the smells of good earth and blossoming flowers. Everywhere I see handsome, well-dressed people, men and women, all laughing and talking and reading. *Reading.* He slithers against my buttocks, up and down, up and down, but I can only see the books and papers, the gazettes and broadsheets, their warm smiles as they share their words with each other.

"Come with me, Rose," he says. "Come with me and see for yourself."

I am panting like a winded horse. He rubs faster now, whining in my ear—

and then he exhales, long and whistling.

"Oh Rose," he sighs. "No books in the Masterson house, my sweet girl, not even a Bible." His icy tongue laps at my earlobe. "And you do know this sewing is making you blind?"

Forty-two. The rush of the world in my ears: whistling winds, cawing birds, the scuttling of rabbits and squirrels while the trees rustle and creak. I wipe and wipe at my eyes, flicking away clots of opaque muck. The wet patches on my breasts and backside are already drying; still I feel moisture on my face. It takes me a moment to realize I am weeping.

~*~

At Mrs. Duggan's we make clothes for a shop in the city. An older woman does the cutting and each girl does a different part, a main seam or a bit of finer work, say hemming or turning a collar. I sew buttonholes and Abigail sews buttons—she's a clumsy girl, thick-fingered, but her father deals in lumber so she only works for her own pin money.

Buttonholes are slow, difficult work. In the summer the light is good but the heat wrinkles the cloth and makes my palms sweaty; in the winter the light is so thin I find myself with my face in the cloth, squinting. My dreams now are of an accident: another girl nudges my chair, or Abigail leans in suddenly, and my hand slips; the last thing I see is the needle aimed for my eye. And then I awaken, sweating with terror, not at the pain but at the *dark*.

"Your Tim not coming for the holidays?"

I blink my eyes rapidly until they can focus on Abigail's plump, rosy face, and shake my head. Not for my birthday, not for the holidays, perhaps not ever again.

All his promises. I cannot even think about it.

"Pity," Abigail says. "But good on him, getting accepted to university. Your mother must be so proud." She smiles at her button with its big, wide shank.

Abigail has a good demeanor, Rose. You could do worse than to emulate her. So Mrs. Duggan tells me; so everyone tells me. *She's always so cheerful.* And the greatest virtue of all: *I've never heard her complain a day in my life.*

"It makes you wonder, though." Abigail laughs. "How did he come up so bright? Look at us, a bunch of lumps to the one. You'd never think we'd produce someone with real learning."

"Speak for yourself," I snap. The other girls pause in their stitching to watch us but I don't care. "I got him accepted. I wrote his bloody essays, I did his proofs. It was all *me*. And as soon as he's settled I'm going to join him and start my own studies." I cannot see the shirt on my lap for my rising tears. "The only damn lump in this room is you," I finish bitterly. "So speak for yourself, Abigail Fitzwilliam."

There is silence, then a muffled tittering. A voice says in a too-loud whisper, "I didn't realize we were working with Lady Muck."

"Well," Abigail says, as if we're having a conversation, "I hear he's courting a magistrate's daughter, and he's going abroad to work for a great lawyer. I'm sure he'll look after you once he's married." She smiles at her needle. "Though of course by then Sam Masterson will be looking after you, so you won't need to burden anyone."

Another rush of giggles and whispering. I feel like I might scream. Sam Masterson. They were my compositions, my proofs. Tim was always slow to understand, he mixed words up and he could never *see* geometry, he could never transpose the equations into shapes. Even now, a year out of school, I know at a glance when a merchant tries to rook Mother; I can do the addition in my head quicker than he can write up the bill, and then I tug her sleeve and she makes him review the prices and I am always right.

I'll send my books to you as I finish them. Tim on his last night home, pale and nervous, as well he should have been. *That way you can keep up while I find out what schools there are for women, and a good boarding house.*

And then he went away.

There were many letters at first, carefully addressed to all of us, never replying to my panicked missives. *Tim please they've taken me out of school. At least if I was working in the city I could make more, enough to pay for my own lessons. Can I not come to you? Tell me what I should do.*

Tim, help me.

Instead we learned about the latest fashions, his new friends. One was a magistrate's son and there was a pretty sister and the father said he had great promise and did we have anything to spare for a better suit, so he would not feel ashamed at their table? Father beaming as he counted out our few saved coins. *My boy, courting a magistrate's daughter! Eating off silver, drinking wine with every meal!*

Tim, help me!

And then, two months ago, the package arrived. There was a long letter, explaining he was going abroad for a term: Sophie's father had arranged for him to clerk for a solicitor. The experience would help him go straight into the best firm once he had his degree. Oh, and Sophie had suggested a present for Rose, a belated birthday gift.

I had recognized the shape at once, that firm, solid rectangle. I had all but snatched it from Father, had ripped the paper wrapping to shreds in my excitement. What could it be? Latin, perhaps, or natural philosophy? Breathlessly I turned it over and read the spine:

The Frugal Housewife

~*~

My boy, courting a magistrate's daughter! My boy, eating off silver! My boy, touring Europe!

My boy my boy my boy

~*~

I eat dinner alone that day, all the girls shunning me, huddling around Abigail instead. I weep all afternoon, quietly, my tears pattering onto the cloth. Two months and it still hurts so much. *The Frugal Housewife*. Abroad for a term, he would not be back until midsummer at the earliest, he could not say just when he might visit.

Did he throw my letters away? Did he burn them?

I hold my hand up to my face, move it a distance away, then close again, watching my fingers slide in and out of focus. I have no more time.

The Frugal Housewife.

Perhaps I'll have to make my own economies now.

~*~

"Rose," the each-uisge says, his clammy arm draped around my shoulders. "Sweet Rose, I'm so very lonely without you."

I am counting my steps, trying to think. Eight, nine. There is another way to and from the Duggans', but it is long and winding, down to the village road and around. It would mean rising earlier, the whole journey in darkness, it would mean coming back to cold suppers and still the chores to do. All that precious sleep, lost.

And for once, I want to see him.

"Why did you come back?" I ask.

"Why, to see you, of course." He nuzzles at my ear, smearing his face against my hair. "How has my poor Rose fared all these years, with her family of numbskulls and Sam Masterson ogling her tits? Do any of them even see her, really see her?"

"'All these years'?" I whisper.

"Such long, long years. But I knew from the moment I saw you: you were a girl worth waiting for." He pulls at my coat, peering down at my chest, then laughs as I shove his hand away. "My darling Rose. What does a smart girl like you say to those idiots? All they know is to count the days until some farmboy sticks them full of cock and makes their bellies swell. What does a girl like you say to girls like them?"

Nothing, nothing. Their turned backs almost a relief today, to be spared their teasing: they've started calling me Missus Masterson, they tell me how lucky I am, he's sown his oats so he'll be ready to settle down.

I'm never sure which phrase makes me more ill, *Missus Masterson* or *settle down*. I am Rose. And I haven't even begun.

"You were never meant for this," he says, his fingers trailing slime down my cheek. "I knew it the moment I saw you. You were meant to be a great woman. You were meant to be a queen—*my* queen."

"A king," I blurt out. *King Rose.* I have not thought of those story-dreams in so long. Now they rush through me, quick and hot, quicker and hotter than his hands that are everywhere and nowhere, doing strange things to the layers of my clothes. And on the heels of the rush comes a last burst of miserable sorrow, as I see Tim in my mind's eye, poncing about his college in the suit I bought him, the qualifications I gave him.

"Why not a queen? There are queens who have ruled, Rose. Did no one teach you this? I have whole books about such queens." His hand encircles my wrist. "Come with me and see, Rose. Come with me and I will sit at your feet while you read, and then I will take the book from your hands and undo your dress, button by button."

"The better for you to kill me," I cry, wrenching my hand free.

He steps before me, stopping us.

I have never stopped before. I have never truly *seen* him before. A thick cloudy liquid covers him from head to toe; his skin beneath is a greenish-grey. His face bony and long-jawed, framed by a tangle of dark hair and water-weeds. Still he looks like a man, he wears the clothes of a man. But his eyes are a flat, solid black and the teeth flashing in his lipless mouth are small and sharp and crowded together.

"Never you, Rose. Never you." His voice, his teeth. His *eyes*. "I saw your face that day. I *saw* you. The way you looked at that beastly boy's body, while they wrung their hands and averted their eyes. A queen amongst the rabble."

And I see it: the boy's body on the mossy ground, grey and bloated, the flesh bitten and ravaged. I had felt no fear or shame, just an overwhelming need to touch him, to understand what had happened, what mouth made such injuries, what that boy-flesh had tasted like—

I shove the each-uisge aside and run.

"Rose," he calls after me. "I can free you, don't you *see*?"

It was I who told Abigail about the boy's body, describing the great tears and gouges. Breathless with excitement, fired with my own courage. How had I forgotten? She had burst into tears and told her father who told mine. I had been whipped for it, and I had hated my Father and Abigail both.

"Don't be afraid, Rose." His plaintive voice was becoming small and distant. "Let me free you. Let me free—"

And then he is cut off, and I am in the world once more.

I stop again, trying to calm my racing heart. My head spins with memories: Father whipping me, the long hot strokes on my thighs. His tears, his shouting: to stay home, to do what I'm told to do, to never misbehave, to know my place. How had I forgotten? Too sore to sit at school the next day, all their eyes on me as I stood in the corner. Abigail wide-eyed with her own solemn righteousness, as if she hadn't betrayed me.

With a last, deep breath I straighten my clothes, smooth my hair.

Rose!

The voice makes me jump. Never have I heard him here, in the world. My mind is playing tricks on me, I'm so very tired . . .

I look back towards the lake.

There is a small, squarish shape sitting on the path, just where it levels out. A dark package, tied with plain string.

I whirl around completely, trying to remain calm, trying to scour the trees without appearing to. What might he be plotting, what kind of ambush? The last sane part of my mind says *leave it be, think on the price you will pay.*

Never you, Rose. Never you.

I dash forward, seizing the parcel as I spin about and race back up the rise, nearly tripping in my haste, cursing my heavy clogs, my thick skirts. Even after I have crossed back I keep running, clasping that solid weight to myself. Not until our gate comes into view do I slow, steadying my breath once more, and look at it. That weight, that shape. Only this time it's wrapped in a still-damp oilcloth, the twine soggy with lake water.

It smells of him.

I hide the parcel in the barn, then go in for supper.

~*~

I use the sounds of my parents' snoring to slip outside and run shivering to the barn. Once back in my room I light my candle and tuck it in a corner, shading it behind my bed. Only then do I undo the wrapping.

Not one but two volumes: *Great Queens of Europe*, and *First Latin Primer*.

I thought myself done with tears, but I start crying again. The books are older, but the words are crisp on the page. There are even pictures in *Great Queens of Europe*, pictures of women riding horses, leading armies, standing on balconies before a sea of kneeling subjects.

I knew it the moment I saw you.

Why did no one tell me that a queen could rule?

I spread the books open on my bed, angling them towards the candlelight. The house quiet now, the window shuttered against the cold winds. For a moment I am small again, Tim sprawling beside me, our heads pressed together as we read from the same book. I never knew how happy I was. And if I had known I would lose it all, what might I have done?

I start turning the pages, but I cannot focus on the words. The black marks swim and double; when I move the page close to my face they straighten into letters but my eyes start to throb, the pain spreading swiftly through my temples.

And you do know this sewing is making you blind?

My stomach heaves. I can feel the scream rising and I jam my fist in my mouth to smother it, howling against my cold knuckles as I have not done since I was small.

~*~

At dinnertime Abigail wiggles close to me. She's so bright-eyed she's almost shining, even here in our dingy workroom. "I'm sorry about yesterday," she says.

I shrug, keeping my eyes on my little bowl. What does it matter now? Besides, I have other things to think on: he was not there this morning. Something is changing. I must not let him get the better of me.

"So who is he?" Abigail whispers loudly in my ear.

"Who is who?" For a moment I cannot think who she means. The only *he* I see on a regular basis is Father. Even Sam Masterson is only a face I greet on Sundays.

"Your fellow. The one you see on the way home."

I stare at her, the food nearly falling out of my gaping mouth. I have never thought of him in any context other than my walk; that he can be seen by the likes of Abigail Fitzwilliam—I have a sudden urge to slap her.

"Ah-ha! There is one!" She claps her hands. "So who is it? I couldn't see his face. Not from the village . . . a woodcutter's son?"

"Abigail," I say, in a low growl that seems to come from another Rose.

"Rose, you must tell me, or I shall simply die!" She almost pushes me off the chair, she's leaning in so.

"Abigail, don't."

"I promise I won't tell anyone, not even Sam . . . if you'll do something for me." She giggles. "I'll keep mum if you introduce me. Today. After all, he might have a brother, all big and strapping, eh?"

I feel it then: something inside me, something new and hard and cold, as cold as his touch. A shape just starting to form. I cannot see it but I can feel it, sense it like the blind woman I am becoming.

"Why not?" And for the first time in ages I smile.

~*~

Abigail twitches with impatience. Excitement is making her cheeks flush; she looks almost pretty. That afternoon I had carefully kicked my glove far away, under the hutch that holds the spools of thread, the cushions bristling with small fine needles. Now I stand in mock bewilderment, shaking my head.

"Oh leave your stupid glove," Abigail says. "You shouldn't keep a boy waiting."

I bite my lip, trying to appear on the verge of tears. "Go on ahead," I say. "Tell him I'm coming. You can walk slowly and I'll catch you up."

She hesitates. "I don't know if I should . . ."

"Please, Abigail. I don't want to keep him waiting, but Mother will be furious if I lose my glove."

And that's all it takes: she's off, nearly falling down the path in her ardor. Every boy in the village has already been a victim of her fawning interest, and her mother is equally scheming. A new prospect, who might not have heard of her? It's a wonder she lingered as long as she did.

Slowly I gather up my glove and begin walking home, my steps measured, trying to make as little noise as possible. Like it was fated. Every other choice boxed off, until there was only this path, this inevitable moment.

I walk. The sun has nearly set, the last thin band of light like a smudge of fire on the horizon. Overhead the stars are coming out, the rising moon a white sickle. There are the cries of night birds, the higher-pitched whistling of the first bats.

I reach the curve, and the world falls silent.

Does Abigail still hear noises? Or did it fall silent for her as well, only she was so taken with her foolish hope that she just kept barreling towards him?

As I pass the lake I can just glimpse them between the trees, their two dark shapes silhouetted. I slow but I do not stop. Not like Abigail; she is rock-still by the lake's edge, looking up at him. Her coat hangs open, her bare hands resting on his arms.

He is not that tall when he walks with me. Tall and yet somehow on all fours—? My vision doubles, making his dark shape seem to blur and swell.

She puts her leg back, trying to move away, but she cannot. I see now that she is stuck to him, her torso fused against his broadening chest. He rears back, growing in size; she is pulled along with him as if strapped to him. For a moment they are a towering mass, his dark animal's rearing form and her small body glued to him.

He leaps up and into the water, arcing high in the air and diving in headfirst. Though there is a tremendous spray at their impact, rising up nearly to the tops of the trees, it makes no sound. No water seems to splatter outward, no waves form; the spray merely rises up and vanishes.

The last thing I see are Abigail's small clogs and his dark, elongated feet, the toes rounded and fused together, looking for all the world like hooves.

I start striding now, my head down as if against a strong wind though there is no wind.

"That's my girl," he whispers in my ear.

I step forward into the long somber cry of an owl, into safety, my heart hammering in my chest.

~*~

They find Abigail's body at first light. The knock comes just as I am reaching for my coat, and before Mother can get the door open all the way Bart Masterson is inside, bellowing for Father. In the confusion no one notices when I follow them to the lake. There are several men, filling the silence with their voices, angry and shouting, and between them all the little heap of Abigail's body. She is twisted and bitten, so much so she resembles some animal's carcass, not the girl I knew.

I feel a deep, shuddering wave of pity and regret; my eyes sting with tears; and then it's gone. Before anyone sees me I hurry back to the house. I've learned all that I need to know.

~*~

I am kept home that day, and the next. I listen to my parents arguing, phrases such as *but you said you ended it* and *what about the money she makes?* and I understand. I understand that they are weighing my salary against my life, against the risk of my returning to Mrs. Duggan's.

On the third day they summon me. In winter, to carry us through,

Father mends harnesses; he does this now as I sit down, his fingers teasing out worn reins and straps, cutting and fitting the newer leather.

"Sam Masterson has been to your father, Rose," Mother says. "He has asked permission to call on you."

She says this brightly, but there is no joy in her eyes. I simply look at the table.

"He's really taken a fancy to you," Father says. "He says you're the prettiest girl in the village. He's got a good piece of land already in his name, and his father has a finger in every pie in this county, he's one of the wealthiest men around. Look at how they've ridden out this blight: it's barely touched them. You'd be a real help to them too, now that Bart's getting on."

"You'd be taken care of," Mother continues. "You'd be safe from all this. Besides, look at some of the girls in the village, still at home in their twenties. Ask any of them if they'd trade with you, I know they'd say yes. Ask Abigail Fitzwilliam," she adds, her voice tinged with sorrow.

"I thought—" I speak carefully, perhaps for the last time. "I thought perhaps I could go to school again. To become a teacher."

"A teacher?" Father drops the leather. "What the hell gave you that idea?"

"I know you enjoyed school," Mother puts in hurriedly. "But Rose. That's a special thing, becoming a teacher. Those girls come from money, they come from better families. We don't have a penny to spare, what with Tim doing so well." Her smile grows tight. "Or would you have us ruin his chances?"

I bow my head; inside I feel a last door shutting. Only my path now.

"Now Sam's coming here tomorrow, before supper. He's asked to take you for a walk, and then we'll all eat together." She rises. "I expect you to be nice to him, miss."

Father has already turned back to the harness, but as soon as I shut the door upstairs I hear them again. *Headstrong* and *your fault for letting her go to school so long* and *at least we have Tim.*

They have Tim. And I have myself.

~*~

I wait until they're asleep, then I creep on silent, bare feet out into the icy night. Before me the road to the lake beckons. Soon, soon. Instead I go into the shed, feeling my way until I reach the high hooks where Father keeps the most dangerous tools: the axe, the filleting knife, the skinning knife with the gut hook. I test each one, trying to see them in my mind's eye, their weight and their heft, how easily they can be concealed.

At last I take my chosen weapon and hurry back to bed.

For the first time in years I dream myself in armor.

~*~

At close quarters Sam Masterson is as oafish as he looks from afar, all grinning and hunched shoulders. Thin hair combed at a harsh part, his face and neck washed but I can see the grime below his collar, under the cuffs of his best shirt. He has brought me a bouquet of pine branches studded with cones.

"You can make a wreath out of them," he offers. "My sisters like to do that."

I thank him and curtsey. I can tell this pleases my parents, I can sense them both relaxing.

He talks about the next year's outlook with Father; from the way he rattles on I know he's parroting Bart's ideas. I meekly set the table with Mother, who beams at me. I've been making a good show of it all day, reading to her from Tim's book and asking her timid questions about running a house, watching as she starts the roast even though I've seen it done a hundred times before.

All this, and I even managed to slip away with my coat for a while.

It needs mending, I said to her puzzled expression, *I don't want him to think I don't take care of my things.*

Now she goes up to Father and lays a hand on his arm. He clears his throat.

"Perhaps you'd like to take a walk before supper?" he asks.

Sam nods. Only then does he give me a look, like he's sizing me up.

~*~

Before we are even past the gate his hands are everywhere, his mouth on mine, thick tongue pushing in. I can't get my breath. Not slow circles like *his* hands, but grasping and pulling like my breasts are teats; then lower, yanking my pelvis against his. In the lining of my coat, the skinning knife jostles against my hip; quickly I move his hands back up.

He pulls back, his eyes gleaming. "You are a goer, aren't you?" His hands kneading my breasts like dough. "Abigail said you had a fellow, you were going in the woods with him."

I look away, biting my lip. "Poor Abigail," I say.

"It was terrible," he says, as if discussing the weather. "I wouldn't mind, you know, if you had gone with someone for a bit. I like it when a girl knows what to do." He looks back at the house, then pushes me against a tree, grinding his pelvis against mine. "Just a quick one," he says, trying to work my legs apart. "We'll be married soon enough, it's not wrong."

I manage to wiggle free, but just; he's stronger than I thought. As he grabs me again, his hand trying to get under my coat, I say "not here."

That makes him pause. "Oh?"

"There's a place in the woods, by the lake." I frown. "Only Father says I mustn't go there, what with Abigail and all."

"Did you go with one of my mates?" he asks, and there's an edge to his voice now. "I'll bust their heads, I will. Everyone knew I fancied you."

"No, no one you know," I say quickly, trying to think and appear coy at the same time. "Just the one boy, from the far side of the county. And we never did . . . that. Only other things. I didn't even want to," I add, looking down at my clogs. "Only he wouldn't listen, he made me, I couldn't stop him."

And when I look up at Sam's moonface, my gaze slowly traveling up, over his breeches twisted with his lust—when I look up at his face, I know I have him.

"Show me," he says.

~*~

Through the woods and into the silence. I lead Sam by the hand, smiling at him over my shoulder. Every now and then he stops and grabs me, pushing his tongue in my mouth again, groping at my backside; I shudder not in pleasure or disgust but at the stopping. We need to get far enough that Mother cannot call us back.

We step off the road and onto the damp ground, near the edge of the lake. I tense, waiting for *him* to appear. But there is only the mud sucking at my clogs and Sam Masterson pushing me backwards until I stumble against a log and fall to my knees. At once he's on top of me, pressing me under him. My head scrapes against the log as he kisses me. He weighs so very much, he's pushing all the air from my lungs.

"No," I gasp. "No, wait."

My skirts up now and he's yanking at my drawers with one hand, squeezing my breast with the other. I have no words for what he's doing with his tongue.

I try to get away, try to push him off, but my clogs just dig deeper into the soft dirt.

"I knew you'd feel like this," he says. "Touch it nice. You know how."

"No," I say to the sky as he grabs my hand and moves it. Not like this.

Anything but this.

Somewhere in a bright-colored world Queen Rose steps out on her balcony into the sunlight and her people cheer her name *Rose Rose Rose*.

"Rose," Sam huffs against me, shoving his pants down. "Rose I can't wait, stop trying to close your legs damn it."

All I can see is his face leering at me, like I'm someone else, like I'm nothing. He wedges my knees apart, his fingers digging into my flesh.

A greengrey hand, its skin shiny with moisture, wraps across Sam's face and wrenches his head to one side. There is a crack, so loud it makes me scream.

"Rose, Rose, Rose," he chortles. "Lovely Rose, I'm starting to think it's you who wants me."

He wraps his squelching arms around Sam, drawing Sam's limp body up against his own. Only then do I feel how my thighs are trembling; it's hard to push myself up onto the log, to turn aside enough to work my drawers back up. And then I keep my body angled away from him, feeling inside my coat until I find the slit in the lining.

When I seize the knife I start to cry.

The each-uisge is swelling and rising, his body expanding with each breath like a bellows. His elongated head blots out the stars. The Sam stuck to his chest is no longer Sam but some still, glassy thing. I can still taste his spittle; I see that his pants are hanging off his hips, his penis small and flaccid, and I cry harder now.

"Rose," he says thickly, nuzzling Sam's head. "My poor Rose, I'll just be a moment. Why don't you lie down again, and when I come back I'll make everything much better."

"You said you would free me," I say, my voice quivering.

"And I will, pretty," he coos, taking a step backwards. "I just have to take care of your swain first, and then I'll show you a different way to read."

"You promised me," I say again. "You said you would make me a queen."

As he starts to reply I lunge forward, seizing Sam's shirt with my free hand like it was the handle of a shield. My shield. We topple backwards and I swing the cruel curved knife out wide and around, driving it into the softness behind Sam's body, burying it to the hilt in his cold flesh. I can feel him scream but we're already beneath the water, sliding into a strange thick darkness, falling down, down, down.

_*_

He trudges along the road, somber in his crisp black suit. As he crosses into my lands he pauses, looking around. I would know him anywhere, even now with his pretentious lace cuffs, the white cravat that would be soiled by the simplest chores.

My brother, the gentleman.

Tim comes to the edge of the lake and looks around again, his eyes gleaming with tears. He bows his head and begins to pray.

For a moment I think to let him pass but his praying irks me, his clothes irk me. As if he were clad in my very tears. Would he even be here, now, would he even have bothered to write, had I become the good Missus Masterson? Like hell he would. Like hell.

I rise up out of my waters. My waters, my lands. My *realm*. As are the books in my library, as are the roads I fashion between my waters, roads that take me through the world. I am practicing languages I did not know existed, I have seen cities unlike anything I ever imagined.

That creatures great and small shun my roads—it is a small price to pay. That I still have a higher power I must bow to, that I must appease from time to time with the sweet, plump essence of three victims—

well, it is a far cry from sewing buttonholes, or having to give service to Sam Masterson.

Tim finishes his prayer and raises his eyes to me and screams. I am gratified.

"Rose," he gasps. "Rose, what have you done?"

"Darling, lovely Tim," I say, smiling. "*Flectere si nequeo superos acheronta movebo*." I take a step forward, and another. I can smell his fear and it is marvelous. "It's Virgil, Tim. 'If I cannot deflect the will of Heaven, I shall move Hell.' Whatever do they teach you in that university of yours?"

"Your eyes," he whispers.

"Whole and well and *mine*. Already they have seen more than you will ever know." I stretch my arms out to him. "Never to be taken from me. Never, Tim. *Vivat Regina*."

I take him with me into my lake.

~*~

Editor's Note: I wanted "lush settings, beautiful prose and complex characters" for *Fae* and this story delivers on every point. L.S.'s writing in this story is so gorgeous that at times I felt like I was reading a poem rather than prose, and every single one of the characters has the sort of depth you often only find in novels. I love that at the end of the story I'm left with conflicting feelings about Rose. I'm glad that she triumphs, yet a little dismayed about the way she achieved her victory. But perhaps when dealing with fairies unsettled is the perfect way to feel . . .

~*~

Ten Ways to Self-Sabotage, Only Some of Which Relate to Fairies

Sara Puls

1. Flea Market Snap Traps

Elly raises snap traps in the basement of her tiny bungalow. She bought the first two at a flea market on a whim. The proper name for these carnivorous plants is Venus Fly Trap or, to get even more technical, *Dionaea muscipula*, but the previous owner called them snap traps and the name stuck. They live in peaty soil and require less humidity and attention than one might think.

Originally, Elly's plan was to cultivate the plants for sale. She would sell them to grocery stores and flower shops, to sad little soccer moms wanting to feel "exotic" and to patrons leaving the local natural history museum. She would be productive.

But then, by the time she got them home—to her house that hadn't been cleaned since she was fired from the post office, and that would probably have the electricity shut off in a matter of days—she lost all motivation. Her limbs were too heavy, like dead tree stumps, and all she could think of was sleep.

After searching for open counter space and finding none, Elly stuck the two potted plants in the basement.

At some point—days or maybe weeks later—she returned to the basement in search of the box of vintage hats she kept for when she needed an escape, for when she needed to be someone other than herself.

The cracked-concrete room smelled of fermenting laundry; visible particles of dust clung to the air. Elly pressed a switch and the light flickered on. Once her eyes adjusted, she discovered that the two snap traps looked just as good as the day she brought them home.

Elly was so surprised she hadn't killed them that she allowed herself a smile. After that, tending to the plants became something of a hobby for her—something to take her mind off other things. Like, for example, her grabby new boss at the Saves-A-Lot, where she took a job as a part-time cashier.

As the snap traps fed on flies and slugs, Elly lied and told herself she needed nothing more.

2. Lina

It wasn't until Lina came along that the fairies appeared. And it wasn't until Elly had tried several other extermination methods— vinegar, hot water, lemon juice mixed with salt, even sticky tape—that she started feeding the fairies to her plants. She knew there had to be a better way to get rid of them but she couldn't stand the sight of them, their delicate touch, or the sugary scent they left hanging in the air.

Elly and Lina met at the Half Price Books on South Lamar. Lina had been standing in the History section, holding open a paperback. The book, something about Constantinople, was upside down.

"You're not reading," Elly noted.

Lina raised her head and looked over at Elly. Her eyes were dark and deep, like two black holes. Immediately, Elly wanted to be sucked into them, to be pulled to some other place that wasn't Earth.

Lina smiled and shrugged. "Yeah. I don't read much—not for leisure anyway. But a friend told me I need to date someone sensitive this time around."

Elly raised her eyebrows.

"I tend to date real jerks, you know? So I thought I'd hang around here."

Elly did know. She only ever dated jerks. Not intentionally, but inescapably. Lately, though, she hadn't dated anyone at all. "Well if you're looking for sensitive, you'd better your chances at the library. It's closed now. But tomorrow maybe."

"I see."

"Yeah. Bookstores and libraries don't attract quite the same crowd. Your friend should have told you that."

Lina smirked. "Maybe it's good he didn't."

Elly felt her heart flutter, as if it had grown two tiny wings. She pointed at the book. "Want me to show you how to read that?"

Lina pushed her long, thick hair from her face and smiled. Her hair was always in her face, Elly would learn, always refusing to be tamed.

Then they were back at Elly's place, hands all over each other, stumbling towards the couch.

A week later, Lina moved in. This is what she brought with her: Four antique couch legs that were shaped like gargoyles but no couch; a standing ashtray that looked a bit like a space ship; one flower-patterned suitcase that couldn't have weighed more than ten pounds; two unicorn-shaped bookends; three cartons of cigarettes; and zero books.

Elly helped Lina find space for the ashtray and bookends. They put the gargoyle couch legs in a closet filled with ten years' worth of Elly's junk. Elly cleared out two drawers in her olive-green armoire.

"Here," she said, pointing. "Use these."

Lina thanked her and put her few pieces of clothing away. Then they made love on the couch. On the floor. In the bed.

When they finished, Elly rolled away from Lina's warm body and let the doubt creep in. It whispered that she didn't deserve this. That this too would end.

3. The First Fairy

One day later, the first fairy showed up.

Elly found it hovering above a glass of water she'd left on the kitchen table. It couldn't have been any bigger than a grasshopper. But it looked far more delicate. Far prettier, too.

Still, Elly's skin itched as she watched the tiny creature flit about without a care in the world. She hated the sight of it. Intensely. It was just—too perfect.

She mixed together a little dish of lemon juice and salt, and then set it on the counter. The fairy went to the dish and tasted the juice. In an instant, the thing pulled back in horror. Then, sputtering and coughing, it fled through an open window.

"Serves you right," Elly said, leaning her head out the window. "And don't come back."

The next morning, Elly awoke to a soft giggling sound filling the bedroom. Sitting up, she saw that yesterday's fairy had returned, bringing three more pale green creatures with it. She groaned and threw her pillow in their direction. She missed.

She groaned again, this time waking Lina.

"What is it?" Lina asked, clearing her throat of sleep.

"We have fairies!" Elly complained.

"Oh, is that all?" Lina closed her eyes again. "They won't hurt anything. Don't get so worked up."

Elly whimpered as she rolled over and wrapped her arm around Lina's waist. "Well what do they want? Can't they bother someone else?"

Lina kissed Elly's head and let an amused laugh escape her lips. Elly rolled her eyes.

Later, and every day that week, Elly poured vinegar into a spray bottle and set to chasing the fairies away. Day after day they returned, multiplying in number as they did.

Elly decided she was cursed.

4. The Idea

After all her other extermination attempts failed, Elly went to where the fly swatter hung from a purple thumbtack on the wall. Grabbing it, she swatted a lily-white tree fairy dead with just one try. Its blood, a too-bright green, sprayed across the counter and left a trail of splatter on Elly's shirt. Despite the blood's distinct vanilla scent, Elly wrinkled her nose in disgust. The flattened creature reminded her of the roaches she crushed beneath her shoes. Because of course a fairy problem wasn't enough. She had to have a roach problem, too.

Carefully, she peeled the fairy off the counter with two fingers. With her free hand, she wiped up the gooey mess with paper towels. A moment later, the idea came to her. She would feed the fairies to the snap traps. She had fourteen plants by now—more than enough to take care of the problem.

Elly bounded down the steps into the basement. "Eat up, Mo," she said as she dropped the fairy into her favorite plant's stomach. She should have felt bad, unsettled, disturbed. Fairies were more like people than bugs after all. But all she felt was . . . relieved.

A second later, Mo snapped shut and set to work devouring the tiny creature. Elly laughed. "Better than slugs, right?"

Upstairs the front door creaked open. It was Lina, home from the store. Elly wanted to tell her what happened. She didn't want yet another relationship filled with secrets and lies. But she had a suspicion that Lina would not approve. And so she said nothing.

5. A List

As with people, there are many types of fairies:

A. Within the water fairy family, sirens and selkies and mermaids are the most common. At least, these are the ones Elly most often finds spit out through the faucet into her tub. They're smaller than she would have guessed. And they have green wings that remind her of kelp.

B. The air fairies consist mostly of ill-tempered Tinker Bell types. They're always whispering about what needs fixing around the house. And they act out something fierce when Elly and Lina crawl beneath the sheets. Elly learns quickly enough that it's straight to the basement with them.

C. Fire fairies. The untrained eye sometimes mistakes fire fairies for lizards. They get along with no one, save the air fairies.

D. The earth fairies that frequent Elly's bungalow most often are tree nymphs and trolls. She finds the tree nymphs tending the potted plants in the kitchen. The trolls sneak into the refrigerator to eat up all the rotten vegetables.

E. House fairies. These fairies supposedly live only to help with household chores. Elly finds such a claim more than a little suspicious. She trusts these fairies less than most. Why would they want to help someone like her? What did she ever do to deserve it? It has to be a trick.

F. There are also goblin-like fairies that speak mostly Spanish and some Portuguese. These are called Duende. Elly has considered taking up the study of Spanish in order to understand their whispers. But she hasn't found the energy.

G. The Moon fairies appear only during a full moon.

H. The soul catcher fairies. Whenever they're around, Elly feels like something is eating at her from the inside out.

I. As a child, Elly had heard that fruit fairies help crops grow. This, she has learned, is true. But there is a limit to how much fruit one can eat.

J. Music fairies. These are Lina's favorite. But Elly can't stand it when they sing.

K. Finally there are the ice fairies. They think it's funny to freeze the water in the pipes. Despite their name, Elly has learned that they do not limit their appearance to the winter months.

Lina likes lists. She tells Elly that making lists might help her take more control of her life. Two months into their relationship, Elly has made several lists. But she still hasn't revealed how she rids the house of the fluttering, singing, sugar-smelling fey.

6. A Normal Day

Elly wakes up and starts shooing fairies while Lina has a cigarette or three.

"Why can't I get rid of them?" Elly always complains.

"Maybe you should ask them what they want," Lina keeps suggesting.

But Elly doesn't hear her, not really. She goes on swatting and shooing and yearning for the moment of Lina's departure, so she can herd the fairies to their deaths. She only ever kills them—or rather sends them to be killed—in private. It's her little secret, and by now she likes it that way.

When Elly takes a rest, or when Lina begs her to stop, they have coffee at the kitchen table. Then Lina jumps in the shower. She's a geologist and works as a researcher for the University. Pretty much all she does there is read and write—that's why she prefers TV at night. Elly still works second shift at the Saves-A-Lot three times a week. She could do something else. She has a degree in economics, after all. But she assumes she'd just be fired so doesn't bother to try.

Before Lina leaves for the day, she always says one of two things. It's either "I love you, babe," or, when she's feeling playful, "I lava ya." Elly never responds. Even to the playful confession of love. Sometimes, as Elly hears Lina start her car, she thinks about this and wonders why Lina sticks around. But she doesn't think about it for long.

She doesn't because she can't. Because she has fairies to kill.

Elly has developed a nice little routine. First she captures several fairies under household miscellany—like hats and mugs and old honey jars. Then she gathers a batch in her hands, as she would a bouquet of flowers, and takes them down to her carnivorous plants.

Sometimes she watches the snap traps as they eat. It doesn't make her warm inside like Lina's eyes once did. But it still passes the time. Regrettably, because of the plants' slow digestive processes, she can only feed each snap trap about one fairy per week.

When Elly is feeling all right—when she doesn't feel threatened or hopeless or ambivalent or insecure—she lets the fairies be and feeds the snap traps grasshoppers and slugs. But this doesn't happen very often. Mostly she just complains about the tiny-winged creatures, about how they're ruining her life.

7. The Mermaid Fairy

When the mermaid fairy appeared, things between Lina and Elly took a turn for the worse. Like regular mermaids, the fairy had both tail and gills. The gills were very small, hidden beneath her hair and behind her ears. Lina didn't like this fairy. Not one bit. She said it reminded her of another woman she'd dated, and that things between them hadn't ended well.

Elly didn't know what made her do it—spite, perhaps—but she let the mermaid fairy live. Later, she almost enjoyed seeing Lina uncomfortable in her own skin. Other fairies kept showing up—most of all little trolls with stupid, goofy grins and dirty toenails—and Elly sent them straight to the snap traps. But she wouldn't get rid of the mermaid, no matter how much Lina squirmed.

And the longer the mermaid fairy stayed, the less Elly and Lina spoke. When the fairy was in the room with them, Elly said nothing at all. Lina just chain-smoked cigarettes, angrily stamping them out in her spaceship ashtray.

"It's not the mermaid that's the problem," Elly said whenever Lina complained about her emotional distance.

"I didn't say it was," Lina would respond.

"It's all the rest of them."

"No, Elly," Lina said gently, "That isn't the problem. *They're* not the problem."

"Yes they are," Elly snapped. "They're a curse."

"I know what you do with them," Lina finally said one day. Her voice held no emotion but her caramel-brown skin seemed to grey as she spoke. "I followed you into the basement yesterday. I guess you thought I was still asleep."

Inside, Elly's organs twisted and turned. Outwardly, she only shrugged. "So?"

Lina's eyes went flat, cold. They were no longer those deep and warm pools of black. This was when Elly knew her girlfriend would leave.

The next morning, Lina packed up all her things. Elly sat on the couch as unmoving as that first squashed-dead fairy. She refused to apologize or cry, to give Lina what she wanted. She had no reason for refusing, other than that she was somehow more at ease when her life was a mess than when it was good.

8. Why Lina Left

It is possible that Lina left because of the fairies. It is possible Lina left because Elly refused to say, "I love you." And it is possible Lina left because she sensed that Elly wanted to sabotage herself. All of these things are possible.

But Elly blames Lina's departure on the mermaid fairy entirely. Feeling sorry for herself, she makes a game of throwing objects at it.

These are some of the things she throws: a "Free O.J." magnet she found at the thrift store for twenty-five cents; a small glass jar filled with volcanic ash that her grandmother sent from Mount St. Helens; a pillow shaped like a kitten; a juice glass with pink giraffes painted on it; a plastic fish she found beneath a heap of clothes.

Eventually, the mermaid fairy grows tired of bruises and broken wings. Just like Lina, she leaves through the front door and doesn't return. Elly considers calling Lina but goes to the freezer and takes out a half-full bottle of vodka instead. She drinks the whole thing.

9. A Fairy Feast

Something Elly learned after Lina left: if you let your clothes pile up on the floor until you can't tell the dirty from the clean, if you leave noodles in the sink until they once again become dry and hard, if you let dust form in thick layers on the bookshelves until you can't go three minutes without sneezing, your fairy problem will increase.

In Elly's case, she soon had somewhere between fifteen and thirty fairies milling around the house—they never sat still long enough for her to get a good count. The fire fairies picked fights with the trolls and dryads, and left burning mounds of debris in their wake. For a while, Elly spent more time putting out fires than anything else.

What Elly did about the fairy problem was this:

She got out the vacuum cleaner—which was also caked in a layer of dust and grit—and connected the hose-like attachment. Then she went from room to room, sucking the fairies into the machine one by one. She saw the sadness on their faces. But if they screamed or whimpered, she didn't hear it. When all the fairies had been caught, she hauled the vacuum cleaner into the basement. Then, one by one, she plucked the nearly unconscious creatures from the bag.

"Here," she said to her plants. "A feast." There was no emotion in her voice. She worried she'd never feel, really feel, ever again.

A few weeks later, feeling only slightly better, Elly returned to the basement. After thorough inspection, she determined that all the fairies had been devoured. Then she pulled the snap traps by the stems from their earthy homes. She put them in a big black trash bag and tossed them to the curb. Next she took the ceramic pots outside and heaved them into the air. She left the debris lying in the street.

10. What the Fairies Meant

With all signs of Lina, the fairies, and the snap traps gone from the house, Elly collapsed onto the couch, closed her eyes, and wished for sleep. Sometimes, when you feel only darkness and sadness inside, it's easier not to think.

11. Another List

After wallowing in self-pity and filth for a whole week, Elly gets up and turns on the shower. She steps inside to find a fairy sitting on the bathtub ledge. This time, after so much solitude, it's the most welcome sight on earth. The fairy smiles and everything clicks: many of the fairies, like Lina, had been there to help. And all of them had something to say—to teach.

Elly showers quickly. After, she makes a list. She doesn't give the list a name or even write it down. Because she knows she won't forget. But if she *had* written it down, it would have been called *Ways to Stop* and it would have said this:

A. That she should have cultivated and sold the snap traps like she originally planned.

B. That she should have told Lina about the first fairy she killed and about how killing it made her feel strangely warm inside. That she should have asked Lina's advice and maybe sought professional help.

C. That it's okay to need help.

D. That she should've let herself cry as Lina packed her things to leave.

E. That she should've asked Lina to stay, to give her a second chance.

F. That she should live as though second chances don't exist.

G. That she should have tried harder to understand the fairies, to listen. That, at the same time, she shouldn't have neglected everything else.

H. That she should learn to apologize.

I. That she should have said I love you. That she should have said it a hundred-thousand times. That she should remember how to love herself.

J. That she should've kept her snap traps.

K. That she should have been brave enough to admit the fairies were never the problem at all.

~*~

Editor's Note: Dude! (Wait, can I say dude in an editor's note? Well, I'm going to because, dude!) This story. I love this story. If you want to read it at just the surface level it's a great story about a woman dealing with a new relationship and a fairy invasion (and oh, the many types of fairies!). But if you want to dig deeper, there is plenty more to this piece than meets the eye. It's a fantastic literary story that I've read again and again as I've worked on this anthology, and each time I find something new in it to adore.

~*~

ANTLERS

Amanda Block

(Death)

The garden is a crypt. Vines grasp at the walls, pulling themselves upwards, right towards the throats of the tallest trees, which bow forward to meet one another, branches clasping branches.

Inside, there is no breeze, and the air is thick with the musk of pollen and damp, dark earth. The birds that remain stand still in the shrubs, their songs low and mournful.

At the centre, lies the Lady. Under the netting of shadows, her skin seems to shine and shift, like moonlight upon water. The only colour is at her breast, opening up like a red flower thrust forward through time, blossoming around the arrow that has pierced her heart.

~*~

(Birth)

She was pulled from the dying Queen, strong and squalling, and they quickly shushed and rocked and coddled her. Her mother, quiet at last, gazed only once upon her girl, before her eyes rolled back in her head.

There was no time to be respectful, to even check, before they cut into the Queen's belly and dug around for the other child. It was a small, sinewy creature slipping like entrails through their fingers; the wrong colour, too quiet. They stood back while the midwife snipped at the cord and then, at the sound of the rasping, rattling breaths, surged forward once more. The healthy girl child was snatched from the wet nurse and replaced by her brother. Her screams filled the chamber, but no one heard her.

~*~

(Growth)

The twins were both pale, raven-haired, he and she versions of the same doll, though everyone could tell them apart. The girl was her mother's daughter, tumbling outside at dawn and only returning at dusk, covered in grass stains and chattering about the lark's nest above the gatehouse or the frogspawn in the moat. The boy was weaker, more wary, preferring to play his own games with his own rules. Sometimes he watched his sister through the arrowslits in the castle walls. He knew of the moments that had passed between the beginning of her life and his, when she had tried to steal his birthright by pushing herself first from their mother's womb. It angered him, as it angered him to see the servants slip her cake, or their father gift her with the private garden within the castle grounds, which had once belonged to their mother.

As the old King faded, his daughter bloomed, and his son wavered somewhere in between. The Prince hated that the people loved her, the rosy almost-queen, and by the time his father died, and the crown sat heavy upon his brow, there was nothing in the kingdom he loathed more than his own sister.

~*~

(Death)

Dawn: the Lady is in her garden, knotting together two ends of a daisy chain, when the King comes to tell her she must go on the hunt. He loves to ride far from the castle with his men, set them upon a trail, and give chase with horses and hawks and hounds.

She sighs, arranges the flowers in her hair. "Must I go?" she asks. "I only slow you down."

It hurts her heart to see the birds and beasts of the forest fall to the arrows of her brother and his men. He knows this, of course; it is why he insists she come.

"We leave within the hour," he says.

Before he departs the garden, he snatches the crown of daisies from her head and crushes it in his fist.

_*_

Noon: the hunting party is deep in the forest. A barrel of mead has been opened, and a boy with a lute is singing old ballads, although the men are shouting their own bawdier versions over him.

The King's sister sits on a tree stump alone. Two young boar lie at her toes, one slumped over the other, their coarse hides already teeming with flies. Above her head, rabbits, hares, grouse and partridges have been fastened to a rope by their feet, so their long bodies hang down head first. To the Lady, they look like they are frozen in the act of falling, their black eyes bulging at ground they will never hit.

As the men launch into a new song, she rises and slowly, deliberately, begins to walk away. Nobody notices or cares enough to call after her, so she continues on, her hands brushing against knobbly tree trunks, or sweeping aside the branches and sticky cobwebs that tickle at her forehead. She walks and walks, until the spaces between the trees are narrow and dark. She has never been this deep into the forest before, but she is not afraid, for the air is fresh and sweet here, and the songs of men have been replaced by those of birds.

Ahead, the animal path she has been following runs into a tangle of trailing leaves that hang, like a curtain, across her way. Curious, and unwilling to return to the hunt, the Lady reaches forward and draws them aside.

At first, all she sees is gold. She blinks into it for a moment, before she realises it is sunlight, and she has stumbled upon a clearing, hidden away at the heart of the forest. Untamed, knee-length grass is embroidered with pink-tipped wild roses and clusters of bluebells, while the warm air seems to spark as light is caught by busy insect wings and floating clumps of thistledown. The Lady laughs with delight and runs forward, eager to feel the sun on her face.

Too late, she sees she is not alone: a creature is moving out of the shadows on the other side of the glade, far bigger than a wolf—bigger even than a bear. The Lady backs against a tree, only too aware of how helpless she is without man or weapon, too frightened to move or make a sound. The creature steps into the sunlight and her heart is thudding so painfully, her breathing has grown so shallow, it is almost in the middle of the clearing before she sees: it is a stag.

It is the most magnificent beast the Lady has ever beheld, and also the strangest. Its coat has a greenish hue, and is threaded through with lichen and moss, while its antlers are as twisted and gnarled as branches. It looks old, far older than she can even imagine, yet somehow fresh and strong as well. Without her realising, the Lady's grip on the tree at her back has loosened, and her feet have begun to take her towards the stag. Once she meets its dark green gaze, she is unable to look away. In his eyes, she can see the whole of the forest; as it was, as it is, as it one day will be.

She draws close, and the stag inclines its great head to her in greeting. The Lady reaches out a hand and, very gently, runs it across its brow.

At her touch, the creature cries out and sinks to its knees so heavily that the ground shudders. The Lady gasps, frightened she has hurt it, but then she sees the arrow in its side, and when she turns back to the edge of the clearing, her brother is there, his bow aloft.

"No!" She stands between the King and the wounded stag. "Leave him!"

But the King is already pushing her aside and advancing upon on the animal, which is puffing and pawing at the ground where it lies.

"Please!" begs the Lady, now restrained by two of the King's men. "Have mercy! He is no ordinary beast!"

The King does not listen. He stands above the creature, draws his longsword and slices down, again and again. It takes a dozen strokes, to hack off the stag's head.

At once there is a swell of noise in the glade: the King's men cheer, the Lady screams, and birds take frightened flight from all around. Then everything is suddenly quiet, as the King, the men and the Lady see that the blood dribbling from the stag's severed head is not red, but bright green, like liquid emerald.

"Oh, Brother," whispers the King's sister, "what have you done?"

~*~

Dusk: the court is feasting in the dining hall, the stag's head propped up in pride of place at the centre of the long table. The King is gorging himself on venison, and relating a story in which he gave chase to the stag for several hours, finally killing it with a single blow. He does not notice that the meat has a bitter taste, or that many of his guests are dropping it under the table, for the dogs.

The King's sister does not eat. She ignores the chatter of the courtiers and sees only the stag's head, its dark green eyes watching them all.

~*~

The next day, messengers arrive from the North, East, South and West corners of the kingdom. Each man bears the same tidings: the crops have failed. In the fields, in the earth, in the orchards; overnight, everything has withered and died.

The King's advisors speak of the weather, the season, the plague that

59

must have swept through the land. There is no cause for worry, they say, and keep saying it, even when they hear that nothing new is growing.

The King laughs. "We shall all feast on flesh," he declares, and doubles his effort in the hunt.

The King's sister dreams of the stag. She is in the clearing again, and her brother has not come, so she is running her hands through the creature's coat, and burying her face in its neck, which smells of leaves and trees and the forest as it was. Or else, she is running with the stag, dodging through the densely-packed trees, and she cannot see her body, but she does not think she is human anymore: she is too fast, too strong.

One night, many months after the death of the stag, the Lady dreams she is looking into his dark green eyes and he begins to weep golden tears that fall to the ground like drops of sunlight. Only, once they hit the forest floor, the grass is scorched. She looks up, tells him to stop, but all of him is weeping now, his whole body is melting away into a golden stream that gushes to the ground, burning away the soil, the Lady, everything.

Awake, the King's sister slips out of bed and creeps through the sleeping castle. In the dining hall, she heaves the stag's head from where it has been mounted on the wall and drags it through the corridors, over the courtyard, and out into the sanctuary of her own little garden. Everything within its walls is as barren as the rest of the kingdom, but the Lady digs through the dry soil until she makes a hole so large that even the stag's antlers can be buried below the earth.

When the King discovers the theft of his trophy, he rages through the castle threatening and punishing all who cross his path. He is so angry, so cruel, that his sister takes him to the dead garden, shows him where she has laid the head to rest. Knowing the worms will have begun their work, and there is little use in digging it up, the King turns his wrath upon his sister.

"If you love the beast so, you may stay with it always," he tells her.

After he is finished with his fists and his feet, he locks the great iron gate to the little garden, trapping the Lady inside.

~*~

(Growth)

The kingdom is a graveyard. Naked trees are breaking apart, the bark peeling off their trunks like dead skin; empty fields are cracking into dust; rivers are clogged and poisoned with the bodies of the starving. More and more people are reaching out to the King, wailing that they have had to eat their dogs and horses and worse, but he can do nothing. "Eat flesh," he tells them, over and over, "eat flesh until the next crop."

The Lady too is close to death. The King holds the only key to the garden gate and has forbidden anyone from scaling the high walls. She has a summer house for shelter, a pond for water, but no food, and so she sits in the skeleton of her garden, and waits for the end.

Instead, something begins: from the freshly-dug mound of earth in which the stag's head is buried, two shoots sprout, side by side. They grow, faster than any normal plant, twisting together into a tree that, in just a few days, is taller than the Lady. The sight of it strengthens her, forces her to her feet, and as she stands, holding onto a branch to check it is truly there, she finds an apple in her hand, red and rosy and ripe enough to eat.

The garden begins to wake. Grass, shrubs and trees rise from their earthy bed, stretching up and up towards the sun. Buds yawn into leaves and flowers. Branches and stems dress themselves in fruits, vegetables, nuts and berries. The Lady falls upon this feast, and she too blooms again.

Some of the plants are exotic and strange, with shapes and colours she has never seen before, and there are fruits she must learn to peel and crack and chop as best she can, in order to scoop out their pulp or seeds with her fingers. Each day holds a discovery: a faraway flavour to be sampled, an impossible new pattern upon petals to be believed, and new growth, everywhere.

Soon, she is no longer alone. Bees and butterflies flit among the flowers; birds squabble over branch space, or tug fat, pink worms from the soil; whiskered, four-legged visitors come in the night, creeping out from under bushes or through gaps in the gate, to snatch at food or one another under cover of darkness. The Lady welcomes them, watches them, and sometimes she forgets to be lonely.

~*~

(Death)

Nobody in the castle knows precisely what is happening within the garden and they are too afraid to dwell on the whereabouts of the King's sister. But vines and the tops of trees are poking above the walls, and people made bold by hunger begin clambering onto one another's shoulders, or prodding at the branches with brooms, trying to reach the plums or pears or sweet chestnuts they can see above. Sometimes, they even dare one another to peep through the garden gate, but it is so overgrown on the other side the view beyond is blocked.

The King has avoided the garden since he left his sister there, unwilling to brood over her fate. Yet he cannot ignore the attention it is receiving at court, the whispers of what is happening within its walls and so, without telling a soul, he unlocks the gate.

Ripping aside the trailing vines that have grown over the entrance, the King steps inside and cries out in alarm: the garden is a living beast, blinding him with colour, choking him with its sweet and cloying perfume, tugging and scratching at his clothes and skin.

"Brother, you do not look well."

His sister stands at the centre of it all, her hands and face smeared with soil, her dress torn and stained, her hair a tangle down her back.

He has never seen her more beautiful, more alive.

Rising from a curtsey, she plucks an apple from the tree above her head and holds it out to him. The King stares at it, at her, his stomach aching. Then he raises his bow, pulls back the string, and fires. The Lady gives a little gasp of surprise as the arrow hits her chest. Her knees buckle, the apple falls from her hand, and by the time her body meets the springy grass, she is dead.

~*~

(Rebirth)

The crypt, then; growing around the dead lady, enclosing her, embracing her. The King too is being cocooned in the garden, along with his twin, she who pushed herself first from their mother's womb. He sees how the very earth is moving to mourn her, and is filled with a fury unlike any he has ever known. He begins to fight this garden-beast, kicking, punching, tearing it apart. He throws his whole weight against it, hissing and spitting and screaming. His head pulses with pain, his eyes sting with sweat, his hands and arms are bleeding, and so it takes him a little while to notice: the garden is fighting back.

It starts with a hum from below, as many roots begin to tremble, and it grows louder as it moves upwards, through stems and trunks. The soil begins to lurch like a storm-tossed sea and the King is thrown off-balance. He tries to grab at a nearby vine to steady himself, but is slapped away. Then there is an almighty crack, as the first tree splits clean in two, and with a bellow, the stag erupts out of the earth.

The King gapes as the animal reborn before him rises up onto its hind legs; bigger, greener, more ferocious than before. He reaches for his bow, but the beast is already lowering its head, already charging, and the King is thrown backwards, slammed against the garden wall, his flesh punctured by the ends of the sharp antlers.

Finally, when the King has stopped struggling, the stag grunts, shakes his great head, and lets the lifeless body at the end of his bloody antlers drop to the ground. He then pays the man no further heed, turning instead to the Lady lying in the middle of the garden, an arrow through her heart.

He is not a stag when he kneels beside her, and maybe he never was. His hair is still threaded with lichen and moss, but now he wears a robe of leaves and cobwebs and evening mist, and he pulls the Lady to him with strong, green arms.

Easing the arrow from her chest, the Green Man throws it aside, and places a hand over the wound. The blood that dribbles between his long fingers turns dark green like liquid emerald, before ceasing to flow altogether. He looks at the Lady, smoothes back the dark hair that has fallen over her face, and he kisses her.

The Lady stirs. She opens her eyes, smiles.

"I knew it was you," she says.

Now she kisses him; hungry, greedy kisses, and she lies once more upon the ground, drawing him down into the grass. The hair that fans around her head turns to spiraled leaves, like a weeping willow, and he pulls up not a dress of velvet and silk, but petals and pollen and morning dew. Her body is shifting under him, with him, and she is older, and younger, and everything in between. She can see the whole of the forest; as it was, as it is, as it one day will be.

Afterwards, they leave the garden. They walk, hand in hand, past the body of the King, through the castle, and out into the land. Those that see them quickly forget: they are distracted by the shoots that are beginning to sprout from the couple's footprints.

‿*‿

Editor's Note: This story felt like an old fashioned fairy tale to me, sort of a grown-up twist to the sorts of fairy tales I loved as a child. For me, reading it was rather like grabbing my favourite patchwork quilt and snuggling under it, only to find a square of fabric that hadn't been there before. And then another. And another. Warm and familiar but new all at the same time.

~*~

ONLY MAKE-BELIEVE

Lauren Liebowitz

Some long-dormant sense between taste and sound woke within me, and I froze with my hand on the library shelf. So much for wondering whether I could still sense someone else's magic, all these years later.

I caught a glimpse of her passing me—brown hair, brown eyes, a few freckles around her tanned nose. In almost all ways, she was ordinary, but the magic hung around her like perfume, glimmering ever so slightly. It was nothing like my glamour, but I knew it was fae, as surely as I knew anything. By the time I backpedaled to catch up to her, she had disappeared.

Frantic, I followed the trail of her magic through the library, past rows of books to the front doors. She waited under the awning while sheets of water drummed off the roof and churned the dirt into mud, filthy rivulets creeping over the cracked sidewalk toward her feet. I pegged her as something of a nerd—she wasn't wearing makeup, and she'd apparently chosen to spend her after-school time at the library.

I gasped a breath. "Hi," I said.

She was taller than me, though I could have towered over her, if I'd wanted to—I could have been a bodybuilder, or a dashing young man with pretty lips and hair swept over my eyes, or anything, really, if I felt so inclined. But that wasn't me. And while the short, skinny, messy-haired self I showed to the world wasn't either, it had some sort of authenticity. It felt right, maybe because I'd been wearing it for years.

"Hi," she said.

"It's really coming down, isn't it?"

Usually I was better at emulating normal people, but a lot was at stake here. Yes, she was cute, but that wasn't it. I'd never had anyone to talk to about me, about magic, about anything—not since my parents left me.

She shot me a thoroughly unimpressed look. I wondered why she couldn't see my glamour, that there was something different about me, the way I could sense it all over her.

I tried again. "Look, I promise I'm not hitting on you. I just really need to talk to you about something."

"What's that?" Her delicate chin lifted in challenge.

"Magic." Speaking the word out loud to someone made me dizzy.

Her eyes narrowed, crinkling the bridge of her nose. I could like freckles, I thought. "You're full of it," she said, but she leaned closer and I knew I had her.

I held out my hand.

She stared at it, then at me. I wondered if I'd crossed a line, but then she placed her hand in mine.

If I blew it, she'd probably avoid me forever and I would go mad knowing I'd been so close and lost my chance. I pursed my lips, exhaled, then pulled her after me into the rain. I could barely bring myself to look at her in case it hadn't worked.

But it had.

The rain fell around her, but her hair, her clothes, were perfectly dry. She spun in gleeful circles. From the look on her face, she'd clearly never seen magic before. Maybe she'd been left here even younger than I had.

"This is crazy," she said. "There's no way."

"You believe me?"

"I've waited my whole life for magic." Her voice quavered. "How did you know?"

"You've got magic of your own. I knew it when I saw you. That's why I had to tell you."

From the curb, a car honked. She bobbed in an impatient,

frustrated dance. "Aw, crap. I have to go."

"Tomorrow?" I asked. "This weekend?"

"Friday. After school. I'm Nadia, by the way—"

"Robin." I waved at her, dropping the glamour on her as I did, and she shrieked as she realized the water had soaked her clothes. It was a good-natured short of shriek, like children jumping through puddles, and she actually stuck her tongue out at me before dashing through the rain toward her car.

~*~

"The first rule of magic," I told her, "is that you have to believe in what you're doing. If you don't believe it, how can you expect other people to?"

I'd met her at the nearby high school, where I sometimes pretended I was a student. We traipsed down residential streets with mosaic sidewalks. My little display of magic had won her over completely, and she seemed to think nothing of walking with me, a stranger, toward the park where I lived.

"I've never heard that before."

"Well, maybe it only applies to glamour." I honestly couldn't remember how my parents had explained it, whether this rule was general or just ours.

"But the rain—"

"I convinced you that you were dry. It's the same principle. It's all about trying to trick you into thinking something is real." I spread my hands, walking backwards to face her. "I'm sure this makes me sound shady, but I promise I've never hurt anybody. I just use it to get by."

"How?"

"I'll show you," I said. "In the park."

I knew she'd have questions for me, but I meant to give her time for those later. So instead I asked her about herself.

She'd just moved to Austin. She didn't have many friends; neither did I, and I'd lived here almost as long as I could remember. She was an only child, adopted, of course. She loved books—Narnia and L'Engle and Cooper and the other classics. She liked the idea of ordinary kids going into a magic world because it made her think it could happen to her. She'd had no idea she was magical herself, and I could tell she was still skeptical about that.

My parents picked a good place to abandon me—I'd heard some cities took swingsets and water fountains and maybe a picnic table and called it a park, but this one went on for over a mile of trees and undergrowth, with my home buried deep inside.

I used an illusion to cover my camp and keep passersby away. When I stuck my hand through it, Nadia gasped. "I've seen that in movies, but it's kind of weird to happen in real life."

"I guess I take it for granted."

I didn't, really. Abject loneliness constantly reminded me how alien I was. But she drank up every word I said, as though I were an expert gifting her with secrets she'd always longed for, and that was kind of nice.

I'd never bothered to make my home appealing to anyone else. As a kid, I'd lived in a proper house cut into a hill. Now I just had a little hut made of branches and stones.

"It looks like a fairy village," she said, sitting on a fallen tree. "Are you a fairy?"

"Not exactly." I clenched my hands at my sides as my stomach turned flips. "Do you—want to see what I really look like? What I really am?"

She nodded, wide-eyed, and sat very still. I took a deep breath. It felt a lot like stripping naked in front of somebody, and I was suddenly shy and awkward, because nobody had seen me without glamour in almost ten years, and she was cute, and she'd probably write me off as a weird freak or an animal or something once she'd seen me. Or maybe not. Now or never, I thought, and I dropped the glamour, like plunging into water.

"You're a *faun*!" she exclaimed, clasping her hands together.

"Something like that." I wondered if she'd ever had a crush on Mr. Tumnus. I could probably rock a scarf, I thought.

I made myself uncross my arms from my chest. Soft fur covered my legs, down to my feet-that-weren't-feet. Between those and the nubs of my horns, it was either faun or satyr. Maybe. She didn't have to know I wasn't entirely sure.

"So you can see why I need the glamour." I fought the urge to cover myself with it again. Nadia's fascination made me feel like a picture in a book, or an exhibit at a museum, rather than a person.

She shook her head. "Why not just frolic through the forest and be, I don't know, a wild spirit or something?"

I gave her a disbelieving look.

She seemed undeterred, making a face of open distaste. "Yeah, but . . . a nerd? When you could be anything?"

Frankly, I was alone in a world where I didn't belong, with no one to show me the ropes, and I fit better with outsiders. But I flashed what I hoped was a winning smile. "I like nerds."

She smiled back, and suddenly the years alone seemed worth it.

~*~

I seized the opportunity to parade my talents—such as they were—for her. When I learned she liked horses, I set a tiny unicorn galloping across the leaf-strewn ground, glitter streaking from its heels as I struggled not to let on how tired the illusion left me.

"It's not really much," I said. "My parents used theirs to tell stories. They entertained at court sometimes—my mother was the best of the best. She'd show the story while my dad told it, and the whole thing came to life like you were there. I can't do it. I've tried."

I *had* tried, so many times, but it was hard to deconstruct it when I only barely understood what little I could do.

"What happened to them?" She stroked the unicorn's mane.

"I don't know," I said. "I think a war broke out. They sent me here to be safe until they came for me, and, well, it's been a long time."

Nadia pulled her knees to her chest. "I used to wait for my birth parents to come get me, too. It was a closed adoption. I thought maybe I was a princess, when I was a little kid, or—what do you think I am? I'm not a faun like you."

I might have guessed a dryad, but the magic I sensed on her felt more powerful than that. "Someone from the court itself," I said. "Maybe you really are a princess."

She laughed. "A fairy princess? Me?"

"Well, princess or not, magic is your birthright as much as it's mine. Are you ready to learn?"

Nadia clasped her hands in delighted surprise, but then her face fell. "I don't know."

"Do you believe in me?"

"Well, yes." She poked my not-foot with her sneaker, emphasizing my otherness, even if she didn't mean to. I swallowed.

"Then believe in yourself, because I know you can do this."

Her trust felt nice, and for once I didn't have to feign confidence. I could be her rock, I thought, and her tutor.

~*~

Her magic came slowly at first. More than once, she tried to give up, but I pushed her. I almost quoted Yoda, and in truth that's kind of how I felt—I got to be the expert, even though all I knew was what my parents had taught a five-year-old. I was so used to glamour that I slipped easily into assuming more wisdom than I had. Eventually, early spring warmed the forest, and Nadia frolicked through the trees wearing shimmering wings she'd made herself.

I'd never been happier, until the day she invited me to dinner. I did a double-take. "Wait, what?"

She dug her toes into sun-warm grass. "With my parents. They want to meet you."

"Why?"

"Because I've told them about you." My eyes must have bugged out because she laughed, clapping her hands over her mouth. "No, I haven't told them you're a *faun*, don't worry! But they wanted to know what I've been up to, so I told them."

"What exactly did you tell them?"

"That I've made a new friend." She looked at me slyly. "That he likes books. I told them you were writing a novel and I've been helping you."

"I don't write."

"They don't have to know that! It'll give you something to talk about. Tell them about the Faerie Court and they'll think you're brilliant for making it up."

~*~

Against my better judgment, I agreed. I spent a long time deliberating over how to present myself, as nervous as if I were meeting a girlfriend's parents. Though reason pointed out that we weren't dating, I worried that my being male would bring all sorts of baggage to the literal table.

I'd never seen Nadia in a dress before—it looked good on her, so good that I started feeling optimistic. But my first mistake was following her upstairs to her bedroom so she could turn her music off, a move that did not endear me to her parents.

The rest of the evening wasn't much better. I'd expected to talk about books and my make-believe story that was neither make-believe nor a story. Instead, her parents grilled me about school and my family, and I stumbled through a series of lies. My mother was an artist, I said, and my father was a storyteller. When Nadia's father asked if they had day jobs, Nadia told him to stop. She seemed as tense and uncomfortable as I was. After dinner, I thanked them politely, and though Nadia's eyes asked me to stay, I left.

It was well and good to be a magical forest creature with weird legs hanging out and practicing glamour in the park, but that didn't mean I belonged with normal people like her parents. I wished I could be what she thought I was, some sort of wise forest spirit like I'd read about in books and stories or seen in movies. But I was only me.

~*~

After the debacle of family dinner, I stayed home for a week. I thought maybe Nadia would forget about me or decide she was better off without me, but instead she tracked me down one evening while I was patching up the side of my house.

"Robin?" She waited outside my barricade. "Are you avoiding me?"

"No," I lied.

"I'm sorry my parents were jerks to you," she said. "They liked you, though."

I tried to think of a response to that, and something nasty caught on my tongue—*yeah, they seemed to get off on interrogating me, at least*—but it wasn't her fault, so I bit it back. "It doesn't matter."

"What's that supposed to mean?"

I shrugged. "I probably won't see them again, anyway."

She finally stepped inside, but her eyes avoided mine. "I meant it about my parents," she said. "You have to filter what they say to get what they mean. They wouldn't have asked you so many questions if they didn't care."

I scoffed. "Why would they possibly care?"

"Because you seemed intelligent and like you had potential. They hate it when people with potential have big ideas that won't go anywhere."

Not for the first time, I wondered what my own parents would think of my little camp. At least they'd been civilized, with a house, friends and neighbors, and a proper role in the world. They'd been respected. Loved.

"I've got a surprise for you," Nadia said.

"Yeah?" I couldn't bring myself to sound enthusiastic.

Nadia frowned in concentration, sticking her tongue out, a sure tell that she was making magic. It took me a moment to realize that what she was building around us was supposed to be the fairy court. Not as I remembered it, but as Nadia imagined it. Glitter, mother-of-pearl, and gleaming marble, with dozens of lords and ladies flitting about in all shapes and colors.

I'd dreamed of it many times, of clinging to my parents' hands and trying not to wake up. I wondered whether the court even existed anymore or if the whole thing had been obliterated and that was why they hadn't come for me. Maybe they were all dead, even the queen and her consort—even my parents.

Nadia's face was radiant, a little slick with exertion but proud. "Surprise."

Farther down the hall, a banquet covered an enormous table, and I could swear I smelled it, like I thought Thanksgiving dinner would smell. Fairy food was sweet and floral, or dark and earthy—nothing like this.

"It's not perfect," Nadia admitted. "Not just the court but the glamour, too. But what do you think? I was up half the night trying to fix it for you. It took me all week to figure it out."

All week. She'd done in one week what I had spent years trying to do. "That's great," I said.

She frowned. "What's wrong?"

"I get that you feel bad for humiliating me in front of your parents," I said. "So thanks, I guess, for trying to cheer me up."

"Obviously it's not working."

"I'm sure they'd be glad to know that their daughter is playing magical make-believe with a fairy boy in the forest. There's a bright future in that. Top salaries, snazzy suits, fancy cars. You'll be an executive in no time."

Nadia stared at me like I'd thrown up on her lap. In a way, maybe I had. "What?"

"Just don't tell anyone about the unicorn rainbow glitter. It might get in the way of climbing the corporate ladder."

"My father is a *professor*," Nadia said tightly. "He doesn't want me to work at a corporation, but he wants me to do *something* with my life instead of throwing it away."

Which, I assumed, was what he thought I was going to do. I wondered if that was how she felt, too. "Wonderful. Maybe you can be a movie special effects artist, then. Make your mark on the world that way. Keep your fairy bits secret unless you want to wind up in the tabloids."

"What's wrong with you today? Are you that mad about my parents, or are you jealous, or what?" Her eyes widened. "Is that it? I can do something you can't do, so you're going to act like a five-year-old and throw a temper tantrum? Maybe if you got over yourself, you'd be able to do more magic than just pretend."

"I'm not the one making excuses for my judgmental parents!"

"At least I *have*-" she said, but she cut herself off before she finished it, covering her mouth with her hands.

I was shaking, literally shaking, my face burning. "Get out of here," I said. "Maybe you can conjure yourself up some real friends, while you're at it."

She looked like she was a moment away from yelling or crying, with neither of us sure which it would be. Instead, she fled, crunching through the undergrowth like any other unwieldy human who didn't belong in my forest.

~*~

I alternated between wallowing in self-loathing and anger at Nadia, replaying our conversation again and again in my head because I couldn't for the life of me figure out if either of us had been in the right.

At first, I told myself I didn't need someone who would say such hurtful things. Never mind that I'd been less than kind myself. I picked up my old hobbies—I snuck into movies, pretended to be a student at the high school, tried on a hundred different faces to see what kind of reaction I'd get for each. Suddenly all the stories I'd ever read about breakups made sense. And we'd never even dated.

I wasn't really kidding myself, and I knew it. I went to the movies I thought she'd like and hung around the lockers at her high school because I thought I might see her, though the one time I caught a glimpse of freckles, I hid in the boys' bathroom.

"Great job, idiot," I told the reflection of a face I didn't recognize, though it moved in time with mine.

Every night I went home and sulked in my hut, alone. I even stole ice cream from a gas station because I'd heard it might help, but all it did was make me hate myself a little more. Normally I foraged for nuts or berries or leftover French fries. My parents wouldn't have approved of stealing. Nadia wouldn't have approved of stealing. *I* didn't approve of stealing. Yet here I was.

After a while, I started getting weird looks sometimes when I went out. It didn't take long to realize that even my pathetically simple glamour was beginning to wane, or at least waver often enough for people to notice something odd about me. And how surprised could I be? I had the skills and talent of a not especially patient five-year-old, and I was never going to surpass what I'd learned as a kid, let alone do something as wonderful as my mother, or even Nadia, was capable of.

I was stunted, magically speaking, and I was losing even that. Sooner or later, somebody would find me and I'd wind up in a lab or sideshow without enough magic to free myself.

I decided to resign myself to my fate with dignity, but first, I needed to see Nadia one last time and apologize.

~*~

At midnight, I set out for Nadia's house, hoping anyone who caught a glimpse of the real me in the flickering streetlamps would think I was some sort of theater performance artist, or just another resident kook.

Pebbles marked the edge of her parents' flower beds, and I scooped up a handful of them and tossed them at her window. Her window slid open, and though I couldn't see her, I could hear her voice. "Who's there?"

"Robin," I stage whispered.

A light clicked on in her bedroom, and I could make out her form, if not her face. "Oh my god, are you okay?"

"Yes," I said. "But I need to talk to you."

"Hold on. I'll be right there."

I crossed my arms over my chest again and tried to figure out how to say everything I wanted to tell her. Then Nadia stepped through the front door and shut it gently, and I forgot what I was planning to say. She was wrapped in a bathrobe and wearing bunny slippers, which I thought was pretty adorable.

She stopped on the steps. "What are you *doing* like that? Here?"

"I've come to say goodbye."

That seemed to stun her. "What?"

"Goodbye. You know? What people say when they won't see each other again."

"Why?"

"Because I'm an idiot."

"If you're trying to say you're sorry, I accept your apology. I was a jerk to you, too."

"It's not just that," I said. "I've been leading you on. I don't really know anything. I can barely do any magic at all, and the little bit I can do, I'm not good at."

"Robin . . ."

I felt smaller with every word I said, and rather than look at her face, I decided to memorize the way her thin ankles tapered above her slippers. "I know you think I'm some kind of fantastic forest spirit-"

"You *are* a forest spirit," she said. "And aside from saying some not very nice things to me last week, I think you've been pretty fantastic."

"I acted like I knew what I was talking about—that was a lie."

"You think you're the first guy to have played up what he knows to impress a girl?" Nadia asked, smiling, and when I glanced at her I thought she might be blushing.

"Well, I'm incompetent. I can't even keep my glamour up anymore. So I'm going to go away for a while. I wanted to apologize to you before I left."

She finally came close enough to touch my horns gently. It was an odd feeling, not entirely unpleasant. "Is that why you're, you know, like this?"

I nodded.

Nadia covered her face with her hands. "Oh, Robin. You really are an idiot, aren't you?"

Even though I'd said it myself, it hurt coming from her. "Harsh. Not unfair, but harsh. What am I doing this time?"

"The first rule of magic," she said, putting her hand on my bare chest. I swallowed. "Come on. You managed to survive here for, what, ten years on your own?"

A light flicked on beside the door, temporarily blinding me. Nadia, too, froze. But in that moment between the light and the door opening, I could feel the buzz of her magic—soft, sweet, but strong, like her—fall over me.

"Nadia." Her mother stood on the doorstep, clutching her own bathrobe, looking so much like Nadia that a lack of blood relation didn't matter. "What is going on." It wasn't a question.

"My fault," I said, nervous under her disapproving stare, as Nadia withdrew her hand but not her glamour from my body. "I, um."

"I can't blame you for your taste, but consider courting my daughter at a sane hour of the night." Her look silenced the retort forming on my tongue. "I'll allow you this one strike because you seem like a good kid. I won't even call your parents. But let's not have a second time, all right?"

"Understood," I said, and then for Nadia's benefit I added a "ma'am" that seemed to go over well. Well enough for her to give Nadia a meaningful look and then go inside, leaving us alone with the porch light on.

Nadia stood awkwardly in her robe. "Robin . . ."

"Thanks for covering me. Literally and figuratively."

She rolled her eyes. "You didn't need me to do that for you, you know. You were just fine before you met me."

I wasn't, though I hadn't realized it until she showed up in my life. But I didn't have a chance to say that to her. The words died in my throat as she leaned her head toward mine, not a smooth confident motion but awkward, jerky. Her eyes started to close. Hands at my side, I focused on my glamour, trying to make myself handsome, taller, better dressed.

Nadia reached out and pulled the glamour from me entirely. "Stop that."

"What, you've got a thing for fuzzy legs?" I squeaked.

She laughed. "No, you idiot. I've got a thing for you. Really you. I don't want you to feel like you have to be someone else for me."

"I'm not even the same thing as you . . ."

"That doesn't matter. I don't even know what I am, and I don't care. We'll probably break up in a year, anyway. We're in high school. So don't sweat it."

I should have been offended that she talked so casually about breaking up, as though anything between us was petty and ordinary and high school. But then I realized you couldn't break up with someone unless you were in a relationship with them, and while my brain tried to catch up to my ears, she kissed me.

~*~

79

Editor's Note: I adore Robin. Regardless of how many years he's been alive, he seems very much like a teenager to me. A sweet teenager whose heart is in the right place but, well, he hasn't quite got everything all figured out yet. So he lashes out in anger when his feelings are hurt, and he stumbles and fumbles his way through this relationship, but despite all the mistakes he makes and the things he doesn't get exactly right, he really does mean well.

_*_

F.C.U.

Jon Arthur Kitson

Fairies don't age like other creatures, so Orchid's reflection in the gold bands covering the dungeon wall told him nothing. He ran a hand along his smooth face, down his sharp chin. Days, weeks, or even years could have passed since he'd been captured and imprisoned in this strange place.

His hand dropped and, for the hundredth time, reached around his back, around the translucent wings folded against his bare flesh, and found the end of the red rope affixed to the base of his spine. The other end of the rope—the end he'd pulled from the wall only an hour earlier—dangled limply against the dungeon floor.

It was smooth, like the skin of a frog.

He wrapped his hand around the rope and pulled. He felt pressure, but just like all the times before, it didn't give. He let go and crumpled to the floor.

In the dim light, Orchid sighed. He wondered if, back in his tiny village nestled along the stream bank, the rest of the Fae already told stories about him. What did they say? Had he drifted into legend?

Orchid thought he knew:

There once was a fairy who wanted so desperately to know what made the sky beyond the Forbidden Mountain glow that, despite the danger, he took wing and went to see. The foolish fairy never returned.

And, for the young girl-fairies feeling the first pangs of love, they would add:

The woman he loved begged him not to go, but he didn't listen. Unable to be without him, she followed. She, too, has never returned.

Orchid remembered the day well. So well it gave him hope his time in the awful prison had been brief.

They took to the sky as soon as the morning dew dried from their wings. Lilly, still apprehensive, turned every few minutes to watch the valley retreat behind them. She paused on the limb of an elm that marked the boarder of their homeland.

"My love," she said, holding out a hand, "are you sure about this?"

He landed and folded his hand in hers. Gently, he kissed her cheek.

"If you're afraid, little blossom, you should turn back. I won't be angry." He looked toward the mountain. "But I have to go. I have to see."

"I won't leave you," she declared. "We belong together, wherever we are." Her eyes followed his up the mountain. "But no one has ever returned."

Orchid smiled.

"Then we'll be the first," he promised and pulled her into the air.

In the dungeon, he sighed again.

It looked like he'd made a promise he couldn't keep.

Lilly's trepidation soon gave way to wonder, just as the familiar flora of the valley gave way to the unusual plants growing squat against the mountain slope. They flew through the day, buzzing around the craggy bushes and sampling the nectar of the strange new flowers. As night fell, they reached the summit. The clouds beyond glowed bright from whatever mystery lay beneath them.

Trembling, they peered over the crest . . .

. . . and down on a sprawling village. An impossible city of stone, metal and light.

Then they heard voices. Much too close. Before they could dart into hiding the lightning sting of a net fell over them, then . . . nothing.

Until he awoke here.

Alone.

Orchid's hands balled into fists, fingers stinging against the welts on his palms from the hours, or maybe days, of pulling at the rope. The pain cleared his exhausted head. He looked around his prison.

He only knew of dungeons from legends of the Old Times; the long ago days when the world—and fairies—still contained magic. In those times the Fae flew boldly amongst the other beings of the world. If the legends could be believed, fairies were revered for their wisdom and ability to see the hidden connections of nature. So much so, the other races sought their counsel.

Sometimes the Fae gave it willingly; but not always.

Countless stories told of fairies captured and forced into servitude. Many of those tales mentioned dungeons; cold, wet prisons of stone and iron.

This dungeon was nothing like that.

The floor and walls were not rough rock; they were smooth, unnaturally so. Orchid rapt his knuckles on the floor. A dull, hollow knock echoed back, similar to wood, but different. And it was dry. The entire cell. Not a drop of moisture in the warm air.

Orchid stood and looked at the walls.

They were green, but not from moss or slime, and made from the same substance as the floor. Bands of gold were pounded flat into their surface, tracing intersecting paths, all straight lines and sharp angles, over the span. Strange objects broke the golden maze at irregular intervals.

Most of them were illuminated orbs—some blue, some green—casting shadowy light around the cell. They showed no evidence of flame or smoke and were cool to the touch. Along with the orbs, a collection of cylinders and boxes—squares and rectangles—protruded from the walls. Orchid inspected one of them.

Black -most of the objects were, except for a few of the cylinders which were shiny metal—and smooth. Crowded silver prongs extended from its sides, like the legs of a centipede, holding it to the wall. Symbols covered its top:

F.C.U.6723-48

Orchid scanned the walls. All of the objects contained similar, but not identical, labels; only the F.C.U. repeated around the room.

A curse, he guessed.

Orchid chose one of the golden trails. His eyes followed it. The path, all of the gold paths, led to—or originated from—one spot. Orchid stared.

A shudder traveled his body.

A ring of dull gray sat in the center of the golden lines. Gingerly, he lifted the rope dragging from him like a tail and brought the end to his face. It terminated in a ring identical to the one on the wall.

The shackle that had held him in place.

And, he suspected, tortured him.

While the rope had tethered him to the wall, cursed dreams swirled through his head. Bizarre images—rigid fish swimming through a night sky, the only words to describe them—blew through his mind like a hurricane. And numbers; nonsensical combinations twisted in his head and burst from his mouth. Like invading vines, they had squeezed at his consciousness, choking it away.

Then, suddenly, they subsided. Their hold on his mind weakened and slowly he regained control of his body.

It all stopped when he ripped the rope from the wall.

Free.

Orchid looked at himself in the gold bands.

If this was actually free.

One wall contained a rigid opening. A doorway with no door. The dim light of the orbs spilled out it, revealing a passageway as strange as his own cell. He knew he should run, complete his escape, but he couldn't muster the strength.

Or nerve.

Instead, he reached out a hand and traced a line of gold. His finger tips brushed their own reflection.

He thought of Lilly.

"Where are you, little blossom?"

"Orchid?"

Her voice came from outside his cell, weak and dry. Orchid ran toward it, into the passageway without hesitation. The cursed rope rattled along the floor behind him.

He found her in the next cell.

Lilly laid face down on the hard floor, her radiant butterfly wings spread around her like a carpet, covering most of the space. She was naked, except for the metal ring attached to the curve of her back. A smooth, red rope—just like the one trailing from his own back—snaked from the ring and into the nearest wall.

"Lilly!" Orchid shouted.

She groaned, but didn't move. On the wall, the light nearest the rope briefly glowed bright, then dimmed.

A shiver ran down Orchid's spine.

Unable to fly in the tight dungeon, he carefully stepped on Lilly's delicate wing. The scales were silky smooth under his bare feet. He loved her wings. So full of life, even laying weak on the floor. And colorful, like a rainbow on her back. He extended a foot over one of the large green dots that dominated each wing corner. From the air, when Lilly coasted on the wind, the dots caught the sun and flashed. They almost rivaled her emerald eyes, which perpetually collected light and sparkled. Always. Even on a moonless night.

Even now, when fear should have extinguished their preternatural glow. Orchid cradled her head in his hands and gazed in her eyes.

"Orchid," her voice rattled like fallen leaves over stone, but her lips curled into a smile. "It's really you."

"Yes, little blossom, I'm here," he said. A lump filled his throat. "I'm so sorry."

"I could feel you," she said, "in my head."

"You could?"

"Yes. But I could feel, and see, other things, too. Things I don't understand." Her eyes turned up. "Oh Orchid, where are we? Are we dead? Is this Hell?"

Orchid flushed. "No!" His voice echoed through the cell. "This is not Hell. Some cruel, evil magic, but not Hell." Then softer, he said, "They would never let you into Hell, little blossom."

Softly, he lowered her head back to the floor and picked himself up. Skirting the edge of her wings, he went to the wall, where the rope extended to Lilly's back. He inspected it.

It was the same as the one that had bound him. Two metal rings, one on the wall, the other at the end of the rope, connected to each other. Orchid wrapped his hands around the one on the rope and pulled. His hands found purchase for a moment, but then slipped. He fell backwards, sliding across Lilly's smooth wing.

It tore.

Orchid stared at the palm sized section of wing that had ripped free. His stomach turned. Even if he could free her, Lilly wouldn't be able to fly. Not until the wing healed. He couldn't carry her, his own wings weren't strong enough. Even if they made it clear of the tight dungeon, they would be on foot.

Fairies traveling on foot didn't live very long.

"Orchid, my love," Lilly said, making him jump, "leave me. Save yourself."

Fairy wings, like those of the insects they imitate, have no nerve endings. Lilly had no idea how much more hopeless their situation had just become, but still, she offered to sacrifice herself for him.

Him; the one responsible for her imprisonment.

Tears welled in Orchid's eyes.

"Don't say that," he said. "I'm not leaving you, Lilly. Never."

Careful not to further ruin her wing, Orchid stood. He entwined his hands around the rope. Legs braced wide, toes digging into the floor, he pulled.

The rope strained against the wall. It began to give.

Lilly's scream pierced his ears.

The rope, still attached at both ends, dropped from his hands. He scrambled to Lilly and lifted her head. She was stiff.

Her distended eyes stared ahead, unseeing. They looked past him, into a void he couldn't see. Her mouth moved.

"One-One-Zero-One-Zero-Zero-One—"

The numbers came without emotion, like a trance. Orchid's eyes darted around the room. The orb above the rope glowed bright. The others around the room blinked in time with Lilly's voice.

"Lilly," he yelled, inches from her face.

"—Zero-Zero-Zero-One-Zero-One—"

"Lilly!"

The numbers continued.

Frantic, he grabbed the rope and yanked. Holes ripped in the bright wing scales beneath his feet.

It didn't give.

"—One-Zero-One-Zero-One-One—"

Orchid's clear dragonfly wings unfurled, filling the cell. They beat the air as he strained. Tattered shards of Lilly's wing swirled like snow in a blizzard. Rainbow snow. Sweat stung his eyes and dripped down his arms, covering the rope.

His hands slipped free.

He collided with the wall, tripping and tumbling over Lilly's unmoving form. His wings crunched beneath him. Now neither of them could fly. His chin dropped to his heaving chest. Quietly, barley above a whisper, he said:

"Lilly, I'm sorry."

She fell silent. Either because the curse had, for now, run its course, or because she heard him. He didn't know. It didn't matter.

The dungeon shook. A grinding squeal came from the ceiling. Slowly, exhausted, Orchid looked up. Involuntarily, his eyes closed tight as the ceiling pulled away and light streamed in.

"Yep," a man's voice boomed from above, "there's your problem. One of the Fae Cores broke free."

"One of the fairies?" Another voice, a woman's, asked. "Well, can you fix it?"

"Depends," the first voice answered. "Let's see."

A shadow fell over Orchid. His eyes opened. A hand, a giant hand, reached for him through the opening. His wings beat weakly against the wall, the shattered tips whipping uselessly through the air.

"It's still alive," the man declared, seconds before his hand engulfed Orchid. What remained of the fairy's wings crackled like autumn leaves as the hand lifted.

The dungeon spread beneath him.

There were no other cells but their own. Lilly laid in hers, silent and unaware of the horrors around her. The passageway that connected the cells turned then abruptly ended in the same green walls, seemingly going nowhere. Bundles of the cursed ropes—some red, but others yellow and green—filled the perimeter of the dungeon, contained by a bare, white wall. More ropes, thicker and in blacks and grays, extended from the outside. What could only be the dungeon's ceiling sat discarded to the side. Bold, black symbols covered its top:

F.C.U.

"Alive; are you sure?" The woman asked.

"Oh yeah," the man said. "See."

The giant fingers unfolded, all but the thumb, which squeezed Orchid tight against the giant's palm. He struggled, kicking and pounding against the embrace, but the thick flesh sprang back from each strike without a mark.

"Plenty of life left in him," the man laughed.

Spent, Orchid slumped against the palm. The air, much colder than inside the dungeon, quickly dried his sweat soaked skin. He shivered and watched a rain of Lilly's wing scales fall from him. They fluttered into the air and around the impossible room.

This, he thought, *may be Hell.*

The cavernous space was enclosed, but lit like under a noonday sun. The light came from flat, glowing panels on the ceiling. Orchid stared until his eyes watered. He turned away, and saw more lights. These were weaker and multicolored, much like the dungeon's orbs. They covered most of the walls, blinking in their own time. The woman sat at a short counter extending from the wall. Her fingers rested next to a plank covered in symbols and buttons.

"So, can you put it back in," she said, "or do you need to replace it?"

"If it stripped its cord I'll have to replace it. But hopefully the connecter just came loose from the circuit board."

"Why?" Then she groaned. "Please tell me you have a spare."

"I've got spares," he said, "in cold storage, but they're all farm raised. This one's wild caught."

"Does it matter?"

"Some. The wild ones are a little faster. They can handle a few more binary calculations per second."

"Whatever," the giant woman said. She pointed across the room. "You see that line of starships? They can't dock with the station until you fix my computer. And my shift doesn't end until they dock."

"Okay, okay," the giant man said. "Let's see what the problem is."

He rolled Orchid in his palm.

The fairy hardly felt the pressure on his back as the giant tugged at the rope. A burst of air whistled between the man's teeth.

"You're in luck," he declared. "The cord looks fine. Must of just come loose. It happens sometimes."

With that the giant lowered Orchid back to the dungeon, back to his cell.

A *click* reverberated up his spine as the man reattached the rope to the wall. The nightmare images flooded his head.

Mustering what strength he had left, and fighting to hold the invasive images at bay, Orchid spun, his hands coiled around the rope. It snapped taut as he pulled and jerked.

It didn't give.

Above him, the giant chuckled.

"Not this time, fella," he said. "That cord's connected good and tight." Then to the woman: "Go ahead, try it now."

The numbers exploded in Orchid's head like thunder.

"One-Zero-Zero-Zero-One-One—" They burst from his mouth of their own will. His teeth ground against them, but they spilled out. "—Zero-One-One-Zero-Zero—"

"Binary calculations are running at full speed," the woman announced. "Good job. I'm already getting docking data. Thank you."

"Hey, no problem," the man said.

In his cell, Orchid collapsed to the floor. The orbs blinked along with the curse issuing from his lips. He watched them as his consciousness leaked away.

"Lilly, I'm so sorry," he managed between the ones and zeros.

Orchid, I'm here.

Her sweet voice sang in his head. It swirled amongst the images of the unnatural sky-fish and drew him in. He let it.

I'm sorry, little blossom. I tried to free you, but-

Shh, she whispered, *it's okay. We're together, that's all that matters.*

But we're trapped-

No, we're together, she said. *Now fly with me, Orchid. Fly with me forever.*

And he did. They took wing in his head, in her head, through the ropes binding them in place and in the maze of gold along the walls.

A shadow fell across their limp bodies as the ceiling lowered back in place.

They didn't notice.

~*~

Editor's Note: I don't think I specifically asked for high-tech fairies, but I'm super pleased to include one in this anthology. Computers powered by fairies. Honestly, is there a more obvious (yet awesome) way of combining modern and traditional in a fairy story? I don't think so. Plus? I love this description: "*Tattered shards of Lilly's wing swirled like snow in a blizzard. Rainbow snow.*" So beautiful. So sad. and so not an image I'm ever going to forget.

Water Sense

Adria Laycraft

The handle slipped out of his sweaty hand. Everything went into slow motion as the bucket hit the ground and tipped. Tom reached for it, willing the water to stay put just like he'd seen Marie do. A useless effort, as always. He could not stop the dark stain spreading through the sand. In his frustration, he didn't even hear Charlie coming.

The first blow knocked him off his feet. He scrambled up, not wanting to give Charlie a chance to get the boots to him, but the second punch took him down again. The kick followed fast, and Tom groaned as it hit a tender spot only just healing.

Tom's hands curled into fists, catching up sand and rock from the dry valley floor. He hunched his shoulders, closing his eyes against the sight of the wasted water and the next blow.

It never came.

Tom opened one eye to risk a look. Charlie stared at something beyond, and Tom swiveled his head, fearing a wild cat had come down out of the mountains. Instead, an old man dressed in rabbit furs stood staring back. At him.

"To find your value, you must understand who you really are."

What? Tom looked back at Charlie, whose face had paled to a sickly shade. When Tom turned back to ask the old man what he meant, the hillside was empty.

Climbing cautiously to his feet, Tom eyed Charlie for clues as to what just happened. His guardian only grunted, pulled his smokes out of his jeans pocket, and lit one with shaking fingers. He puffed, drew, coughed a bit, and drew again.

"Next time you spill the water, you can go thirsty for the rest of the day." His words seemed to hang on the air like the smoke he exhaled with them.

Tom licked his cracked lips. "I'll get more," he said. His throat burned, wanting to ask Charlie what he'd seen, what he'd heard, but he didn't dare. One beating today was enough.

~*~

"And then he was just gone?"

Tom nodded, always a little at a loss for words around Marie.

"It must've been an inipi," she said, her eyes as wide as a startled deer.

"Inipi?"

She bent over her basket weaving, her black hair tucked behind one ear. The baskets sold well to the white tourists, making her useful. Tom wished he was useful for something.

"Ghost spirits. My grandma told stories about inipi that made people crazy and sick until they died. Don't tell me you never heard the same stories."

He wanted to say he'd never have asked if he had, but he kept his mouth shut. Seemed the smartest way to get by these days, whether with a girl or a bully.

"Was it looking at Pa?" She looked worried and hopeful all at the same time.

"No." Should he tell her? Would she worry for him?

Her head came up and she studied him, eyes narrowed. "Was Pa roughing you up again?"

"No," he lied. To tell her the truth would be to admit his clumsiness with the water. Around here, a drop was never spilt, never lost, and every Kawaiisu could find water in uncanny ways or make it stay where they put it. Everyone had a special way with water, except him. The elders just shook their heads at him, and the mamas clucked their tongues and felt his forehead, poking his ribs and trading looks.

"Maybe they came farther than we first thought," one mother said once, only to be hushed by the others.

"Don't matter now," another said. "He's ours and nothin' to be done about it."

Right now Marie's look said she didn't believe his lie. "Well you never mind. Do you know where the blue sage grows by the canyon rocks?" He nodded. "Gather some and keep it with you. Mix in some tobacco . . . not cigarettes, mind you, the real tobacco the elders chew."

"Why?"

"'Cause it's more powerful, duh."

"No, I mean why do I need that stuff?"

"Oh." She hesitated, then she reached out and squeezed his hand with hers. It was cool, soft. Her brown eyes were worried and serious. "Those inipi, they're also called devils. They're evil, Tom. If you see or hear one, you toss some sage and tobacco at it and tell it to leave you alone."

Tom looked up from where her hand touched his. "That's all I have to do?"

"That's it."

_*_

"Who are you?"

The shouted words brought Tom wide awake, his heart hammering against his rib cage. Was it the dream, or did someone call? He tried to quiet his breathing so he could listen.

Coyotes yipped, way far off. Charlie snored, like usual. Marie made no noise, like usual.

Then Tom heard whistling. It came from behind the house, as if someone wandered by. He rose and went to the open window, but he couldn't see anyone there despite the bright moonlight. He peered out at the scrub brush and sand and the rising mountains beyond. The junk scattered around Charlie's shop made weird shadows.

A deer trail went up the ridge where the old man had stood. He could follow that trail, find the man, ask what he meant about Tom finding his value. Even if Marie said he was an inipi ghost. Even if Charlie had told him to stay off that mountain on the threat of the worst beating of his life.

What did a threat like that matter if Charlie hit him anyway? Everyone turned a blind eye, but Tom was growing up. Pretty soon he would fight back. Or maybe he should run away. Trouble was, that wouldn't help Marie. He'd seen the marks on her arm, spots just where fingers would fit turning purple and yellow. It made him want to kill Charlie, seeing that. Which wouldn't help Marie either.

He shivered as his sweaty t-shirt cooled. The sound of the whistling came to him again, far off like the coyotes. He slipped his jeans and shoes on, swung his legs over the window ledge, and jumped down into the rocky dirt. With slow careful steps he avoided the nettles he knew were there and moved out into the moonlight. He patted his pocket to make sure his blue sage and tobacco mixture was still there.

If he knew what value he had, or how to find it, maybe he would finally discover his water sense. Maybe he would be able to finally put Charlie in his place, and protect Marie.

Tom hummed the whistled song as he walked past Charlie's shop and through the scrub. He hesitated at the beginning of the trail, right where it led up off the sandy valley, wondering if he was being a fool. But the moment he stepped from the basin onto the deer trail he heard the same melody sung in a high reedy voice.

Sun be sun, rain be rain,
Neither alone can bring the grain.
Earth, water, wind, sunfire,
Each sense comes from the sire.

Tom climbed up over the first ridge and down through a slight bowl before climbing again. As he crested the topmost ridge, the sky brightened, and dawn broke in the sky.

"How the hell . . . ?" he said, watching as light changed the landscape to the east, making the high mountains there stand out in stark relief. It had been full night just a moment before. Had he walked longer than he thought? Maybe it had just been too long since he saw such an early hour. He could still make it back before Charlie woke up, if he turned back now.

The song continued, so faint now he couldn't make out the words. He pushed the thought of Charlie's temper aside and hurried on, worried more about losing the song. Tom entered a juniper and pine forest and climbed further as the sun rose, leaving his fear and following his heart.

When he stepped into a clearing and saw the old man, the song stopped. Tom fingered the sage and tobacco in his pocket.

"Were you brought by the music?"

Tom nodded, his tongue too thick in his mouth for words. The old man had built a Tomo-Kahni, the traditional winter house of the Kawaiisu, and wore rabbit skins as before. He crouched at a small fire.

"Then you know."

"Know what?" Tom asked. "All I know is you told me something yesterday, and I want to know more about it. And you scared Charlie."

The old man studied him with bright eyes sunk within folds of wrinkles. "I did not tell you anything."

Tom's anger flared at this lie. "But you did . . . you said I had to find out who I really was to have value."

The old man sighed. "Not my words, but they make sense. Would you like some acorn mush?"

Tom gave him a skeptical look, uncertain now about everything. The old Kawaiisu man went back to poking his fire, humming tunelessly. A pot simmered, and the smell made Tom realize he was hungry.

"What is acorn mush, anyway?"

The man quirked an eyebrow at him. "I am Joe, pleased to meet you too," he said, sarcasm ringing through his words.

Tom flinched. "Sorry. I'm Tom."

"Tom, are you sure you're supposed to be here?"

Tom shrugged, glancing around the tumbled rock and wind-bent pine. The sky above was sharp blue, and he realized suddenly there was no wind. That, in itself, was unusual, but the whole experience seemed like a dream already. It gave him a spark of excitement, like he was really living for a change.

"Charlie will be mad I'm not there to bring the water up from the creek," he admitted. "I don't know why it should be my job. I can't control water the way everyone else can." He moved closer and hunched down across the fire from the old man who had somehow been able to stop Charlie from finishing his beating. Joe handed him a rough clay bowl of mush, which Tom sniffed at. Sunflower seeds specked the brown grain porridge-like mixture. He tipped the bowl and sipped, giving an appreciative grunt.

Joe watched, his brown hands beating out some unheard rhythm on his knee. "You don't know where you are," he said finally, as Tom lowered the empty bowl. "You haven't the faintest clue."

"Sure I do. I'm up the mountain behind Charlie's shack, talking to the guy that actually put the fear of God into him."

"Gods . . ." Joe murmured.

"What?"

"Boy, you aren't up some mountain. You're in the Otherworld."

Tom didn't believe him. He stood and retraced his steps, the old man following, until he looked over the valley he'd called home for as long as he could remember. The valley he saw had no houses, no dirt road leading to town, no nothin'. It looked like it might have looked hundreds of years ago, before the white man came and the Kawaiisu stopped being hunter-gatherers.

"What have you done to me?" he demanded, facing Joe. "Where are we?"

"Told you," Joe said. "The Otherworld. Don't you listen?"

Tom pulled out a handful of his herb mixture and threw it. "Leave me alone!" He stumbled back, trying to watch for a reaction and check the valley below for his home again.

Joe scooped up a bit, sniffed it, and sighed. "Good waste of tobacco, that," he said, his voice sad. "Do you have more, by chance?"

Tom swallowed on a dry throat. "Why am I here?" he whispered. "How do I get home?"

"Ah, both very good questions. First, you have to actually want to go home. Then you need to find whatever blocks you from your water sense. It's like you have resisted being at one with your people, and so you are now apart."

Tom looked down from the ridge and thought of Marie's smile. Of course he wanted to go home. But Charlie's face was there, too, and the thought of her having to bear the brunt of Charlie's temper made Tom sweat with worry.

"Why are you here?" Tom asked then, only to discover Joe had wandered back up the trail. "How could this be happening?" he called.

He'd never believed all those old tales, whether they were about Coyote or Rattlesnake or the magical ways of the people in the times of old. Maybe that's why the magic eluded him. Maybe he had to believe. He looked out over the empty valley again. Believing would be a lot easier now.

He heard whistling again and turned to study the hills around him. A cold breeze caught him unawares, nearly toppling him into a thicket of nettles. "Hey!"

Another gust butted him from the other direction, and he went to his knees to keep from going right over the ridge and tumbling to the rocks below. Twisting around, he saw two people standing in the brush, though none of it was broken and no trail was to be seen.

Tom pulled out another handful of sage and tobacco. "Go away!" he yelled, throwing it. They faded from sight.

Tom scrambled away with both hands and feet. Laughter followed him, but when he looked back, no one was there.

He stood and gathered his courage. He went down the mountain and into the valley. There were no signs of humans at all. He climbed up again and hiked to every viewpoint he could find to see if he'd simply gotten turned around and came farther than he thought. But there was no mistaking the direction of the sun, or the familiar rise and fall of the land around the valley. There was no way home.

Joe had no good answers other than what he claimed was the truth. They were in a different place, the land of all those stories that Tom never paid heed to. Joe was friendly and loved telling his stories, and Tom sure was paying attention now. Surely they would reveal the answer. But days passed, and still the valley remained empty.

One night, after a successful hunt, Joe told him a Coyote story.

"Coyote was thinking one day and realized there would be many people. Bug was worried that there would be too many people and they would have to eat dirt. Coyote said no, for if they did, they would eat up all the dirt. So Coyote decided The People should eat acorns, pinyon, chia, and deer."

Then Joe picked up Tom's bowl, filled it with deer stew, and sprinkled dirt over it.

"Hey! What are you doing?"

"As much as we don't have to eat dirt, what I have gifted you with is the track of a wild cat." He handed Tom his bowl, his wrinkles all bunching up in a big grin. "If you mix a wild cat's track into your food, you will become his brother. You will know the ways of hunter and tracker. But you must also find in that bond a deep respect for your brother, or he will send inipi to haunt you and make you crazy until you die."

His words echoed Marie's, and Tom missed her with a physical pain in his chest right then. "The inipi already haunt me," he said, wondering why he decided to tell Joe that now.

Joe's grin faded. "I know. I hear you call out in your sleep."

"Will this stop them?"

Joe shrugged.

"Will it help me get back?"

Joe pursed his lips. "Might."

Tom dug in, ignoring the grit of sand between his teeth as he swallowed down every bit. He even used his finger to wipe out the dregs of the bowl.

Joe worked at his own stew. "Tomorrow we hunt, but not for meat. Tomorrow we hunt water."

Tom stared at him. "There's water in the creek, at least in this season. Or in the dew, like you showed me. Why hunt something we already have?"

Joe's wise eyes flickered in the firelight, almost teasing. "We hunt the water in you."

~*~

As he dreamed that night, Tom heard the words Joe had said before. *To find your value, you must understand who you really are.* But they came now from the two inipi he'd seen on the hill above the empty valley. They stood together, the man's arm around the woman while she cradled something. Tom realized, in that strange dream sense that made no sense, that she held a baby. The song wove through the dream, the words too faint to hear.

They beckoned him to come, and when he refused, they came towards him, the baby gone now and the mother weeping. But they stopped short even as he dug in an empty pocket for his herbs, and he saw that they could not cross the cougar's tracks. He took a step forward, curious now. Where did the baby go? Did they need help?

Joe shook him awake, calling him. "Don't let them take you, boy."

Tom groaned and sat up, peering at the old man. "What's going on?"

"The inipi were calling you in your dream, weren't they?"

"Yeah, but they couldn't cross the cougar tracks."

"Huh." Tom saw Joe's teeth flash in a smile. "Good. Let's get hunting then."

Once they were done with their morning chores and had something to eat, Joe built up the fire. He chanted in a language Tom didn't know, tossing sage onto the fire. Then he gathered something from within a basket and cradled it in his hand. Gingerly, as if handling a precious egg, Joe transferred a ball of fluff to Tom's hand.

"It's eagle down. Put it in your mouth and swallow it."

Having seen what eating a cougar track could do for him, Tom willingly did as he was told. He worked his mouth, trying to get up the spit to swallow.

Something crawled in his mouth.

He started to spit it out, ready to dig at it with his fingers if he had to, but Joe caught his wrists.

"Swallow it! You must swallow it," he said, shouting in Tom's face. "This will protect you from the inipi while we hunt."

Tom swallowed, again and again, gagging a little until all the dry fluff and crawling things were gone.

"What was it?"

"Eagle down."

"And . . . ?"

"Ants."

Tom was on his feet before he could register he wanted to be. "Ants? You fed me live, crawling ants?" His stomach did a little flip, and he put a hand over his mouth.

Joe brought him a drink and patted him on the arm. "It is an age old custom that saved plenty of people from sickness caused by inipi."

Tom sat down, hard. He look a long drink, wiped his mouth. "You never did tell me why you're here, if you're not inipi."

Joe looked over, tipping his head to one side. "Just an old man who got tired of the world the way it was," he said with a little shrug. "I was getting a little lonely before you showed up, though. How do you feel now?"

Tom was staring at the sky, and Joe's voice seemed a long ways off. "What did you put in my water?" he asked, but his words oozed like sap in a cold pine tree, and his mind went away from him.

He saw the inipi again. They called to him, trying to tell him something over a great distance, but he did not understand them.

He also saw a cougar stretched out in the sun. "Good day, brother."

"Good day," Tom replied. It seemed perfectly normal to be talking with this animal in this place. Cougar groomed his front paw.

"What are you hunting?" Cougar asked.

"My water sense."

Cougar gave him a look of disdain like only a cat can do. "You don't have water sense," he said, as if it were obvious.

Disappointment flooded him. "I kinda figured that, but I still hoped."

He came back to the fireside, back to his body. Joe hovered over him, tapping at his forehead and poking him in the belly. "Hey, stop."

Joe sat back with a frustrated sigh. "You are not Kawaiisu."

"I know," Tom said, sitting up. The world spun, tipped, and then settled.

Joe frowned. "You always knew?" he asked, a note of anger in his voice.

Tom blinked at him. "No. But Cougar just told me I don't have water sense, and all the Kawaiisu have water sense. I'm an orphan, and no one can really tell me much about my parents, so my guess is I'm not Kawaiisu."

Joe was nodding, his smile back. "Cougar told you? That is good, very good." His smile faltered. "Except I do not know how you will ever get home again."

⁓*⁓

Tom dreamt of the inipi pair again that night. This time, when they stopped at Cougar's tracks, they knelt and cupped sand in their hands.

They seemed to offer it to him, their faces more clear to him than they'd ever been before.

"What do you want of me?" he asked.

"You must know who you are," they said together. Their voices made gooseflesh rise on his arms and neck, and he shivered.

"I am Tom. What more do I need to know?"

"You are our Tom, and you are not Kawaiisu."

Tom stared and stared. "Your Tom . . ." he said, taking a step closer, wanting to see their faces better.

"Come be with us, Tom. We miss you so much."

"Mom? Dad?" He took another step.

"Yes. Come, you are so close now."

"Tom! Tom! Tom, wake up!"

He blinked, thought he'd suddenly gone blind, then realized it was the dark of night. "My parents! Joe, the inipi are my parents!"

"And you were going to them," Joe said.

Tom was glad of the darkness to hide the tears that sprang to his eyes. "Yeah, I was going to them! They're my parents!"

"They *were* your parents, but they are inipi now. If you go to them, you will wander the Otherworld as a spirit yourself."

Tom wanted to shout and pace and throw things about, but it was dark and cold and as he thought about everything he realized maybe Joe was right.

"They said what you said. That I am not Kawaiisu."

Joe just grunted, obviously now tucked back in his sleeping furs.

"But if I'm not Kawaiisu, then who am I?"

He lay and thought about it until the song birds woke and light changed the world once again. He dozed off then, and saw Marie, her right eye swollen shut and her lip cut. Charlie loomed up behind her, and Tom came awake in the full sun of morning shouting, shaking with fear for her.

"I have to go back," he told Joe.

Joe followed him down the deer path, and when the empty plain did not change Tom rounded on the old man.

"I saw you that day. You made Charlie stop beating me, you scared him. Why? What did you do?"

Joe's lipped thinned out, and his eyes narrowed. He looked angry enough to make Tom let go of him and step back.

"It's not what I did, it's who I am . . . or was." Joe wouldn't meet Tom's eye. "Charlie is my grandson. My daughter died too young, and I did what I could to teach him other ways, but his pa was mean, and Charlie grew up mean too."

"You're an inipi? How did you resist my sage and tobacco?"

Joe shrugged. "When a shaman becomes an inipi, he is a little stronger than a bit of weeds." He almost smiled.

"You have to cross back over and stop Charlie from hurting your great-granddaughter."

"I can't. They don't see me."

Tom stared at him for a long moment. "You have to try."

Joe agreed to try, and they went down to the valley's edge. The inipi shaman crossed into the world and back again to affirm that they were in the right place, but he could not bring Tom over with him. "They do not see me," he admitted.

"Did you see Marie? Is Charlie there? Is she okay?"

Joe looked sad. "She is there. Her pa has just come home with too much beer in his belly. She's hiding behind his shop."

Tom swore softly. "Go scare him again!"

"I told you, they don't see me. It was you that made me visible that day."

Tom growled and scrubbed his face with his hands. "How could it be me?"

"You came here."

Joe's words sunk in, teasing at his brain. He shook his head in frustration. "Then I must be able to go back." He thought of Cougar, and how he ate the wildcat's track. He thought of his inipi parents, and how they offered him handfuls of sand. He thought of the water, and how he never understood the Kawaiisu's water sense.

"But I still don't know who I am!" he shouted.

Then he heard the song, and saw his inipi parents on the ridge singing.

Sun be sun, rain be rain,
Neither alone can bring the grain.
Earth, water, wind, sunfire,
Each sense comes from the sire.
Four Peoples, four Ways,
Each from something depraved.

Four other senses.

He knelt in the sand, the ever-present sand, and placed his palms upon the earth. He could feel the power of it, the way it pulsed deep into the bedrock. He remembered his inipi parents offering him handfuls of sand. He had first seen Joe when he'd been down, his hands in the sand. Joe said he'd made Charlie see, too. He must have come from a wet place, where dry land would be a luxury, something to covet, just as water was here. And in this moment, he had an abundance of earth.

Tom took up two handfuls and stood, then scattered the sand into the wind before him. The air shimmered, and the familiar house and shop appeared. He could see Marie crouched behind the shop, and Charlie calling out for her.

He had found his earth sense. He ran for Marie.

~*~

Editor's Note: This story wasn't actually submitted to *Fae*, it was sent to a different WWP anthology, but the editor thought it might be a better fit for *Fae* and sent it my way. I'm so glad she did. This story is the perfect example of what I was asking for when I said I wanted stories with lush settings, that weren't taking place in Anycity, Anytime. There is so much to like about this piece I don't know where to start, but one of my favourite things is that though it doesn't leave me wanting more from this *story*, it definitely leaves me wanting to read more stories set in this *world*.

~*~

THE CARTOGRAPHY OF
SHATTERED TREES

Beth Cato

Since that terrible night six months ago, Vivian had tolerated her body as a foreign, broken thing. She took care to never look at herself naked, yet as she stepped from the shower that morning, she glimpsed something strange in the mirror and paused. Instead of mere scars, a map adorned her skin. A highway of red traced the curve of her breast and flowed down to her belly button. The flecks and scars of wooden shrapnel had shifted to create the outline of hills and the undulation of a river. Her city rested above the knoll of her heart, thatched by cross-streets and byways.

Her fingers glanced her skin. The scars felt like divots, the fern-like spread of her burns in soft ripples. According to doctors, the Lichtenberg figures should have faded months before. Now those fractal burns had metamorphosed into something more.

Repulsed and fascinated, she followed the red route south to her navel. Did the map go where . . . it happened? Shuddering, she clenched her fist.

"I need to get ready for work," she said aloud.

Yet she still stared at herself, mesmerized. Despite the burns, despite the horribleness, there was something beautiful about the map.

She reached into the darkness of her closet and pulled out her old portfolio. Disturbed feathers of dust were set adrift in the air. She propped a large pad of paper against the bathroom counter and, with glances at the mirror, began to sketch. Her head pounded as it had so often since the lightning strike, and she furrowed her brow as she struggled for focus.

The line veered, gouging at the paper. She flung the pencil away with a wordless scream.

Vivian used to draw, paint, exist for the muse that overflowed from her fingertips. She used to *live*.

Her therapist had told her that if she wanted to create art again, she would find a way, even with the lingering nerve damage. Such trite, arrogant advice from a man with an illegible signature.

She didn't just want art again, she wanted her old life back. She wanted her innocence, for her body to be a clean slate, free of burns, free of the lingering memories of Andrew's heavy hand dragging her down.

Vivian ached to feel whole again, to fill the emptiness that constantly echoed beneath her breast.

She scrambled into her work clothes, smothering the memories beneath cotton and polyester. Her feet knew the path to work. She needed no map.

~*~

The throbbing drumbeat of pain worsened as the day continued.

The pain itself was nothing new; it had been a constant companion all these months. Doctors had bluntly informed her that she could experience dementia, chronic headaches, motor impairment, personality changes, or even amnesia—oh, how she prayed for the latter.

On the contrary, Vivian remembered every detail of that night. The throbbing pain made it easier to fall into the past, when the agony had been fresh and intense. If she could still paint, she would have portrayed it with a foreground of bobbing blades of grass and a high, stark wall of trees beyond. It had been the first day of May, everything green and lovely beneath the moon.

And then Andrew's fingers jerked her down like manacles and the tree trunk scraped her elbows and she screamed, "Help me! Someone help me! Get off, Andrew, get off me—" and a bird's silhouette swooped against gray swirls of clouds and thunder rumbled and . . .

Vivian shivered out of the memory. Chatter continued in the surrounding cubicles, everyone content in their carpet-walled boxes. She was content here too, usually. The mindlessness soothed her. No need to think. Just read, type, code.

Heat flared just above her heart and, like a dragging finger, seared its way to her navel. She curled against her keyboard, gasping through the agony. As suddenly as it had appeared, the pain was gone.

Headaches, she knew. This—this was something more.

Vivian shoved away from her desk. She kept her gaze down, avoiding eye contact that might have raised questions or concerns, and staggered down the hall to a singular bathroom. Another hot wave arced down her chest as she turned the lock. Moaning, she crumpled to the floor. When the spasm passed, she clutched the lip of the counter to pull herself upright. She tugged off her shirt.

The hard line of the roadmap glowed in ugly red. All around it, the divots of her scars radiated blue like stars against a pale sky.

On that night six months ago, lightning had channeled through a tree and blasted into her and Andrew. A brilliant flash and crackle quivered through her marrow as part of the tree exploded, piercing her with shrapnel beyond count. The doctors never removed all of the splinters. Her body would work them out in time, they said.

Now those splinters—or where they once lay—shone like a thousand distant constellations, tiny pinpricks aglow. Vivian splayed a hand against the lights. Her skin felt normal in temperature, the texture as mottled as it had been that morning.

The heat returned, and like a laser beam, the pain traveled from her heart to her belly. The map burned within her flesh.

"I don't want to go there," she whispered to herself, to the strangeness of her own body.

The pain lashed her again. Again. Again. She braced against the counter and rocked with the waves. It was strange, really, to feel something so intensely after such emptiness, but the agony brought no relief, no catharsis. Sweat slicked her fingers and coursed the taut lines of her neck.

"And what happens if I go there?" she asked herself. Vivian had long avoided the sight of her own skin, but somehow she knew the map hadn't been there before today. It had waited until now, until Halloween.

The blue lights sparkled with such intensity that they radiated through the thick cups of her bra.

~*~

Vivian had loved Andrew. In hindsight, she understood it was a naive, stupid love, that she had been desperate for anyone to love her or show the slightest interest. He was a brooding artistic genius in the university fine arts track, the person she admired from afar since their freshman year. At the end of their first date, she dismissed the roughness of his kisses as mere eagerness.

On their second date, May Day, he drove her south. "To find a good make-out spot," he said, as the road curved through the hills.

Suspicion quivered in her belly but she wore a smile. In her senior year high school yearbook, she had been described with one word: 'Nice.' Nice to a fault. Nice in the most gullible way.

Andrew said he liked nice girls.

Now, six months later, she drove south by herself.

At the fringe of the city, she passed children in costume, their treat bags in hand. One little girl wore a purple witch's hat that shimmered in the glow of passing headlights. It almost made Vivian smile. During her teenage goth phase, she had tried to summon spirits on this night with its thin veil between the real and the spiritual. After hours of chanting and giggling, the only thing she and her friends successfully summoned was the pizza delivery man.

As she drove onward, the physical pain withdrew but memories gouged her. She knew these landmarks, not only from the map on her torso, but from that distant night. She recognized the particular bow of an old oak tree, and the gas station with its neon sign screaming CERVEZA. She knew the long curve of the road as it followed then crossed the river, just as the line flowed over the ridge of her ribs as it worked southward.

Vivian's arms, rigid as rebar, gripped the steering wheel. She wanted to stop, but feared if she did the pain would return and paint her world in red dapples. She felt used. Herded. Just as Andrew forced her on this route, now something inexplicable was forcing her again.

The realization caused her to lurch to the side of the road. The car braked with a violent crunch of gravel.

What if Andrew was doing this again?

This was Halloween, the night of ghosts and spirits. What if he awaited her? What could she say to him, what could she do?

She opened her car door and retched.

Andrew never acknowledged that he had done wrong, never had that chance. "I drove you all the way out here. Isn't this a romantic spot?" he said, pointing to the beautiful oak that towered overhead.

"No," she said. "No. I want to go home, I don't want to—"

She had always admired his hands in class. One usually thinks of painters with long, delicate fingers, but Andrew had the wide mitts of a football player. He gripped her slender wrists so tightly his fingers touched.

He had died with his pants wadded around his ankles.

"No," she said, punching her ribs and the map. "I'm not going. You can't make me."

Vivian backed up the car, the tires grinding as she angled them north. Pain crashed into her again. She had enough presence of mind to lay all her weight into the brake. The scars, hidden beneath her shirt, flashed so brilliantly they illuminated the blackness.

"No. No. No." She panted as she leaned on the steering wheel. She had repeated those words to Andrew, and they were just as effective now as then. Maybe *she* was the ghost.

A light reflected against the silver hood of her car. She looked up. A full moon gleamed through skeletal branches, as though it were snared in the spindly grasp of twigs. Watercolor clouds in hues of black, purple, and navy softened the sky.

"I could paint that," she whispered. Fury uncoiled in her gut. She *used* to be able to paint scenes like that.

Vivian wanted to paint again. She wanted steadiness to return to her fingers. Instead of that constant emptiness within, she yearned for the overflow of her soul onto canvas or paper. Hot rage compounded her headache.

Six months ago, she was broken. Tonight she could confront Andrew. She was alive, not him. He had no power over her, not now. She refused to be herded to the scene of her attack. No, she'd go there willingly and face the bastard down.

She turned south again, her rear wheels peeling on gravel as she roared back onto the road.

Vivian took a side street darkened by tall trees. At a right turn, the map sizzled on her chest, and she knew to turn left instead. She wound her way deeper into the hills until she reached a broken wooden fence all too familiar to her nightmares. In the field beyond stood the tree.

She wanted to hate it, but instead, she stared in awe.

The gnarled branches of the oak scraped the sky. The nearest trees cowered as saplings in comparison. Vivian absorbed the eloquence of the tree's composition. Like a bonsai tree on massive scale, it looked utterly natural yet unreal in its asymmetrically balanced perfection— *Wabi-sabi*, as her college Arts Aesthetics professor would have said.

She hadn't been able to take in all of that before. She had been talking to Andrew, her shoulders braced, her hands shoved in her pockets. By the time they were within the tree's shadow, he had grabbed her arm, and the images of the tree became a mixture of utter clarity and terrified blurs.

Vivian stepped over the broken fence and approached the tree along an intermittent muddy path. She remembered the mud. She had crawled back to the car, to her purse and phone, even as her skin zinged in continued electric agony.

Andrew had landed some twenty feet from the big oak. She looked for him there now, her arms clutched close, her throat dry with fear. Acorns and dry leaves crunched beneath her feet and she shivered within the deep shade of the tree's canopy. No stereotypical ghost stood in wait. She frowned. Things glittered in the grass, as though a bottle had been broken and scattered.

"Don't you recognize yourself?" asked a woman's voice, creaking with age.

Vivian whirled on her heel, gasping as the scars across her torso flickered with cold. Not pain, just—strangeness.

The trunk of the large tree stood five feet wide, and from it leaned the body of woman. The branches of her arms flexed and bowed in greeting. Vine hair trailed over her shoulders to the adolescent curves of her chest and down to where her waist melded with the tree itself.

Vivian stared. "What . . . what are you?"

"What are you?" The woman cocked her head to one side.

"I'm . . . I'm Vivian. A woman. Human."

"You are more and you are less," the tree said, her ebony eyes narrowing. "I expected more growth. You're little more than a stump."

"What? A stump?" Vivian licked her dry lips and looked around. "I thought . . . I expected a ghost here."

"A ghost?" The tree sounded incredulous. "You wear part of me within your flesh, its magic lighting your path here on this night of power, and you expect a ghost?" The bark-skinned woman shook her head in clear disgust.

Vivian pressed her hand against her shirt, her mind rapidly trying to take in everything. This being in the tree was something straight out of a fairy tale or Greek myth.

"You're a dryad," Vivian whispered. "Why—why do I see you? I didn't when I was here . . . before."

"You see me because of what you carry. I have stood here for three hundred circuits of the sun. I have hosted picnics upon my roots, blanketed lovers with my leaves, and shared in such joy. And then," the dryad said, her eyes blazing like coals, "one fool human sought to use my trunk, my roots, to shatter you. I will not be used in such a way."

"Andrew," Vivian whispered.

"I thought to spare you, but the damage was done. You beings are so brief and fragile. Part of your soul fragmented like an autumn leaf." The dryad nodded towards the sparkles in the grass. "The pieces are over there, visible on this night and Beltane."

Vivian closed her eyes. She remembered her hands clawing into the roots. Andrew's heavy weight, heavy breaths, heavy presence crushing her. "Someone help me! Help!" she had cried.

Then the lightning came.

"It was you," Vivian said. "You brought the lightning."

The dryad nodded, her leafy hair swaying in the breeze. "It is an easy thing, at my height, to stretch towards the sky."

Heat uncoiled in Vivian's chest, but not the heat of the burns or the map. "Do you realize what it did to me?" she screamed. "Do you know how much it hurt, how it still hurts? And my hands." She thrust them out towards the tree. "I can't . . . do anything." *Draw, paint, live.*

The dryad blinked, unfazed. "I have been struck by lightning dozens of times. I hold no fear of it."

"Well, you're a tree!"

"And you are a human."

Vivian's shoulders shook as she breathed rapidly. "I haven't been the same since that night."

"You expect to stay the same? This day, *my* roots have sunken deeper into the ground. *I've* shed a hundred leaves." Vivian turned away from the tree and swallowed another scream. Her throat burned with the effort. She didn't want to stare at this pompous being, this thing that caused so much pain even as it meant to save her.

She stooped to pick up a piece of her soul. It was the size of a fingernail, iridescent, weighing nothing against her palm. Looking around, she spied a dozen more shards.

She needed to be whole again. She pressed the piece to her lips and swallowed.

Vivian walked back and forth to find and swallow every shard. Heat curdled in her chest again, and she breathed through the pain. She faced the dryad. The heat instantly subsided.

The woman in the tree studied her with an impatient frown.

"Enough of that! Come closer. The night grows older, and your ilk isn't meant to carry my magic. Let's do this and be done."

Vivian stopped, staring down at her body. Once upon a time, she would have been delighted to carry such magic. A blue glow lit her shirt.

"Don't hesitate or I will do this until you come close." The woman in the tree flicked her spindly fingers. Pain shivered down Vivian's torso. "I'm content with my roots planted here. I have no desire to graft with a human."

The pain was all the motivation Vivian needed. She took a few steps forward and the dryad grasped her with a wooden hand.

Pinpricks of cold intensified across Vivian's breasts and ribs. The world glowed vermillion and black as agony rippled across her body, as though the lightning struck again. Vivian blinked and saw tree branches directly above, though she had no memory of falling or closing her eyes. Her hand clutched her shirt and found holes—dozens, hundreds. The map had been ripped from her skin. She held a hand up to the moonlight and didn't see any blood.

Vivian pressed a fist to her stomach, which had abruptly turned queasy. "That's not—that's not all, the bigger splinters were pulled out at the hospital—"

"I lose branches to the wind and it is no loss, but my essence isn't meant to be melded with yours." The voice was fainter. Even its appearance had withdrawn, more fused with the tree.

Vivian sat upright. She didn't feel different, or did she? She lifted her shirt. In the scarce light she could barely see the Lichtenberg figures. Maybe they would heal now. Maybe . . .

Her stomach burbled, and she had just enough time to face the ground before she became ill. Shards of her soul sparkled across the dirt. They were as bright as ever, unaffected by the absence of the dryad's magic.

Above her, the dryad laughed like a wind whistling far away. Her branches clattered. "As if ingesting your soul will restore it. It's a soul, not rainwater." The words were scarcely audible.

Vivian picked up a single fleck of her soul. She turned it between her fingertips. The shard glowed in her hand, its edges jagged yet not sharp. None of the pieces were alike. It was an impossible puzzle.

They could never go back inside. They were never meant to.

An odd sense of peace fell over her.

Vivian sat, gazing up at the tree. She could barely see the dryad at all now, those dark eyes as whorls. The burn scar on the trunk began at Vivian's eye level and extended to the roots. That was where the lightning channeled through, struck her, then passed on through Andrew. Her fingers hovered over the scorched wood.

The tree had taken the blast and survived, even thrived. It stood, magnificent and old, braving the wind and winters and whatever else came this way. The burns and lost branches did not take away from the dryad's perfect imperfection. *Wabi-sabi.*

Vivian scooped up the fragments of her soul and stood.

Her body was ugly. Scarred. But she was alive.

In a violent motion, she flung the shards back into the grass. The fragments sparkled like a hundred prisms as they arced through the air and bounced into the carpet of green. They resembled strange glass flowers with rainbow petals, glowing and iridescent.

She would paint them someday.

If her fingers could never hold a brush, she would use finger-paints. Somehow, someway, she would capture this scene again. The tree would loom in the background, holding up the moon and a dome of stars with its ancient strength. Vivian was just as strong, just as resilient.

"I'll come back someday," she said to the tree. The lower branches bowed in acknowledgment.

Vivian did not need a map to find her way.

~*~

Editor's Note: Those of us who both write and edit end up playing a weird balancing game. We're often critiquing stories for one another at the same time that we're accepting or rejecting each another's work for various publications. It can be a challenge sometimes, but mostly we all find a way to muddle through and separate personal from professional. This story is a first for me and is a wonderful example of that. It's the first story I ever originally encountered as a critique partner and eventually published as a part of an anthology. It's been quite an experience to watch it grow from first draft to final product and, rather than growing tired of it, I've liked it even more at every step along the way.

~*~

POSSESSION

Rhonda Eikamp

Corporal Francis McFarlane was about to drown, and the woman in his pocket couldn't save him.

Black water had cascaded in when the submersible's tip ruptured, the hand-cranked propeller not quick enough to pull them back from the explosive charge they'd rammed into the Union ship, the sea like a steely-cold monster poking its snout in through the twisted hole, and now all eight men were flailing away at the crank *up around up around*, headed for the shallows of the Chesapeake Bay, but they would never make it. The water was up to McFarlane's waist. Private Dunsey was screaming beside him. On every face McFarlane saw the knowledge—clear by the light of the single candle clamped to the ceiling—that they would be dead in minutes, clams at the bottom of the bay.

Moments were tripping in his head like lightning bursts: the old farm, sunlight. Cherish, home in Suffolk with the baby, her eyes red from crying when he left for war. There lay a sadness, worse than the panic closing his throat. They would be alone. His life for the Confederacy, yes, but god help him, his wife and child would be alone.

McFarlane felt the flutter in his breast pocket and fumbled open the button. He knew the others believed he carried a live mouse there, a lucky charm, and he'd let them think that. No use for secrets now. The tiny winged woman clambered onto his palm. Perfect and perfectly nude, her skin a white gold glowing brighter than the candle. Eyes too large for the thumbnail bit of smooth beast face, lids sweeping back and up to her temples, etching the same parabola as the impossible violet wings rising from her shoulder blades, huge as elephant-ear leaves as they unfolded, colors of bruises and winter sky. The men had stopped cranking, the water to their chests. The nearest stared, death-hallucinating, McFarlane knew they assumed, seeing an angel come to lead them home.

He brought her close, basking in the glow. Water washed at his chin. So cold. She stroked his nose with hands like gnats, the subtlest of touches, then tried to hug his cheeks, though her arms barely reached past his nostrils, scratching at him then, animal fury fighting to possess its master, wolf-gone-dog gone wolf again.

"Mine," she hissed and it was the hiss of wind in forests, ancient bodies buried in humus and rising again.

"You can't save me this time, flower," he told her.

Above them the candle, sole beacon of light and oxygen, guttered out.

␣*␣

It was the hottest day the county could recall since 1840 and Frank McFarlane had gotten free of his pa for the afternoon. Thirteen and learning the trade from the rich clayey ground up, expected to take over the farm some day, but the peanuts would do without him for a few hours. The shagbarks behind the slave quarters had drawn him in with their coolness, a green velvet cloak, until he was deeper in the woods than he had ever been before, ready to turn back as the ferns became too thick, when he spied an iron spike that had been driven into one of the trees at shoulder height. An odd sight, with an even odder patch of moss growing around the spike in a butterfly shape, lavender hues that fluctuated with scarlet and which he found hard to look at. Without thinking, Frank grasped the spike and worked it from the bark, and as it came the moss thickened—*congealed,* he would have said, churned like purple butter out of flat milky nothing—until the spike lay in his hand and a miniature woman hung before him, naked, with her back to the tree-trunk, her outspread wings of gauzy skin caught on the rough bark.

Frank reckoned he was dreaming. He'd had some of those dreams already, but the women had been his size and his inexperienced imagination had been unequal to the detail spread before him now. She opened eyes that seemed to take up half her face, black pupils swirling in night irises, and a cosmos of sparks lit up in their recesses at the sight of him. As Frank watched with his mouth hanging open, she rocked back and forth until her wings were free, half tumbling, half fluttering to the ground, and when he picked her up and held her on his palm, his hand shaking, she looked him up and down.

"He," she hissed, almost startling him into dropping her.

A strapping boy, his ma called him. Tall for his age. "I'm male, if that's your meaning."

She fluttered to his shoulder then, caressed his ear and cheek, and a shudder galloped through him, raising the hairs on the back of his neck. A sense of a thunderstorm approaching. *I'm awake*, he thought. *No. I'm waking up.*

She leaned forward to look at him. "Mine," she pronounced.

Mine, Frank's thoughts echoed and the shudder throbbed through him again.

He took her home with him. She became his pocket secret, crawling back and forth between the pinewood box he found for her and his coat whenever no one was looking. All winter and spring, while she nuzzled his fingertips unseen by others, he felt a lethargy that was at the same time a joy, a sense that he had at last come to be weighted down by deep adult truths he'd never hoped to understand. Frank's parents looked at him strangely. Great-grandma Louisa, who left her room at the back of the plantation house only for dinner, would watch him across the table with loving troubled eyes. A year passed, two. His flower, he named his moss woman in his thoughts, telling her secrets she only ever answered in monosyllables, her replies never seeming to match his ramblings, as though she had no real idea what he said.

She protected him.

From work: a voice in Frank's head telling him how to get out of the hardest tasks, his father snapping at him more often, calling him lazy. From the elements: storms, the fire in the barn one winter—some force like iron chains on his legs that kept him from running in to save the horses, though he knew he could have made it.

Teaching him to favor himself.

In the summer of his sixteenth year he was hunting squirrels in the woods west of home when an angry black bear rose before him out of nowhere. Furred death, towering above him on its hind legs. He tried to shoot and his rifle jammed. Of a sudden he saw the blur of violet streak from his pocket to land on the back of the bear's neck. The moss-woman burrowed her face in the fur and the roaring stopped. The bear dropped onto all fours, turned and ambled away. When she flew back to him, he saw her teeth were red with blood. It was the first time he understood what she could do, his little goddess bossing nature around, and wondered whether he should be frightened.

He was nature too.

When Frank was eighteen his great-grandma Louisa died. She called him to her bedside once the doctor said her heart wouldn't see another day and she waited until they were alone.

"You were always a good boy, Francis," she mumbled. He hadn't expected that kind of platitude. They hadn't spoken much in his flower years, but he and his granam had been close once, his child spirit drawn to a like vision in her that saw beyond the farm and the peanuts. She reached out a hand and stroked his pocket, and he understood. Reluctantly he undid the loop.

"How?" Louisa whispered as his flower clambered down his sleeve to gawk at the old woman's wrinkles. Frank told her about the tree behind the slave quarters and the iron spike.

"The Negroes know," she muttered. "This is an old, forgotten thing. Older than me even." She tried to chuckle and had a coughing fit. "They take you, you know. Used to say they'd take you into a mountain for a hundred years." Urgency crept into her face. "But that's not it, Francis. They take you over on the inside. Something in you goes to sleep. This little thing, its morals aren't ours. It'll protect you from danger, but it'll want and want and you'll become beholden to it. If you let yourself start to think like it does, you won't be human anymore." The long speech tired her and she lay back. The moss-woman crawled onto his granam's face, investigating her lips, and Frank removed her and put her back in his pocket.

"Promise me you'll stay yourself," came the dying woman's weak whisper.

He wasn't sure he understood what she meant. "I promise," he said.

He remembered the words, and when he told his father two years later that he wasn't taking over the farm but moving to Suffolk in the south of Virginia to enter the merchant trade, ignoring his pa's stricken look, he didn't know if it was what he wanted or what his pocket wanted. *You go to sleep.* Standing behind a counter and retrieving dry-goods for customers seemed preferable to tracking through peanut fields, waiting for the black-rot to ruin a year's crop and bankrupt him.

He had no desire to better himself until the day Cherish Gaston walked into the shop. He felt turned to liquid at the sight of her brown curls, some strong spirit intoxicating him, burning him when she spoke to him. A spirit that came from a different place than the lethargy. Within a year he had purchased the establishment from Mr. Penderfeld and married Cherish. On their wedding night he ignored the voice in his head crying *No no no* and sat his new wife down on the edge of the bed.

"A husband and wife shouldn't have secrets," he told her. He imagined the words spoken in his great-grandma Louisa's voice. He opened his pocket and his flower climbed out.

Cherish and the tiny woman stared at each other. Cherish was a tenacious girl, but the sight was too much. She reached a hand across the bed and clutched Frank's arm to steady her shock and the moss-woman saw it. "Bad," it spit at Cherish, more a growl than a hiss, and before Frank knew what was happening it had launched itself at his wife's face. Cherish screamed. Miniscule fingernails tore at her cheek, leaving scratches like small shaving cuts before he could bat it away.

To her credit Cherish did not faint. Together they tossed a scarf over the woman and locked it in the cupboard. All night, while Frank delved into deeper adult truths in the shape of his sweet wife, they listened to his flower throw itself against the cupboard door until they thought the wood must break, howling one word over and over.

Mine. Mine. Mine.

He was twenty-three.

When the baby came, he was ecstatic. Leaning over the cradle Frank forgot who and where he was, forgot everything, and when he looked again, his moss-woman had fled his unhooked pocket and attached herself to the rim of the cradle, crawling toward the baby's head. Just as he was about to snatch her back, she paused, gaze roving up and down the tiny wrinkled form, then she turned a perplexed face to him and chirped, "What." A question. He wondered then if they had children at all, or if they just grew out of moss, or out of each other, the way gnats seemed to coalesce from mud.

"Maybe you should get rid of it," Cherish said when he told her in the evening. She rocked the baby and watched him with loving eyes. He felt drenched in the sun by those eyes, rocked the way she rocked their infant son. He had explained the voices in his head to Cherish once and his pledge to his granam. He knew the small mind in his pocket still pulled at him; he had turned into a miserly shopkeeper for his age and a strict employer, even hated by some for his penny-pinching, and yet he and Cherish were well-off for it, never wanting for anything.

"What if I was a different person without her, Cherish?" *Twelve years with an invisible loving thumb on you*, he refrained from saying. *What would that do to you?*

His wife smiled, showering more sun on him. "I married you, Frank, and I love you so. Sometimes though, I think whoever you are is hidden. Maybe that's the way it is for everyone, but . . ." She gazed out the dark kitchen window. "But there's a . . . veil on you at times and it comes from her. Whatever comes through of you seems so . . . thin. I think you wouldn't be a worse person." He was not one of those men who considered women's intuitions silly. His wife was strong and wise and he listened.

After that Frank left his flower in her box as often as he could, putting off any decision to get rid of her, ignoring the animal yowls in his head as he went about his day. Then the war came, usurping every thought, raising its own yowl that was louder than anything he could have imagined.

He had her with him, not trusting to leave her at home with his family, in battles that were visions from hell, while she told him through his fingertips or through a Morse code of his racing heartbeats where he should run or dodge or advance. Francis McFarlane became known for his luck. He advanced to corporal. At Berryville a bullet struck him in the chest, just at the pocket he kept her in, or he dreamed it did, and he went screaming into the dark of pain, but when he woke on the field there was no wound on him, only a scorched hole in the front of his pocket. Her magic protecting him again.

Saving him. Saving her possession.

_*_

"Mine," she repeated.

Corporal Francis McFarlane saw nothing, felt nothing in his freezing body, only the salt water sloshing now at his lips. *Lord, don't let me die in the dark.*

"Breathe," she hissed. It made no sense.

On his cheeks he felt the flutter of gauzy wings stretch to cover his face, barbs piercing his skin in a circle from jaws to forehead. Then beneath that death shroud she forced his lips open and crawled into his mouth.

Violet light flared—no, he could see through the gauze. Luminescent globes that were the faces of men floated beside him, upturned to the last inch of oxygen, then the inch vanished. He was underwater. He could feel her shifting behind his teeth, then air slammed into his lungs—amazing, terrifying thrusts that scorched his throat and withdrew again without his diaphragm moving, a worm sliding back and forth in there.

He scrabbled at the ceiling of the submarine, found holds to pull himself along, their steel edges lit up violet for him, past Dunsey, until he came to the rupture and wiggled his way through the twisted struts. Then he was out in the water of the bay, a stronger violet flare far above that was the burning Union ship to guide him to the surface.

He shed his coat, kicked off his boots. Exhilaration keened *Live live live* and just when he made to stroke upward—inexplicable horror punched a fist in his stomach, as though he stood on the edge of a precipice, about to make the worst mistake of his life.

He was forgetting something.

He fought to think back, through the howls of *Up!* and *You live!* that ate his mind away as soon as he stopped moving, and there it was.

Private Dunsey.

Dunsey beside him in the submersible, flailing at the water, blind in the utter dark. Still alive.

He'd swum right past him, oblivious to all but his own survival.

McFarlane kicked back down and a dead, hateful space opened inside him. He would die, fish would eat his eyes. The man wasn't worth it. The iron chains were on him again, pulling him up this time, as though gravity had been turned on its head, while the submersible, still slave to the old gravity, began to sink fast, its last air cavity gone. But there was Dunsey. Half out, squirming and trapped in the twisted metal, too panicked to free himself in the dark. With a tremendous kick McFarlane reached him, saw where the terrified private's jacket had caught in the torn hull. It would take seconds to untangle him, the sinking mass drawing them both down all the while.

Abruptly his light went out. Breathing became harder.

Is that it, flower? he thought. *Punish me to make me obey? I can do without you, you know!* His heart convulsed at the thought.

In his arms Dunsey went limp.

With his free hand McFarlane ripped the wings from his face and spit her out. Where the barbs tore out of his skin the salt rushed in and he clenched his teeth against the urge to scream. His lungs burned. Another second, fumbling now in the dark, and he had Dunsey loose and was rising with him, boxing toward the surface.

McFarlane's thoughts were turning silky-soft at the edges, shutting down. They broke into the night like breaking through to heaven, the cold air a god, and Dunsey woke and gasped, beating at him before understanding where they were. Before them floated the burning ship, so close McFarlane could hear the Union sailors' cries, and he spun and put it behind him, hauling a weak Dunsey toward what he hoped was shore.

After a moment the dim, peeved glow of a winged figure ignited in the air ahead of him to guide him, beast instinct deciding to help him a little.

Less loyal than a dog.

Pebbles rolled beneath his feet. They stumbled up the shore, Dunsey collapsed again, and McFarlane dragged him to the trees and a thicket that would hide them from any Union men who might make it to shore. The softness in McFarlane's brain iced over and he shut his eyes.

_*_

When he woke she was close. Black lakes watched him and blinked. He felt steeped in the old lethargy, the comfort of being looked after, and for a drowsy second he studied the strange familiar face inches from his. Reptilian or insectile, he could never decide. Then memory slapped him. A cold stone settled in his stomach. When she opened her mouth to speak, he knew what word she was going to say.

"Run," she chirped.

The logic of it was a weight, a sickening turd sliding catty-corner through his mind, seeking a way out. Dysentery of the brain. It was the sensible thing to do. They would think him dead, at the bottom of the bay, his body unrecoverable. Dunsey hadn't seen who rescued him. He could desert and no one would know and when the war was over, the goddamned war they were going to lose anyway—oh how long he'd known that—he could slip home in the post-war chaos, plead loss of memory. Just leave the death and the spilled bowels and the guns behind, as he'd left the men drowning in the submersible, as he'd been about to leave Dunsey. Protect himself and never a thought for honor.

Dunsey.

A sharp cry flew up from somewhere near. His own throat. He rolled and found the private beside him, still unconscious, his thin chest rising and falling, and McFarlane sank his own forehead to the dirt in relief. He tried to remember how old Private Dunsey was. Nineteen or twenty. Nothing but a boy, all of them boys. Wings fluttered at his hair. When he looked up she flew to his face.

"Home."

He managed to shake his head, neck-bones grinding like unoiled gears.

"West." She let her gaze slide to the dark where the trees thinned.

"I could have saved more of them, flower. If you'd of let me have the air, let me risk myself just a little." Her face gave no hint he'd spoken. His words might have been raindrops, or a gust of wind. She flitted to his hand and McFarlane closed his eyes for a while, thinking of skeletons rolling around in a steel coffin at the bottom of a bay, thinking of his next move, until a stinging pain bloomed in his wrist. He lifted his arm and stared.

She'd never bitten him before.

He could see the fangs sunk deep in his vein, pumping, reptilian after all, and with every pulse came a new desire to survive, to run and hide, a yearning so strong his legs twitched with it.

"So I'm a bear, huh?" he yelled at her. "No more freedom than that?"

Beside him Dunsey groaned. The knowledge of what he had to do left McFarlane colder than the seawater. His own jacket was gone. With his free hand he searched Dunsey's pockets, fingers grasping for the object that should be there.

Closed upon it, drew it out.

A staghorn folding knife. He opened it with his teeth.

She fought with the fury of a child that cannot understand its punishment. A wing tore as she tried to twist from his fist, the purple-veined cartilage leaking thin plumes of red smoke. While he sought a tree deep in the thicket she went limp, a possum trick, but when he held her against the bark, bracing his hand over her face so he wouldn't have to see it, she began to struggle again, arms and legs writhing with snake ferocity. He could feel her biting his palm.

Stop bawling, you idiot, he thought, and meant it for himself.

It took two tries to get the knife through abdomen and bark to the hilt and he put his weight into the thrusts. *Stay. Yourself.*

He expected blood, yet there was only her skin-glow going out like a candle, that same smell of a charred wick, or he imagined it. His hand slipped from her face and she saw him. "Love," she gasped. Another trick. Then there was no mouth to speak. She flattened, detail leaching away, smoothing out and draining inward, until there was nothing left around the knife but a butterfly-shaped patch of lavender moss.

Back near the shore Dunsey was awake. He'd heard the struggle. McFarlane helped him to his feet.

"Was that a Yankee back there?" Dunsey whispered.

"No," McFarlane replied. "Just an animal."

They stumbled south, staying hidden in the trees, toward the secret launch station and their unit. Toward Cherish, McFarlane thought, and a baby that was not made of moss. Toward a war that could last another hundred years, the bullet that might kill him tomorrow. Toward life. He felt thickened, real.

_*_

Editor's Note: For this anthology I wanted stories that *belonged* in, a specific place and time, rather than taking place in some nebulous idea of a time or place. I wanted stories that happened where they did because they couldn't possibly take place anywhere else, and "Posession" is exactly that. You couldn't take this tale and tell it during the second World War and have it be the same. The technology would be different, the characters would be different, the fairy would be different. The story would be different.

I love it.

I mean, how could you not love a story that begins with a fairy in a submersible?

_*_

AND ONLY THE EYES OF CHILDREN

Laura VanArendonk Baugh

You've probably heard of the survival of the fittest? It's where things first broke down. An immortal doesn't have to be fit for anything; he's going to survive anyway. Immortality was evolution's biggest screw-up, and any ecosphere worth its salt is going to do its best to make sure an immortal never breeds.

But they try.

Oh, how they try. And sometimes they succeed, after a fashion, and they spawn *things*. And those things become stories, because they're too horrid to be real, so they must be stories, they *must*, and thus we have fairy tales and horror films and unconfirmed internet stories of shocking infants in third-world countries, with photos quickly taken down after human rights advocates protest that no one should be gawking at tragedy like some sort of modern day freak show.

"Human" rights. Heh.

But though the immortals try to breed, they generally can't. And thus, the Fae fascination with children.

It even hits me sometimes. Right this moment, for example, I was completing a perimeter check of a park playground and settling on a bench. I pretended to check email on my phone, but I wasn't really seeing anything on the screen because I was too busy sneaking peeks at the kids playing on the slide and swings. There were five of them, three girls and two boys, and most were strangers to one another until the game of tag started through the autumn leaves. It was all I could do to stay on the bench instead of jumping up to join in.

I didn't, though. A hundred years ago, a stranger could stop a stroll and play a few minutes with kids and everyone would have a good time. Nowadays people start calling police and shouting "Stranger danger!" if you so much as wave at a kid or give him a high five, forget chasing him giggling around a park.

And that's kind of a bad thing. Not only for all the little kids who grow up paranoid and nature-deprived and utterly dependent, but because all those jonesing Fae can't get their tiny little hits of *child* through frequent, harmless interaction, and some of them finally snap and just take one.

Almost two thousand kids a day go missing in this country. Think about that a second, okay? Every forty seconds. If you're reading this at average speed, that's six kids since you started. (Sorry; Fae personalities also tend to obsessive counting.) About half of those are family abductions, and half of what's left are acquaintance abductions. We don't have anything to do with those; that's your own mess, humans.

But about twenty-four percent of kidnappings are stranger abductions, and a very few—okay, three percent if we're counting, and I always am—are Fae-related. Most of the time, those children are found a few days later, unharmed and a little confused (or assumed to be). Most of the Fae who like kids—really like them, I mean, and not just to eat—are pretty good about returning them nowadays.

But the other stranger abductions are entirely human in nature, and that's where I come in.

My phone rang—Blondie's "Call Me"—and I took the opportunity to look across the park and watch the kids in a totally natural manner as I answered. "Hello, Jimmy."

"Have you seen the news?"

I hadn't. I have a Google Alert set and of course Twitter on my phone, but I was watching the kids. "Not yet. What is it?"

"Amber Alert just went out. Little girl, age seven. Taken from her front yard."

Not a typical abduction, or Jimmy wouldn't have called. "Where?"

"Out this way. I actually know the family a bit; they come in every week or two."

Jimmy owns the Steer & Beer, a little dive over on the east side. He serves more root beer than beer, and he makes a mean Black Cow. He also fancies himself a marksman. Actually, he shoots Expert at local matches, which is two ranks above Marksman, but whatever.

"You know them enough to figure this isn't a family matter?"

"Her parents are together, and while I obviously don't know much, the police don't seem to be looking for any relatives."

Bells and breadcrumbs, this was likely to be a serious one. And by serious, I mean there was a decent chance she'd been taken by some pervert-pander for sex trafficking. It's a bigger thing than most people want to admit. "Are you at the Steer now?"

"Meet me here?"

"I'm on my way."

I hung up and stood, and no one noticed. I'm one of the rare half-breed freaks myself, though not of the type to get an *OMG!!!1!* photo on the internet. No, I'm lucky enough to pass on a human street—which conversely means I'm pretty unlucky on what passes for a street in the Twilight Lands. So I tend to spend most of my time here.

Exactly here, in fact. This is a good place for us. What, you don't think of Indianapolis as being a particularly supernatural city? That just means we're keeping under the radar. I know, New Orleans and Chicago and places get all the arcane press, but think for a second. Indianapolis has two affectionate sobriquets: "the Crossroads of America," for its prominent location on first the National Road and later several interstates, and "the Circle City," for its efficient, nearly ritual, circle and grid layout.

Crossroads and circles, people, right in the advertising. If you can't find the Fae in that, I can't help you.

I made my way to the Steer & Beer, where Jimmy had an enormous fried pork tenderloin waiting for me. As I walked in, he removed the overturned plate keeping it warm and then mixed ice cream and Coke into a Black Cow, setting it on the counter. There's no land like the Old Land, but there are certain advantages to the American Midwest.

"What are we looking at?"

Jimmy nodded toward the small television hanging at the far end of the room. "Not a lot of details yet, but it looks like she disappeared about an hour and a half ago. From the front of the apartments, like I said."

The screen showed a smiling black girl, her hair in braids and beads, a candid photograph scavenged from a phone or Facebook to get on the news as quickly as possible. *Alexis Foster*, read the footer text.

"Cute kid," I said, and stuffed the tenderloin into my mouth so I wouldn't have to say more. I'm not Fae enough to be swept away in pure and unbridled emotion, but I have enough fairy in me to get choked up over a snapshot of one of today's two thousand kids.

Jimmy left the counter and went to the rear wall of the Steer & Beer. The rest of the joint was decorated in typical drive-in style, old posters and unintentional retro, but the rear wall was papered in children's drawings. Every kid who comes to the Steer & Beer for the first time is offered a free ice cream sundae in exchange for a signed work of art.

There were four drawings signed "Alexis," but Jimmy selected one. He had a digital photo frame of happy customers waving spoons or holding up tenderloins, and many of the photos included children. A light pencil notation on the back of each drawing, obliquely referencing the photo's file number, made it easy for Jimmy to know which drawing belonged to which child's image.

It was the kind of thing that would make many parents paranoid, even though he had no family names or addresses, but to be fair that wouldn't be hard with some facial recognition software and a credit card database or something. But Jimmy was one of the good guys. Only he and I knew the drawings were marked with anything more than the date, and we both hoped never to need them.

When they were needed, though, they were awfully handy.

Jimmy slid the drawing over the counter, and I studied it without touching. Alexis had drawn a pony with what I assumed were sparkles trailing from its mane and tail, and a wizard or college graduate or something to one side. Hey, I like kids, but I'm not good at following their art. At the lower right was her name in red block letters.

I finished my tenderloin and drained the last of the Black Cow. Jimmy made another, this time in a foam cup to carry out, and called back into the kitchen that he was going out.

I picked up the picture for the first time and carried it out with us.

Jimmy drives an SUV of some sort. I'm not good with cars but it's old, noisy, and solid. That comes with a lot of steel so I tend to ride leaning away from the door with my feet elevated on a couple of phone books he keeps for the purpose. He drove us to Monument Circle and wedged into a passenger unloading zone.

The Circle is named for the Soldiers and Sailors Monument. It honors veterans of five wars, it has neat fountains and an underground Civil War museum, and it's nearly as tall as the Statue of Liberty. And most importantly, it sits at the very heart of the city, in the center of the Circle and all those precisely-drawn streets.

I got out of the car and went to the Monument. I paid the two dollars to ride the elevator. The stairs are free, but I was going to need all my energy.

No one else was at the top, which was just as well. I don't need a lot of theatrics, but it's nice not to have to deal with distractions. I took Alexis' drawing in both hands, pulled up the photo of the smiling, braided girl via the alert on my phone, and concentrated.

Scrying a location is a really complicated thing, and trying to describe it is kind of like trying to describe seeing colors. It really only makes sense if you already know what you're talking about. Having a face isn't enough; you need something personal, something connected to a soul. Art is about as personal as it gets, and Jimmy's ice cream exchange is brilliant.

It doesn't give me an address, of course, but I can get a sense of direction and distance. After that, a little work with the maps app on my phone can narrow it down to a few hundred yards, and that's a pretty fair working prospect.

There's an obscene number of calories in a traditional fried tenderloin sandwich and Black Cow, but I stumbled out of the Monument with blurred vision and a racing heartbeat. I had to blink and concentrate to remember where Jimmy would be, and I hurried toward the car like an addict toward his stash.

Jimmy opened the door as I neared—I can generally manage a door handle, even on a steel door, but it's pushing it after a scrying—and handed me the foam cup. I sucked at the straw greedily and shoved the phone at him, in navigation mode, without speaking.

Jimmy pulled two energy bars from his jacket pocket and dropped them in my lap. I threw him a grateful glance and stopped gulping long enough to say, "Bless you." The shakes made it awkward to manage the wrappers, but the ice cream and Coke were kicking in and my hands soon steadied.

So anyway, kids. Fairies like 'em. Some like to play with them, like the Cottingley Fairies (not the cardboard and hatpin ones, the real thing). And some like to have them, like the Queen.

For those of you who slept drooling through English Literature and woke up just long enough to giggle-snort at *A Midsummer Night's Dream* because he said "ass," you're probably thinking of Titania. That would be fine—she's had a lot of names, and she's not particular about which get used—except that Shakespeare was a great writer but a lousy historian, and a chauvinist to boot. Have you ever actually paid attention to the fairy side of the story? Titania's all like, *I'm raising this little boy, I knew his mother*, and Oberon's all like, *No, I want him*, and they spat a bit, and then Oberon pranks Titania in the ugly shape of Nick Bottom—"ass," hur hur—and so Titania's like, *Ooh, that was so embarrassing, I guess you can have the little boy and I love you*, the end.

Seriously, who would buy that, besides a bunch of rowdy men

feeling rather threatened by a female monarch? Shakespeare knew his audience, I'll say that for him, and none of them knew the Fairy Queen.

Jimmy pulled into an empty parking lot and put the car in park. It was a business strip near middle-class neighborhoods, not exactly a part of town you'd associate with human trafficking—but you don't get to be a thirty-two billion dollar industry without developing effective protocols and safeguards.

Jimmy nodded toward a corporate accounting office at the end, adjoining a wholesale warehouse which sat behind the strip. "Everything else here is a boutique or retail, something anyone could walk into. But no one strolls into corporate accounting without an appointment. And they could have easy access to warehouse space."

I nodded. "Looks like a place to start, anyway." I could scry again, if we got stuck, but that wouldn't be such a good move right away if I wanted to be any use later. Better to use brains as well as magic.

Jimmy didn't bother to check the Sig Sauer P220 he wore under his flannel jacket; he'd loaded it right the first time. It wouldn't come out unless something went very wrong. "I'm just going to go in and ask about some accounting then," he said. "See if I spot any red flags."

I nodded. If the office were legit, no problem. If it were a front, they'd give him a polite brush-off and we'd call in an anonymous tip.

It'd be a lot easier to call in a tip in the first place, but I think I mentioned that scrying a location can be inexact. Search warrants can be tricky to get, and the last thing you want is a police visit next door. By the time they can get a warrant for the right property, the stash house is empty and the kids are in another state, maybe. Better to pinpoint and nail them the first time.

Jimmy looked at me. "Stay in the car."

I smiled. "I'll bet you say that to all the girls."

"That is so wrong, coming from you." He shook his head and got out. Jimmy doesn't have much of a sense of humor when things get serious. Me, I keep mine lively at all times. It's my nature to be either flippant and playful or deadly cold, and the former is more comfortable.

I'd finished the ice cream float and the energy bars, and I felt nearly normal again. I tipped my head back against the seat.

It was only a few minutes before Jimmy came back, casual and calm. When he got into the SUV, however, he slammed the door too hard. "They took my name and number and offered to have someone call me Tuesday."

"But?"

"But I could hear cartoons coming from a back room."

Candy and cartoons go a long way to keeping captive children quiet. The stuff you see on the news about tiny, filthy rooms and physical restraints is real, too, but cartoons are a cheap sedative in a holding area. I flexed my fingers deliberately to keep from clenching them into fists. "Drive. I'll make the call."

I had my phone to my ear, ringing, when the bread truck pulled into the parking lot. Jimmy slowed the SUV, watching the truck in his mirror. "Are you thinking what I'm thinking?"

The truck pulled alongside the accounting office, its painted bakery logo at odds with the cheap imported goods in the warehouse.

"Bells and breadcrumbs," I snarled.

"Anonymous Crime Reporting Hotline," said a voice from the phone.

I gave her the address as Jimmy turned the SUV. "I saw Alexis, the Amber Alert kid." I'd scried her, close enough, and that would get the fastest response. "I think it's human trafficking. And they just brought in a truck, they're going to move them now, so you need to hurry. I have to go." I hung up on her questions; she had what she needed, she didn't need to know more about me, and we had work to do.

Exposure was what the traffickers would fear most right now, so the mere presence of a couple of outsiders might be enough to make them sit tight for a while. Jimmy pulled his SUV into the lot and angled across two parking spaces. He then held his phone up at eye level and gestured angrily at it. "How long do you think they'll be?"

I pointed with equal fervor at my own phone and then up the street. "Hard to say. Telling them they were moving the kids now bumps it to probable cause, I think, so they can act faster, but I wouldn't want to bet anyone's life on it."

Arguing over directions is a pretty good cover in a lot of places, but it was less convincing when Jimmy had just been asking about accounting a few minutes before. It wasn't long before we noticed a face at the office window. "I think we've been spotted," Jimmy said unnecessarily.

I shifted my feet on the phone books and drew a pair of light leather gloves out of my jacket pocket. Three men came out of the office, and two walked to separate cars. The third came toward us with a friendly smile. "You guys lost?"

Jimmy put the window down a few inches. "We were having something of a debate about the fastest way back to the interstate. But it looks like we've got some time to kill, anyway, before we meet my folks for dinner. Might sit here a bit."

The friendly smile faded. "I'm afraid you can't loiter here."

Jimmy grinned in a good-old-boy way. "Aw, we won't be any trouble."

"This is a private lot. If you don't move on, I'll have to call the police."

The bread truck began to back along the building, probably heading for a loading dock or door, and Jimmy's grin faded too. "Well, if you feel you should."

There was a moment of silence. Jimmy had called his bluff, and it suggested we knew more than we should. It was a dangerous play, and Jimmy knew better, but like I said, no sense of humor, and the truck was right there.

And then the man gestured, and the two cars pulled in on either end of the SUV, blocking us in.

I yanked the handle and leapt out of the car, skimming around the obstructing car and bolting across the parking lot. I'm not quick like some of the Fae, but I can move pretty well, and I reached the warehouse before the guy who'd told us to move on or the guys from the cars could catch up. They all chased after me, leaving Jimmy alone except for one goon who somehow tripped as he passed Jimmy and went down hard on the asphalt. Humans can be so clumsy.

The truck was backing into the warehouse area behind the accounting office, and I dove through the gap between truck and wall. Apparently the guy inside wasn't expecting me because he went down under our impact. I wasn't expecting him either, unfortunately, and our tangled limbs slowed us as we both tried to get up first.

Children laughed. Not a lot of them, as they were across the warehouse and behind the office and most were still watching the cartoon screen, but a handful laughed at us. I stared. There were so many of them—maybe three dozen. This wasn't a small-time pedo ring, this was major business, probably into resale.

Looking at the kids had been a bad idea. The goon's right hook staggered me and I hit the warehouse floor. The two chasing me through the parking lot arrived and kicked me hard in quick sequence.

Fights aren't like what you see in most movies. They're nasty, brutal things, and once you're on the ground and outnumbered you're pretty much done. So I was glad when Jimmy leaned around the edge of the loading door and shouted, "Freeze!"

They looked at him for a moment, and that was all I needed. I twisted off the ground despite my ringing head and dented kidney and I bolted. The warehouse was full of steel shelving and racks of plastic-bound pallets, and I skimmed up like a squirrel on meth.

No, really, it's one of the things we're good at. Speed and grace are in all the old stories. Lots of the great parkour artists have a little Fae in them, and one of the world's top rhythmic gymnasts actually dopes with fairy blood; there's just no test for that yet.

Oh, and the steel? Good thing I was wearing my gloves. My hands tingled a bit, but I'm used to that.

Jimmy had retreated around the door again, and apparently the goons realized he hadn't actually declared *police* or flashed a badge. They scattered, two heading for the kids while a third began circling the steel shelving, looking up.

If you haven't been in a warehouse like that, that shelving is pretty tall. I was probably twenty-five feet above the floor, crouching on a pallet of boxes marked "Hella Catty." Cheap knockoffs don't even try anymore. I stayed in the middle of the pallet, so it would be hard for him to see me unless he got me silhouetted against one of the overhead lights. A little glamour would have been really useful, but that genetic lottery is pretty hard to win.

Another goon came in, a little scuffed, which meant Jimmy had gotten out of sight somewhere. With any luck he was calling 911, reporting an assault in progress and speeding up the police arrival a bit. On the other hand, the last time I called—to report what looked like a heart attack I'd spotted through a bus window on the highway—the dispatcher told me they'd get someone out when they got to it. So my hopes weren't exactly pinned on the cavalry arriving.

As long as I was up here, I might as well be doing something useful. I slid my phone from my pocket and took several pictures of the kids in their group around the television, the warehouse, and the creeps who were keeping them there. And then the office door opened, and I took a picture of a woman.

It shouldn't have surprised me; lots of women work in trafficking. Some of them were victims themselves once, and some are just twisted, perverted sickos. Don't get me wrong, it's awful when a man does it— but when a woman exchanges maternal instinct for predatory, it's somehow worse. Maybe that's not politically correct to say, but Fae feelings go back a lot further than the PC style guide.

I took another picture of her, all neat department store clothing and smooth dark skin and middle class, and then I shoved my phone back into my pocket. She strode through the kids and pointed to the truck with a smile. "Okay, it's time for our ride! You get to ride in the back, and we're going to all go get ice cream."

The kids cheered and got to their feet, mostly. A couple were slow to rise and didn't look enthused, and my half-Fae heart squeezed in me. They acted like they'd been someplace bad for a long time. Easy victims, already broken.

Sometimes, in the old days, the Fae stole children from homes that weren't homes.

If these guys got the kids into the truck, they could take them just about anywhere. We had to stop them here. I eyed the truck, but from this high angle I couldn't see the license plate, or it was on one of the doors which hung open.

The kids started moving in a cluster across the warehouse, a few looking over their shoulders at the cartoons still running. The floor was littered with empty chip bags, microwaved popcorn bags, cookie packages, pizza boxes. Cheap fodder for the livestock.

Shakespeare did get a few things right, and one of them was that Titania (she's fine with that name, really) took the orphaned boy for his mother's sake and meant to raise him well. She's like that. But she wouldn't have given him up, not for Oberon or all the equine-headed peasants you might throw at her.

Not clear yet? Imagine all the motherly tenderness and protectiveness you've ever seen in a human. Now refine that in whatever crucible you like until it is a pure elemental force of the Fae, raw power honed to maternal instinct. Getting the idea?

Changlings are one thing, because they're usually taken to be coddled and petted and raised as fairy's own. But Titania is displeased when a human child is stolen by human predators.

And so she deputized me.

I slid to the edge of the pallet, looking down, and reflected that I hadn't seen the driver yet. That meant he was still in the truck, and he could drive away with any kids who got in. I hoped Jimmy would do something about that—maybe a little carjacking for a cause—but I couldn't count on it.

And then one of the goons shouted and drew a gun. His first shot skimmed over my left shoulder and into the light behind me.

I ducked beneath the showering glass—at least my silhouette was gone now—and bared teeth in a savage snarl-cum-grin. A snarl, because he'd just pulled a gun and started shooting in front of children. A grin, because he'd just escalated the situation to my level of competency.

The Fae are specialists. There are some who could have walked into the warehouse and spoken with the traffickers and walked out leading all the children skipping in a neat line, with the traffickers clutching a five-dollar bill and pleased with the deal. My bloodline isn't the kind that's good with words.

I whipped my slim Walther from its leather holster inside my waistband and shot into the empty floor of the bread truck. I know, it's illegal—can't shoot unless it's life or death, and if you can afford to shoot anywhere else it's obviously not life or death—but I wanted to scare them off the truck and I wasn't quite ready to kill them yet.

I was close. I mean, child sex traffickers are kind of like really ugly spiders, only without the ecological benefits. But not quite.

The lead goon jerked backward, because running toward a truck with bullets flying at it is kind of mentally hard to do, and kids were screaming and covering their ears. Two of the men started shooting at me, but the light was gone and I slid back, so they had to shoot the whole pallet of Hella Catty figurines while I crept over to the Hella Catty T-shirts, which would do a better job of stopping bullets anyway.

Gunshots are loud, and echoing in a warehouse makes them worse. I flattened against the T-shirt boxes and shielded my ears, waiting for the idiots below to get bored. The gun felt warm through my jeans in a way that had nothing to do with the shot, and I rotated my arm to hold it away from myself. Polymer firearms are a kindness, but the barrel is still steel.

The third man ran for the office, probably intending to grab incriminating paperwork or computers and get out the front door. I didn't care; I had his picture, his skeevy partners were still here to rat on him, and I don't even kill spiders when they're running away.

The woman knelt in the center of the kids, pulling them close to her. At first I thought she was comforting the scared kids, the hypocritical monster, and then I thought she was just getting low in case of a ricochet. But then I saw her looping their clasped arms over her neck and boosting one little girl—Alexis—onto her shoulders and pulling two boys to her torso, and I realized what she was doing.

Middle-class sex trafficking bitch struggled to her feet, weighted by eight or so terrified little kids clinging to her for security, and started toward the truck, protected by her meat shield of children.

And that's when I lost my sense of humor. There's a line, and using children as a bullet shield for your getaway is a few steps past it. I slid along the Hella Catty T-shirts, squeezing the polymer grip of my Walther and pressing my index fingertip hard into the frame.

The two guys below were still aiming high, looking for me. They'd have a clear shot in a moment, but I wouldn't give them long to take it. Moving shots—at a moving target, or from a moving position—are a lot harder than Hollywood makes them look.

She would reach the truck in another dozen steps. The goons between us were about fifteen yards away. I took a deep, slow breath, wrapped both hands around the Walther, sighted on the first gunman, and jumped.

I fired the first shot just as my legs straightened. He was aiming high, leaving his chest exposed, and I put two rounds where his heart would have been if he'd been in a different profession. More shots boomed across the warehouse as his fellow goon tried for me, but as I was jumping through my downward arc at thirty-six feet per second and his ammunition traveled eight hundred fifty feet per second, he'd need to aim about twenty-three inches ahead for his bullet to have a chance of finding me. And he wasn't that good.

I was. I switched targets and put a round into the other gunman, enough to take him out of the fight if not out of the world. I landed, rolled, and came up with my sights on the woman. "Drop the kids."

The kids stared, wide-eyed and too afraid to move. She laughed. She boosted one kid higher in her arms, to more completely shield her face, and so help me, she *laughed*. It was nervous laughter, but it was still all kinds of wrong.

Headshots, contrary to Hollywood and video game lore, are tricky and unreliable. The skull exists for the sole purpose of deflecting impact away from the brain, and it's shaped to do exactly that. There are only a couple of points where a bullet will reliably penetrate, and this waste of breath was wearing children like human mufflers.

But she'd left one eye exposed to watch me as she started again for the truck.

Low-velocity hollowpoints don't make the biggest holes, but they're a lot less likely to run through the intended target and hit someone on the other side. Kids screamed and tumbled as the woman collapsed where she stood, but none were actually hurt.

Don't ever try that, by the way. It's not the kind of thing humans should risk. The Fae are specialists, and even in your post-modern ultra-science reality, your kind still knows it. Every elven ranger in a basement D&D game, every computer-generated battle sequence featuring Legolas trashing orcs is tribute to our ancient and arcane skill. Humans have their own advantages—my aching temple and kidney could testify to that—but when it comes to projectiles, you'll never quite match the Fae.

The driver must have been watching, because he slammed the truck into gear and pulled out, rear doors swinging. I didn't do anything about it—there's no good way to stop a truck, and there were three dozen crying children in front of me. I holstered the gun, knelt, and held out my arms.

The kids should have been terrified of me, after seeing me jump out of nowhere and shoot three people. But maybe they knew something was wrong about their captors, or maybe they recognized something in me, or maybe it was just any friendly adult in a storm of distress, because they came to me and hugged me and each other, some crying, some unnaturally quiet.

I just sat there, their warmth and youth and life all around me, and wept.

Jimmy came in and hugged some kids, too. He stood and went to the open loading door when the police arrived, waving them in. They had a full team, even counselors to collect the kids. I stood slowly, hands spread to show I meant no threat.

They took the kids outside, away from their prison and the bodies, and bundled the injured goon into an ambulance. Then they started on the dead man and woman. I described most of what had happened, pointing out the shattered light, my bruising face, the dent where a swinging truck door had struck the loading door's track as it raced away.

The officers listening to me were having trouble keeping up. Maybe I was talking a little fast and not quite calmly. "Hold on one sec, sir," said one. "I need to get this more slowly."

His partner gave him a pained look and turned back to me. "Sorry, ma'am." He paused, now uncertain. "Er, what's your name, please?"

I gave a tight little smile. "Robin Archer."

I could see by their faces that the name didn't help. Well, sorry. Best I can do.

"Can we have some ID? Including your permit?"

I shook my head. "I don't have my wallet with me, left it at home. Didn't exactly know I was going to happen into all this. I can show it later."

Jimmy knew the drill—he didn't really know me, I ate at the Steer & Beer sometimes but that was it, he just happened to be near when I told him there were kids in danger. Interrogating him about me wouldn't get them far. And I really would show my ID later—if there were a later. I'm legal, but we kind of don't like getting tangled up with human authority.

"Look, I really want to go to the bathroom." They would understand that. "There'll be one in the office area. Can I go?"

The officers exchanged glances and nodded. "He'll just stand outside," one said, "where he can see the door, okay?"

I nodded.

If the officer who followed me was hoping to see which gender I chose, he was out of luck, because it was a single unisex restroom. Ah, well, one more thing for him to puzzle over, along with why I wouldn't be there whenever he finally forced the door. Portals to the Twilight Lands are much harder than scrying and not to be made lightly, but I'd rather be in bed for a week than sorting details with the police for far longer, and they pretty much have to detain someone who shoots a woman in the face, no matter how much she deserved it.

I pushed back the unlatched door and waved to the waiting officer. "I'll be out in a minute." Not exactly a lie, as I would be out of the room. Just not this way.

I was startled by the boy curled into the corner of the bathroom, squeezed between the toilet and the wall, maybe ten years old. He looked at me with dull, frightened eyes, like a street dog who half-expects to be kicked and isn't certain if it's worth trying to avoid it.

I held a finger to my lips and squatted before the toilet. I whispered. "You didn't go to the truck."

He shook his head.

"You knew what they were?"

"Guessed enough." His voice was flat.

I should have sent him out to the officer, but his eyes were too lifeless. "You were going to run home?"

He shook his head, as I knew he would.

I nodded toward the warehouse and the swarming authorities. "Is anyone looking for you?"

One shoulder twitched, hardly a movement. "Not sure. Left th' foster home. Sixth."

There would be a report for him somewhere, but he was deep in the system. It was a system which tried its best, but it dealt with tough situations, and it couldn't save every kid.

Sometimes, in the old days . . . .

I held out a hand. "Come away, human child?"

He looked at me, curious with the first flicker of emotion. "Where?"

"The wood, the water, the wild."

He was old to be taken, but he had little holding him. He looked at me a moment, and then he reached for my hand.

~*~

Editor's Note: "YES! Now *this voice* is a reason to have a first person narrator. And to top it off, this story isn't just set in Indianapolis, it is oh-so-incredibly-Indianapolis, right down to the pork tenderloin sandwiches . . ." That was how the Editor-in-Chief of World Weaver Press, Eileen Wiedbrauk, responded to this story when she read it in my shortlist. This is one of my favourite stories in this collection and I don't think I could describe it any better than Eileen did. YES!

~*~

SEVEN YEARS FLEETING

Lor Graham

I first saw her watching me from the hillock where the garden became the beach. Mam didn't let us go down there alone. I just saw the flash of red curls, and then those huge brown eyes swallowed me whole.

I was seven years old, and I had just fallen in love for the first time.

It took me three days to say hello.

She was better at hopscotch than my little sister, and better at skimming stones into the sea than me. She joined us when Mam took us down to the beach for picnics, and charmed her without trying.

I was seven, and I was in love.

On the days the rain battered the bothy, and that happened a lot that summer, she would turn up at the door, water streaming from her curls. We dried her out by the fire, peeling vegetables for Mam to make soup.

Those were happy days.

When we sat on the shore, in the quiet moments broken only by the skreel of the gulls, she would stare out at the sea, as though desperate to return. Yet she never joined us swimming, preferring to sit on the rocks and smirk at our attempts at the strokes.

She was strange, and I loved her for it.

We laughed a lot that summer, at each other, at and with my sister, and at the sheep in their field. To us, the bothy with its flock of sheep, the garden left to grow over since Father had left and the beach beyond were the entirety of our world. To us it was enormous, a fitting home for our expanding imaginations.

We were pirates, storming up from the beach to take the fort made of branches in the middle of the garden. Removing the splinters that evening was painful.

We were soldiers, re-enacting the Normandy landings on the beach, being brave like Father, all the time hoping he would return to us soon. Mam watched these games with wet eyes and a sad smile.

We took the dog out one day, and attempted to round up the sheep. My sister, only four at the time, ruined the fun by breaking her leg, and getting us banned from the field altogether.

All of this time we never thought to ask where she came from, or why she would only talk to me.

I was in love, so to me none of it mattered. To me, her being there, joining in my games, was the best thing in the world. I decided she only spoke to me because she was in love with me too.

And then summer began to wane, bringing with it a chill in the breeze, and the talk of returning to school. To me this was a disaster, the removal of my time with her every day was the end of my world. She giggled when I told her this, and raced me to climb the apple tree in the garden to take my mind off of it.

She never mentioned going to school, and I never questioned it. In my world, she existed for adventure.

The first morning back at school arrived, with the earlier than usual start for the two mile walk to the school house. I watched for her all morning, for she would have to walk the same road I did, but there was no sign of her bright red curls, or her brown woolen dress.

She wasn't in my class, and there was no hint of her in the playground. That afternoon, I ran most of the way home, glad my little sister was still at home with her broken leg, as that way she couldn't slow me down.

Mam hadn't seen her, and I spent the rest of my afternoon sitting in the apple tree, watching for any sign of her approach.

It was a week before I resigned myself to the fact that she was gone.

I was seven years old, and I was heartbroken for the first time.

_*_

I was twenty-one, and I was bored.

I knew I had only gotten this scholarship because of my good grades, and that I should be grateful for the opportunity to study further, but I hated the city, and I hated the people in my classes. They were from the wealthy families, and had made it clear from the start that I was an outsider.

I embraced it.

On Saturdays I took the train out to the coast, and spent my days fishing in the sea. I knew I could get to this place as we'd been here on a field trip, to see the new bridges they were building. I knew I was never going to apply my engineering knowledge to building bridges, but they were interesting nonetheless.

This place was better without my classmates.

I didn't hear her approaching, despite us being the only two people on the cliffs. One moment I was alone, the next she was sitting next to me, red curls twirling in the wind, bare pale feet poking out from below her dress as she sat cross-legged.

I didn't know what to say for the longest time.

She began to sing, a beautifully sad song of the sea. I knew then that I was right, that the things I had read in the library were true. I asked her of her nature, and she merely smiled in return. I found I didn't care, I was lost in her large brown eyes.

I was twenty-one, and I was in love with her all over again.

I began to skip classes in order to go to the shore and see her. I knew from experience she wouldn't be around for long, and I wanted to spend every minute possible with her. I was young and impulsive, and in love. It was a dangerous combination. I didn't care about eating, about sleeping, I just wanted to be with her, to lie with her, to give myself to her.

I fell ill, and the day I was admitted to the hospital was the day she disappeared. I know, because my hospital room overlooked the cliffs where I fished, and I watched them all day every day. I never once glimpsed her long red curls, her brown woollen dress, nor did I hear her sad song of the sea.

I recovered, slowly. The doctor said I had contracted pneumonia, a result of spending so much time by the sea this late in the year. He warned me I had to rest and I had to stay warm, and then he let me leave.

I took one last look at the shoreline as I left my room, but I knew in my heart I wouldn't see her again. Her time here was only brief, and in making the most of it I had made myself ill. I promised myself I would never be so foolish over a girl again, and headed to the station to get the train back into the city.

I was twenty-one, and I had had my heart broken for the second time.

⁓*⁓

I was thirty-five, and I was tied down.

I sat at a table outside of the café on the promenade, pushing the baby's pram back and forward gently, trying to lull my son to sleep. We had come to the seaside as a family, but late in the season as it was the only time I could afford the room and board.

My wife had been struck down by a cold after our time on the beach the day before, and I had offered to take the lad out to allow her to get some rest. The poor mite was at the end of colic, so sleep was sparse for him too.

People often commented that I had left it late to have a family, that I ought to have been married much earlier, but I just told them that I hadn't found the right woman until I was that bit older.

Truth was, I hadn't been able to let go of the fantasy that I might be able to keep her with me until I had grown up a bit.

The thought seemed to summon her, because I looked up from my crossword and there she was, smiling across the little table at me.

Despite everything, my heart leapt at the sight of her.

She cooed over the baby, slipping a coin under his blanket, and commented on how he had my eyes, as everyone did. All the while she had that smile across her face.

I was thirty-five, and I hated her.

I asked her why she had never said goodbye when she left, why she kept coming back, but would never stay with me.

She didn't reply, she just looked at me with those big brown eyes, the sorrow glistening in them.

She said I was better off without her.

I left then, just got up and walked away with the pram, remembering at the last moment to throw down some money on the table to pay for my tea and scone. She trailed after me, shouted after me, but it was easier just to walk on, to smile down at my son and calm him after his fright.

We got strange stares from passersby, but they were easier to ignore than she was.

I was angry because now she had turned up again, I knew I wasn't giving my whole heart to my wife and son.

I was thirty-five, and I was torn in two.

Eventually I had to stop, I was just too tired to keep up the pace I had set, and I collapsed on to a bench. I was at entirely the opposite end of the promenade from our hotel, so it was going to be a long walk back.

She sat down next to me, and held my hand as I cried. I cried for what could have been, for what was and for what was going to be. I was stuck in a job I hated for the sake of my family, and she had just reminded me that I could have had so much more.

She kept popping up over the next couple of days, thankfully never approaching when I was with my wife, because I had no idea how to introduce her.

The only other time she spoke to me was late one night, when I had gone to the pub for a drink, and was making my slow way back to the hotel. We were to leave the next morning, and whilst I told myself that I just wanted to make the most of the sea air, I knew in my heart I was just hoping to see her again.

She was dressed as she always was, in that brown woollen dress, barefoot despite the wet left from the evening's rain.

She was wary now, apparently scared to come too close after my outburst a few days before. We just stood looking at each other for the longest moment. Eventually, although I had no idea where it came from, I had the courage to step closer. I took her in my arms beneath the full moon, and we stood there until we were both cold though.

I was thirty-five, and that was the first time I had held her in my arms.

~*~

I was forty-two, and I was burying my wife.

We stood on the hill overlooking the sea, the grave gaping open at our feet, my son's face buried in my thigh. My trousers were soaked through with his tears. The sun shone down on us, and up on us, reflected in the surf. It was mocking us.

It had been sudden, a car accident whilst on the way to pick our son up from school, and a night in the hospital on the best machinery they could muster, but it wasn't enough. The doctor said her brain had shut down to try and repair the damage, but from what they could tell, it wouldn't be a battle she could win.

She looked so small lying in the hospital bed.

The lad had become withdrawn in the days since we had received the phone call, telling us she had left us, not speaking a word to me and grudgingly eating his meals. He would hide away in his room, and didn't know I had overheard him talking to his teddy bear, telling Alfie how much he missed his mummy already.

I was forty-two, and my world had been shattered.

Naturally, that's when she chose to appear.

I just stared in the beginning, not sure I was really seeing her, almost wishing that the sun was just playing tricks on my eyes and casting images into the spray. I blinked, hard, trying to clear my vision. She was there.

I looked down at my son, hand on his shoulder, and managed to pry him off of my leg. He looked up at me from under his sandy fringe, green eyes swimming with tears, and sniffed. I did my best to smile for him, and nodded down the hill to where the rest of the family were milling about the gates, comparing their grief before heading to their cars. I told the lad to go and catch his aunt, and get her to get him some squash and a sandwich when they got to the social club where the wake was being held.

He clung to my trousers, wanting to know why I wouldn't go with him. I looked up at her, wordless, and then he looked up too. He looked right through her, I could tell by his continued pleas. I didn't know what to tell him. Thoughts rushed around my head, and I had to fight to calm them.

Eventually I told him I wanted to say a last goodbye to mummy, alone, and he sniffed again, but nodded. I watched him stumble down the hill, looking tiny in his formal black coat, and then turned back to look at her.

She hadn't aged a day since we were twenty-one, and that almost hurt more than the fact she had chosen today of all days to show up.

She held out her hand, and led me away from the grave, to the low wall that marked the boundary of the graveyard. It also marked the cliff, the sea churning against the rocks a dizzying drop below as we sat down.

I was forty-two, and I suddenly felt seven all over again.

She told me she was sorry for my loss, and I thanked her for the thought. The wind whipped her hair around her face, hiding her eyes from me. I don't know why, but that was even more unsettling than seeing them.

I could lose myself in them when I could see them.

From I don't know where, she pulled out a little box, a plain brown box, and held it out to me. I took it as though it was electrocuted, belatedly realising, as I teased it open, that this was the first time I had noticed her own anything other than her brown dress.

The box contained a small patch of fur, the same brown as her dress, curled like her hair, and damp with sea spray. I felt my brow furrow as I looked at it, my mind seeming to run despite me grief.

She told me if I accepted it, she would stay with me forever. I just stared at it for a long moment, my head a foggy mess.

I stood up, and hurled it into the sea.

I was forty-two, and I had just had my heartbroken for the last time.

~*~

I was fifty-six, and I was dying.

It had started as a migraine the summer before, instilling in me a weakness that left me scared. It had taken several days lying in a dark room to recover. The lad had been home from university, working for the summer, and his eyes said it all when he found me, collapsed on the kitchen floor that afternoon.

As soon as I could move about again he insisted I visit the doctor. So we went, and spent the morning sitting in a waiting room full of coughing, whispered concern, crying babes and stifling heat. The lad couldn't sit still, shifting in his seat as though his backside were on fire, and running back and forth to the reception desk, asking constantly how much longer until we're seen, don't you know my Da is ill?

I was fifty-six, and not for the first time in my life, I was scared.

The doctor, when we eventually saw him, was exhausted. A nasty bout of summer 'flu, he said, the surgery had been backlogged all week, all the staff having to work extra hours to deal with the demand. And then he smiled, a wan smile but a smile none the less, and asked how he could help.

As I had expected, he said it was just a migraine, and whilst it was more unusual for them to come on at my age, it wasn't unheard of. I just had to rest, and take painkillers as soon as I felt a headache coming on, just in case. The lad opened his mouth to protest, cranky beyond belief after the morning we'd had, but I caught hold of his arm, squeezing it, and thanked the doctor for his time.

The lad nearly burst my eardrums in the car home, and brought on another headache. He stormed out of the house, the door rattling in the doorframe after him, and I have no idea if he came home that night.

The next time it happened I was at the wheel of the car.

I woke up in a bed in Accident and Emergency, the harsh light biting into my vision the moment I opened my eyes. I screwed them shut, and felt something squeeze my hand, hard. Blinking to clear my vision, I opened my eyes again to see it was the lad, eyes red in his pale face, knuckles white as he clung on to me. I shook him off, massaging my hand to get the feeling back, and he managed a weak laugh.

And then the doctor came in.

I was fifty-six, and I was given a death sentence.

Inoperable brain tumour, a year at most to live.

So now here I lay, after a major seizure, hospital bound by doctor's orders, to live out the last few days of my life in perpetual boredom. The pain came and went, and I slept around it, regardless if it were day or night. The lad came and went too, around his classes and homework. I was almost glad when he left; I couldn't stand the almost constant tears.

The pain woke me one night, a stabbing above my left eye, into a world lit only by the full moon from outside the window, and the blinking of the heart monitor I was attached to.

She was there.

She still hadn't aged, was perfect at the age of twenty-one. She smiled, silent tears streaking down her cheeks, and told me she was sorry to hear the news. I asked how she had gotten in, past the staff, and she said they had taken her to be my son's twin sister. She said even if they hadn't, she would have found a way.

I asked what she wanted, and she leant forward, kissing me on the temple.

I was fifty-six, and for the first time in my life I admitted to myself that she was the woman I loved over everything else. I smiled, a tight smile against sudden hot pain, glad I was able to see her one last time.

My vision faded amidst the flatline beep of the heart monitor. The last thing I remember was the scent of the sea, an oddly sad scent.

I was fifty-six, and my time was up.

_*_

Editor's Note: She would have stayed with him forever. I'm going to say that again. She would have stayed with him *forever*. All he needed to do was accept her gift but instead he tossed it into the sea. That is what makes this story for me. He could have claimed her, but he didn't. What was he thinking in the moment he decided to throw the fur to the waves? That's the question that will make me keep coming back to this one, reading it again and again, trying to get into his head and really understand.

_*_

THE LAST KING

Liz Colter

A sudden spring rain pattered on the leaves above Anna's head, causing her to look up from the tangle of roots criss-crossing the woodland path. The rain didn't seem able to penetrate the thick foliage. She decided to go on a bit farther as the walk was clearing the clutter in her head that her boss, her job and her lemon of a car always managed to engender.

Already she had gone deeper into the woods than ever before; past the sunlit birch and oak and into the heavy, dark trees near what must be the center of this grove. Her rotten sense of direction and perpetual fear of getting lost yammered at her, but it felt good to push the boundaries of her comfort zone. She had carefully counted every branch since leaving the main trail—three forks, always to the right.

Besides, if this helped rebuild some of the self-confidence Sam had stripped from her, then it was all for the good. Hard to believe it had been three months since she had moved from Chicago to England to escape her psycho boyfriend—long past time to rediscover the person she used to be.

Anna distracted herself from thoughts of getting hopelessly lost by recalling the story her landlady had told her; a local myth about a fay king and his trooping fairies that came to this woods once every hundred years. With the rain on the leaves sounding like tiny feet, Anna could almost picture wee-folk running through the tree tops, playing in the foliage, and watching her from behind the large boles.

Turning to note the landmarks behind her, she realized the woods were getting darker. Probably from the rain, she thought. Unless the sun was setting. She wasn't wearing a watch and *had* walked farther than she planned. Resisting the urge to panic, she did a quick calculation and told herself it couldn't possibly be sunset yet.

She had only gone a few feet farther when she heard a sound like soft whispers beneath the rain. Turning first one way and then the other, she stared between the thick trunks. From the corner of her eye, she thought she glimpsed movement in the shadows. Gooseflesh pricked her arms and made the fine hairs of her neck stand on end.

"Quit it!" she said as firmly as she could, trying to convince herself that nothing was there, but the eerie feeling continued to grow.

The creepiness won out over her desire to prove her confidence, and she suddenly very much wanted out of these woods. Forcing herself not to hurry, she turned and started back. The little feet playing in the treetops abruptly became thousands of feet, drumming a loud tattoo on the leaves. Big wet drops found their way through the canopy.

Anna began to trot, stifling nerves that told her to run full out. She came to a fork she didn't remember. Veering left, she continued to jog, pulling up short when she reached a dead end of thick, thorny gorse.

"Oh, crap! Calm, Anna, just be calm." Her heart beat in great, heavy thumps and she tried not to hyperventilate. "Think, God damn it!"

She turned and hurried back the way she had come, scanning for the fork again. The trail narrowed without branching until it was no more than an animal track. Anna stopped, staring at the dark trunks, like sentinels all around her, crowding her to stillness. Her body was stationary but her heart kept running, beating a hard, fast rhythm against her ribs. She had no idea what direction might lead her home.

"Are you looking for something?" a voice said.

Anna jumped so hard her shoulders jerked and a choked noise popped out of her mouth. She whirled. A man stood just a few feet away. Adrenaline coursed through her body, making her lightheaded, but the man remained perfectly still. Anna's heart and breath limped back into sustainable rhythms. As she calmed, she became aware just how beautiful he was. Not handsome. Beautiful. So beautiful that she couldn't stop staring.

He was of medium height, with a face and body like a work of art. His skin was pale, even for England in March, but radiant with health, and she guessed him to be about her age, late twenties. He wore a light jerkin and breeches with soft, high boots, all in shades of brown. She knew that should seem odd, but his clothes fit him as naturally as bark fit a tree. He wore his black hair longer than current fashion, and even in this poor light she could see the blue of his eyes. Her landlady had warned her that Gypsies sometimes camped in these woods, and she wondered if he was one of them.

Anna realized she hadn't answered him, but she couldn't seem to pull away from those eyes—deeper than sky blue, brighter than bluebells. Heat rose in her face and she forced herself to say something, anything. "I . . . I was walking by myself. I got scared, and when I turned around I got lost. I was trying to find my way back."

Wrong, wrong, wrong. Where had that little regurgitation of facts come from? She was pretty sure her Women's Self Defense class in Chicago would have advised against telling a strange man in the middle of the woods that you were alone and lost and scared. "Um, what I mean is, I missed my turnoff back there."

He smiled. She wouldn't have believed he could be more handsome until she saw that smile. She tried to collect herself but her thoughts were becoming less and less coherent. Physical attraction had always been her downfall—the first catalyst in each of her disastrous relationships—but this was more. Much more. She felt like a twig in a strong current.

He crossed the distance between them, coming so close she could feel the heat radiate from his body. His skin had a sweet, clean scent. Her breath quickened. She wanted him to touch her. She could imagine it as clearly as if it was happening; sliding his fingers under her hair, his strong hands cupping her head. His mouth moving to hers.

His warm breath on her face just before his tongue slid past her lips.

She blinked. He was watching her with those fathomless blue eyes, he hadn't moved, hadn't lifted a hand to her. *What was happening? Why couldn't she think straight?*

"Come. Walk with me," he said.

He extended his elbow and she slipped her arm through his without hesitation. His skin below the short-sleeved jerkin was so warm it felt fevered. Touching his flesh sparked a sensual reaction, like an electric shock that ran from her arm down her body, leaving a residual pulse lingering in her groin.

He took them deeper into the woods. One part of Anna craved his physical touch so much she felt she would do anything for it but a deeper, quieter part of her was terrified. Images of the two of them together, naked bodies twined, kept flitting through her mind. The little pocket of fear suppressed deeper with every step.

Anna had always been pretty enough to interest men, but she felt plain and dull next to him. He moved so gracefully that she felt clumsy. She should have worried about where he was taking her, but instead she worried that he might not be as attracted to her as she was to him.

"Let me show you a favorite place of mine," he said. Anna thought she heard a Scottish brogue in his soft voice.

She would never be appealing to him if she stayed mute. "You know these woods well." Her voice croaked, ugly and harsh compared to his.

"Every root and branch," he replied. "Though Andredsweald is a poor fragment now of what it once was."

Andredsweald? Her landlady called this Glover's Wood. Not that it mattered. Nothing mattered except being with him.

He brought her to a small clearing, surrounded by trees so huge that three men together wouldn't be able to encircle one of their trunks. Their long, leafy arms reached across to one another, touching in the middle like dancers in a reel.

"It's wonderful," she said.

Green grass grew within the circle, making a soft mattress, and he helped her down. He lay on his side next to her, propped on one elbow with his head cradled in his hand, those blue eyes looking right into her soul. He asked her name.

"Annabelle Jane Clayton," she blurted out, wanting him to know everything about her.

"Annabelle," he rolled the name on his tongue, making it elegant where she had always thought it old fashioned and silly sounding. "I am Tamlane." He looked expectant. The name meant nothing to her and she worried that it would disappoint him.

The fingers of his free hand pushed a lock of blonde hair from her shoulder. He traced her neck and collarbone, making her shiver. She stopped trying to make sense of things. She didn't care. All she wanted in the world was to feel his touch on her skin.

His hand moved lower, following the V of her neckline. She gasped when his feverishly warm fingers slid beneath her sweater and bra. The electricity returned to her groin with new intensity. Removing his hand from her breast, he deftly slipped it to the belt at her jeans. Anna moved to accommodate him. "I shouldn't," she managed to say. The distant, frightened part of her knew it for truth and fought to surface.

"But I have chosen you," he said, as if that settled everything.

He chose her. This beautiful man. The bubble of fear drifted away.

She heard a light giggle from behind the trees. Childish faces, blue-tinged in the gloom, peeked around the large trunks. She saw a hint of nearly transparent wings. She didn't care that they were being watched . . . or by what.

Tamlane shifted his weight. One hand continued to work at the belt while his other pulled her sweater and bra to the side, uncovering her breast. His mouth lowered. She closed her eyes in an ecstasy of sensations too powerful for her body to reconcile.

Anna opened her eyes again to a shadow gliding just above the high branches, black against the gloom of the sky. The shape was that of an enormous bird but instinct told her it was no bird. Tamlane glanced up as well and, in one quick move, threw himself over her, hiding her beneath his body. The heat and scent of him smothered her. His phallus was hard, though there was nothing sexual in what he did now. He lay over her no more than a moment before he rolled away. The shadow was gone.

Fear and confusion pierced Anna's desire for Tamlane like a pin to a bubble, and left her sick and shaking. *What had she been doing? She didn't even know this man.* She didn't understand what that strange thing overhead had been, or why he hid her, or anything that was happening. Tears rolled down her cheeks and she sat up, fumbling to pull her clothes together.

"I would rather he doesn't discover you just yet," Tamlane said, by way of explanation. Seeing it did nothing to reassure her, he continued, "Soon you will be one of us and this will all be easier." He stood, grinning, suddenly expansive. "I will plan a feast for you tomorrow. A celebration to welcome you to our host." It rang from his lips like a pronouncement.

His words washed over her, making no sense. The heat of desire was gone and the empty place where it had been left her disoriented and numb.

Holding a hand out to her, he helped her up. He glanced upward, casually. "Come," he said, "let's get you home for now."

He led her along the dark paths until they came to the end of the old forest. Dusky twilight bled through the thinner trees ahead and she recognized where she was.

Tamlane turned to her and gently brushed a leaf from her hair. Placing his hands on her shoulders, he held her gaze, serious now. "Come back tomorrow," he said. She felt his words settle in her bones like a weight.

Anna nodded and turned to go, still numb and confused.

"After your feast, we can finish what we started tonight," he called after her. She could hear the smile in his voice. She nodded again without looking back.

~*~

She hurried up the trail, worried that it would be full dark before she was out of the woods. She was lucky that man had been nearby to help her find the trail when she got lost.

That man. Had she even asked his name? Funny, she couldn't remember, only that he had led her back to the path. She couldn't remember his face either, though he'd been stunningly handsome. Now he was like a charcoal drawing that had gotten smeared by the rain. Oh, well . . . good-looking men always muddled her brains.

The next day at work Anna watched the clock so often, a few times she thought the hands had stopped moving. She wasn't sure why she was so anxious to get home and take a walk, but it was all she could think about. At four-o-clock on the nose, she was packed up and headed out the door.

Once home, Anna changed quickly into walking clothes. She left her cottage and followed the footpath through the sheep pasture and into the trees. Taking the main path a short way into the woods, she turned off on a little-used trail. She veered right at every fork, hurrying on until she came to a stand of ancient trees, taller and darker than the surrounding woods. Drawn forward by an urge she couldn't define, Anna stepped under the gloomy arch.

Suddenly, she remembered.

All of it.

Getting lost. Tamlane. He had taken her deeper into the forest and he had . . . she had nearly . . . *Oh, my God*. She needed to get out of here. If she ran only a few yards, she would be free.

Her mind raced, but her feet didn't move. She looked back at the lighter woods behind, wanting to leave but unwilling to go. Other memories came to her now, memories which heated her blood. Anna brushed the breast where his mouth had touched her and she shuddered. She wanted him more than she had ever wanted anyone.

Run, Anna. The part of her mind where self-preservation dwelt screamed at her. The part that had made her move all the way to England to get away from Sam.

"So," a deep voice said. Her head jerked to the right at the sound, afraid and excited that it might be Tamlane. It wasn't.

The speaker was leaning in the shadow of a trunk. He pushed upright and came toward her. "You must be the treasure Tam Lin is hiding."

Tam Lin? He had pronounced it Tamlane last night and she hadn't recognized the name. She backed a step as the man neared. Something about him . . . the blackness of his hair and clothes, the way he moved, the sense of danger he carried . . . convinced her he was the shadow that had passed over her last night, though that made no sense.

His skin was light, but his features were hooded. The only trait she could clearly make out was the bright yellow of his eyes. They held no whites and had coal black pupils at their center. There was a mischievousness in those eyes, but it glittered with something familiar. A thing she had seen in Sam's eyes. A cruelty that bordered on madness. Fear lanced into her at the recognition and sliced at the seductive pull that had drawn her back to these woods.

"Beautiful," the shadow-man said. He stopped in front of her. "I see why he wants you for himself." He reached out and stroked her face. It was like cold seaweed brushing her cheek and she shuddered.

"I could do so much more for you, though." He sounded amused. "I could give you a ride if you wish." He shimmered into a huge, ink-black horse, still with piercing yellow eyes. The image lasted only a heartbeat and the man stood before her again.

"Or I could ride you," his voice was deeper, softer, imbued with a menace beyond her ability to imagine. He took a step closer. She wanted to scream, but her throat was too tight. "I could ride you better than *he* ever could."

He wrapped one powerful arm around her waist and pulled her roughly against his body. She pushed at his chest but she might have been a mouse fighting an eagle's talons. She stopped struggling. Her rapid, frightened breaths filled her nose and lungs with his musky scent.

"Tam Lin is nothing so special, you know," he said. "He was once human, like you, until the Faerie Queen took a shining to him. He escaped her once, but came running right back to her when she called. Just as you have come back to him."

The shadow-man was so tall that Anna came only to his chest. His voice grated down at her. It rumbled against her body. She closed her eyes and willed herself to wake from this nightmare.

"Do you know that his kind pay a tithe to Hell?" the shadow-man continued, almost conversationally. "One of their own. It comes due this Hallow's Eve. If he brings you into the faerie host, I think perhaps you will not be with us for long." She forced herself to look up into those yellow eyes and saw truth in their hardness. "Stay with me until the next equinox. Be mine for that time, and I will free you when we move."

She was trapped in a bizarre dream, where fairy tales were real. There was nothing to rely on except instinct. But instinct had saved her before—in Chicago. "If I say yes," her voice shook as she answered, "what then?"

The shadow-man took her by the shoulders and pushed her back to look into her face. The yellow of his eyes pierced her. "Do you desire me?"

He said it like a challenge but she heard the need. He wanted her to choose him over Tamlane. Instead of flattery, she gave him honesty.

"I want to live."

His eyes narrowed to slits of neon yellow and darkest black, weighing her.

"Well enough," he said curtly. He glanced behind him, as if hearing something she couldn't. When he turned back, he spoke quickly. "Tam Lin prepares a feast. You must eat or drink none of it or you will be tied to him. Come to me at the end of the feast. Once we consummate, Tam will lose his power over you."

"How do I resist him?" She had no intention of having sex with this thing, but she needed information. She remembered how helpless she had been in Tamlane's presence.

The shadow-man shrugged. "Some can. Some can't. You must believe you can."

That was hardly the help she had been hoping for.

"After the feast," he continued, "convince him to have one of his foolish processions, it should be easy enough." His lip curled in contempt. "Leave while he is occupied and come to me here."

Forced to couple mindlessly with Tamlane or willingly with the shadow-man. Tithed to Hell. She was thinking more clearly with every new threat.

"Perhaps we should meet outside this forest. I think maybe he can't follow me there." Tamlane had made her come to him. He might be constrained by these old woods. Either way, there was more chance of help outside this unnatural place.

"No." He grabbed her chin in his powerful hand and forced her eyes to meet his. "You must not leave our land again until we have moved on. Tam Lin wanted to keep you from me last night and he was overconfident, as he often is. It would take so little to undo us—a leaf, a twig. You must not risk going back to your world. Do you understand?"

She didn't. She tried to nod 'yes' anyway, but his grip was too strong.

He relaxed and let go of her jaw. "All you need do is meet me here." He glanced over his shoulder again. This time she also heard the soft footfalls.

"Phooka!" She recognized Tamlane's voice. It rang with authority. "Leave her be, Phooka," he said more quietly, emerging from the trees, "or answer to me."

Never taking his eyes from the shadow-man, Tamlane said, "Forgive me, Annabelle. I was detained, seeing to your feast." He reached out and took her arm, pulling her to him.

The shadow-man held her arm a moment longer, like a wish-bone between them, then released his grasp, his sharp, yellow eyes still fixed on Tamlane's blue. He turned, finally, to smile at Anna. Unlike Tamlane's enchanting smile, there was nothing of beauty in the shadow-man's grin. It held a promise of seeing her again, later.

His form shimmered. She had a brief glimpse of a huge bird before it leaped into the air and became a blacker-than-night shadow that skimmed through the high branches and away.

"There, my love," Tamlane said. "He is gone, and I will see that he troubles you no more. I am his better, and he knows it well."

He was dressed in brocades and silks, and he was gorgeous. He brought her close and she couldn't help wrapping her arms around his neck and pressing herself into his sweet warmth. Going from the phooka's embrace to Tamlane's felt like salvation. She wanted to give herself to him right here. She kissed him, feeling his soft, warm lips yield to hers. Something deep inside her rang with alarm. There was something she must not forget.

He saved her from herself. "Not yet, my love," he said. "There will be time aplenty after the feast, but others wait for us now."

He unwound her arms from his neck and took her hand. Together they walked to the ring of trees with the grassy center. A huge table was covered with a white linen cloth and laden with food. Platters of meat, venison she guessed, were held aloft by racks of antlers. Carved wooden bowls overflowed with fruit. Nuts and currents filled side dishes and a silver pitcher sat in the middle of the table. Half a dozen tall chairs covered with brocaded velvet surrounded the table and a gossamer canopy was strung between the great trees.

Tamlane led her to a chair at the head of the table. As she sat, Anna felt the momentary roughness of a tree stump beneath her, the realization forgotten almost as quickly as the sensation itself. Winged, blue-skinned pixies ran naked, chasing each other in the grass. Four men and women entered the meadow, all dressed as elegantly as

Tamlane. She looked down in embarrassment at her sweater and jeans. The four took their seats at the table and Tamlane sat opposite Anna.

"Eat, friends," he said, "and drink. Welcome Annabelle to our host." He poured a cup of red wine from the silver pitcher and raised it to her. The pitcher was passed down, and the man on her left poured wine for Anna. All of them watched without partaking, waiting for her to drink.

Anna reached for the glass. It seemed much smaller than it should, and rough, like a walnut shell, but the thought was so fleeting it was gone before she could hold it. Tamlane was watching her. She didn't care about the feast. All she wanted was to be with him. Forever.

Something tickled at the back of her mind.

Forever.

Would there be a forever for her? The faerie men and women were staring at her. They clenched their wine cups and narrowed eyes the color of gemstones at her hesitation. The shadow-man had warned her of something. *What was it?*

Tamlane's blue eyes urged her to drink. He was a king here, she could see it in the deference of the others. He loved her and she loved him. Why would she not want to do as he asked? She lifted the cup of gold and jewels.

Sam had loved her too, she remembered. He had loved her so much he had cut her off from family and friends to have her all to himself. He had controlled every aspect of her life and when she tried to leave him, he had stalked her and threatened her until she left the country.

The words came back to her. *Tam Lin prepares a feast. You must eat or drink none of it.*

They were still watching her. More than eager, they were anxious. She smiled and lifted the cup to her lips, careful not to let the odorless liquid touch her. She pretended to swallow and they all smiled. Her mind cleared a little more with her rebellion.

Tamlane clapped his hands and sat back, grinning.

The man on her right plucked a green grape from a bowl and held it to her mouth. He was as beautiful as Tamlane, though older and blond.

Anna shook her head. "I'm too excited to eat. Perhaps later."

"I insist," he said.

Sam had wanted to feed her once. He promised it would be sexy. She had done it for him and hated it. The fairy man pushed the grape to her lips. It made her angry. Tamlane's hold over her lessened a bit more.

She took the grape between her lips, feeling a hard texture. She slid the whatever-it-was under her tongue and pretended to chew. The others cheered and toasted again.

When they weren't looking, she wiped her mouth with her linen napkin and spit the thing into it. Whether or not the napkin was a frond of soft pine needles, as she suspected, it would not hide the thing that wasn't a grape. She leaned forward and let it slip out of the napkin and down her sweater, hoping it would roll through and come out under the table. It lodged in the notch of her bra instead.

She had to get away from the table before they caught her at this. Before her mind fogged again and all she could think of was Tamlane. Just looking at him made it hard to concentrate.

"I hope I will be as beautiful as all of you someday." She forced a smile.

"You will, my love," Tamlane said, "soon."

"Everyone looks so elegant. It's a shame you can't have a dance or . . . or a parade or something."

Tamlane's eyes brightened. He stood, the feast forgotten. "There shall be a procession!" he announced loudly, to the forest in general.

He walked around the table until he stood beside her and smiled that incredible smile of his. His approach wound her body tight, like the surface tension of a pond waiting for a single touch that would send ripples across the whole. She took his hand. The feel of his flesh on hers made her gasp. She fought with everything that was still her, still Anna, to hold onto the clarity she had gained.

"Come, we must gather the others."

"There are more of you?" she asked, glancing at the men and women also getting up from the table.

"No," he said sadly, his mood mercurial again. "But there are other races here, and a procession calls for an audience."

He seemed so melancholy at her question that her heart ached for him. She wanted to touch his face, to kiss away the pain. She fought it as they walked hand in hand from the grassy circle.

"Ah, Annabelle," he said, "you should have seen us in our glory. Oberon and Titania to the north, Finvarra of the Celts and the lovely Oonagh, Midar, and all the others; our kingdoms spread across the isles. Music and pageants and feasting every day." He looked at her face. She thought how plain and human her features must seem to him.

"What changed?" she asked.

He shrugged. "The world changed. Mankind increased and the fairy began to die off. The forests diminished. Those of us that were left were forced to crowd together, all the varied races . . . and these few of us, the last of the fairy aristocracy."

She looked into the blue depths of his eyes, at the knowledge there, the power, the age, the pain. The intensity in his face was far greater than when they had nearly made love. That had been casual for him. This was intimate.

She could never imagine the phooka, nor some of the other dire creatures they passed, playing audience to the faerie procession, but the smaller beings were starting to gather. Tamlane gave her a light kiss that made her head spin and took his place at the front of the pageant. The pixies flocked around his legs as he moved.

The procession was nothing more than a stately walk through the forest to show off their faerie splendor. Despite the absurd vanity, Anna could hardly take her eyes from it. All of them together, dressed in gossamer gowns and fine tunics, were breathtaking. Tamlane most of all. Her heart ached at the sight of him. But soon, she could be in that procession, vain and purposeless as the rest of them. And in half a year she could be tithed to Hell.

Her plan was not much of a plan, considering she had no idea where in the forest she was, but this was her best and, likely, only chance. Tamlane glanced at her occasionally, making sure she was appreciating his majesty, but soon he became caught up in the pageantry, trusting that the feast had tied her to him. The spectators ran alongside and Anna was left alone. Tearing her eyes from Tamlane, she eased back into the trees.

Anna hadn't explored the whole of the woods near her home, but she knew the general dimensions of it. This oldest section couldn't be very large. The light in the thick trees was too diffuse to know one direction from another, but all she needed to do was run in a straight line. And avoid the phooka, who would be waiting for her across the grassy meadow.

She ran.

Twice, anguish at leaving Tamlane nearly made her turn back, but memories of Sam pushed her on. The further she got from Tamlane, the more the tangle in her mind unbound, and her fear became terror. Terror of the things living in this forest, terror of becoming trapped forever with them, terror that the phooka or Tamlane were chasing her.

She stumbled often but managed not to fall. Her breath came in burning gasps. Branches tore at her face and clothes, like hands reaching to capture her.

"Annabelle!" Tamlane's voice. The authority in it nearly made her stop. Nearly.

She pushed on through the trees, frantic, but he was faster. Within moments he was behind her.

Anna saw the most wonderful thing she had ever seen in her life—sunlight through the branches ahead. Desperate now to save herself at any cost, she plunged the last few feet.

A tree root caught her foot and sent her sprawling, inches from safety. She crawled for the light but Tamlane grabbed her ankle, pulling her back. The touch of his hand was warm and strong. She turned and looked at him. *Why had she run from him? Had she been mad?* But he wasn't looking at her; he was staring at the ground in front of her. She looked where he did.

The grape lodged in her bra had jarred loose with her fall. It went spinning and bouncing over the border, into the brown dirt of the oak and birch woods. The sunlight revealed it for the small, brown acorn it truly was. They both froze, watching the acorn gently roll to a stop.

"What have you done?" he said in a whisper. *"What have you done?"*

The pain in his voice devastated her. His blue eyes were hard. She had hurt him somehow.

"I'm sorry." She got to her knees and reached for his legs. "I'm so sorry I ran," she said. She grabbed at the silk of his pants, but he stepped back.

"I would have made you my queen," he said, looking down at her.

A wind started deep within the old forest. The branches above her head shifted and swayed with it. Anna heard strange, muffled sounds under the deep voice of the wind. Tamlane flashed a look of hatred at her. Then he turned and ran.

"No," Anna cried, getting to her feet. She tried to follow him, but the wind pushed her back so hard she nearly fell. The trees above her were creaking, branches whipping to and fro in the increasing gale. She had to get out of here; she would die if these huge limbs came down on her. She had been trying to escape this forest anyway, she suddenly remembered as Tamlane disappeared from sight.

The wind buffeted her, pushing her the last few inches to the border of the two woods, as if even the forest didn't want her anymore. The muffled sounds beneath the wind grew in intensity and volume to a gurgling, moaning clamor. They resolved slowly into terrible, voices; sounds of howling, crying, fear. Sounds of agony. Anna cried out herself when she heard Tamlane's voice among them.

What the phooka had said came back to her. *It would take so little to undo us—a leaf, a twig.*

An acorn.

She understood finally what he had been trying to say; the world of fairy and the mortal world were separate things. And she had brought them together.

Strange shadows swirled before her eyes amidst the sound of the great wind building stronger still, drowning out the voices. A wind strong enough to bend those huge treetops and break the large branches. A wind strong enough to blow the forest clean. Phooka, the banshee, the pixies that had spied on her making love to the Faerie King. They were terrifying and dangerous and wondrous. And now they were no more.

She wept for the terrible loss the world had just suffered at her hand. Magic had been real, and she had eradicated what little remained. Anna fell to her knees and doubled over with great, wracking sobs. She crawled the last few inches from the old forest into the ordinary, human one.

_*_

Anna woke to bright sunlight. She looked at the clock over the couch and saw she had slept in until noon. Good thing it was Saturday.

She was bone-weary and strangely melancholy, and yet she had a longing to walk to the forest. A funny, urgent sensation, like she needed to check on it, too make sure it was still there for her. Not stopping for breakfast or even coffee, she headed out.

The day was sunny and warm. Even in the forest, the air seemed bright and cheery. When she left the main trail and took the next three forks, she looked around amazed. Funny, she thought she remembered the trees being much larger here, older.

The path was littered with leaves. Branches were hanging broken or lying on the ground as far as she could see. She had a vague memory of a strong wind. The woods felt new somehow, like the wind had cleansed it, like spring had renewed it.

Looking around, though, she had the peculiar feeling that the change brought more loss than gain. She was surprised when a tear spilled over her eyelid and ran down her cheek as she turned to head home.

~*~

Editor's Note: One thing I never realised until I read the submissions for this anthology was how strongly fairies are associated with sex. I mean, I've read the myths, I knew they were connected to some degree but the strength and depth of that connection in the stories we were sent blew me away. As did "The Last King." The sexual aspects are hot but tasteful and necessary to the story, and much like in "Seven Years Fleeting" the thing that made me elevate this in my mind from a "good story" to "a story I must include" was the fact the main character resisted the fae. That in this story the repercussions of that resistance are disastrous just makes it even better.

~*~

Faerie Knight

Sidney Blaylock, Jr.

1. The Knight of the Fae

Mr. Theron heard the subtle sound of a cell phone's keyboard clicking away in Brad's corner of the room. He shook his head—when would they ever learn? Just because he was blind didn't mean he was helpless.

He straightened his dark glasses and moved to Brad's corner, deftly avoiding the media stand and projector in the center of the classroom. The entire class grew silent and Mr. Theron smiled.

"Bradley, you wouldn't be texting in class again, would you?"

He heard the sound of a quick beep—the sound a screen being cleared, but not of a phone being turned off. "No, Mr. Theron."

There was a shuffling of feet in a desk further back in the same row. Lydia. She was one of the good students. Her restlessness told him that she knew a confrontation was coming and that she didn't want to be a part of it.

"Do you really want to be without your phone over the weekend? Think of all the Halloween parties that you'll miss."

Silence. Then a long beep—the sound of the phone going off.

"I appreciate it, Bradley." He pitched his voice louder. "In fact, I appreciate it so much that the homework that I was going to assign just got put off until Monday. Enjoy your weekend and have a safe Halloween."

Right on cue with the silent timekeeper in his head, the bell rang. Desks creaked, books were scooped up, and sneakers scuffed against the floor. When the classroom emptied, he smiled. Once again, experience triumphed in diffusing a tense situation.

He took a deep breath. Experience. He would need all of it in a few hours especially with All Hallow's Eve and a Hunter's Moon falling on the same night. For this one weekend out of the year, he would not be a teacher, but a knight in the service of the Queen of the Fae.

2. The Queen

"My knight, step forth."

"Yes, my Queen." Thomas Theron stepped forward and kneeled before the queen of the Fae.

"The Hunter's Moon rises. Are you ready to receive my boon?"

Always before Thomas had responded with an affirmative. Today, however, he felt compelled to speak.

"My queen," he said, then faltered as his voice stuck in his throat. He recovered. "My queen, I am still your knight, but I am not of the Fae. You took me in centuries ago after my parents abandoned me because of my blindness. You gave me a home among the Fae and for that I will be forever grateful. But, my queen, I'm mortal and I'm old. My bones ache and my speed isn't what it used to be. Please, my queen, do not think me churlish, but I feel that I must tell you that your knight is not the man he once was."

Thomas' insides felt horribly twisted. His heart pounded. Never before had he ever said such words to his queen. How would she take it? He meant it truthfully, but the Fae were fickle. She was benevolent, but she was still a queen and used to being obeyed.

His queen was silent.

The Seelie Court was silent.

That could not be good.

He heard the sound of cloth shifting and felt a light hand touch his shoulder.

His heart pounded.

"My knight, do you trust me?" Her voice was clear and her tone was firm.

"With all my heart."

"Then receive my boon again."

"I receive your boon, my queen," he said using the formula he had been taught so long ago, "I live to serve and I serve to live."

The formula was ancient. Her boon kept the years at bay. Had he not accepted it, he would have begun to age again, like any other mortal. There was another gift that her boon bestowed, however, and it was that one which he looked forward to the most.

She removed his glasses, touched his eyes and suddenly light flared through them. Slowly, sight came with it. Sight that would last until end of the full Hunter's Moon tonight. One day a year, he could see. And once a year, he received the gift of life.

Yet, he had seen so much evil, had fought against so much evil, that he wondered if his preternatural lifespan was a blessing, or a curse. His right knee ached and his hands had begun to curl under the debilitating effects of arthritis. Some mornings he felt as if it was all he could do to get out of bed, let alone prepare his lesson plans and gather his school supplies.

However, all his pains seemed to melt away when he looked upon his queen.

A simple circlet encircled her brow and it shone like starlight, and a long gossamer gown reached down to the edge of the dais. Her features were fox-sharp, but not severe. Her eyes were both greenish-blue, like the ocean. They seemed to shine bluish when she was serene, but flashed green when she was angry. Her ears were elongated and ended in points. Silvery-white hair cascaded down her shoulders like a waterfall shining in the moonlight.

"My brave and true knight, the world needs you. I need you. The Unseelie Court holds more sway in today's world than mine, but I refuse to abdicate my authority there. They are stealing children and turning them away from the light. I need all my knights to fight against the enveloping darkness. All of them."

She lifted him to his feet with a gentle touch and returned his sunglasses to him. "Fight for me, once more, my knight. The world needs you."

Thomas' knee throbbed and the aspirin was beginning to wear off. Soon his hands would begin to hurt as well. How could he serve his queen, if simply kneeling caused him so much pain?

He simply bowed. "Yes, my queen."

3. The Wild Hunt

The Hunter's Moon raged and Thomas felt the thrill of the wild hunt flow through him. The moonlight tingled on his skin like a heat rash and he could feel the power of the Fae as it eddied and pooled around his body. He held out his hand and ethereal tendrils began to coalesce around his palm. Slowly, a shape emerged. It was neither sword nor staff, but an amalgamation of the two. A long flowing blade, reminiscent of a katana merged into a glowing, leather-bound hilt that in turn flowed into another blade that was the diametric opposite.

Silverthorne.

A Vorpal Blade, mind-forged from the magic of the Fae. The top blade shone brilliantly with white-hot moonlight, while the bottom blade was ebon dark. He grasped the hilt, the only truly solid part of the weapon and spun it several times. The blades wailed their distinctive *snicker-snack* cry.

On any other day, he would not have dared draw Silverthorne in public, but this being Halloween, Thomas felt confident that the blade would simply seem like part of his costume. He was dressed in a flowing black coat that reached down to his ankles and wore a dark tri-cornered hat which gave him a decidedly seedy look. The long black cloth mask that covered his nose and mouth completed the costume and made him look thoroughly disreputable and menacing, as was his intent—his costume was that of a highwayman.

He stalked two trolls as they swaggered through the streets of suburbia. They had thick grayish skin and large unblinking eyes, like sharks. Their faces were thick and stone-like. They were not mortals in costumes, but fae, members of the Unseelie Court. Kids in costumes and their adult supervisors passed the trolls completely unaware.

Thomas followed the pair. He knew that his disguise and the fact it was Halloween would keep them from noticing him. He did have to be careful, however, as his fairy sight touched off a sense of unease in Fae. The last thing he wanted to do was spook these two. Thomas needed their leader.

"Hey, man, that's a nice sword! Where'd you buy it?"

Thomas turned. A tall Chewbacca, escorting Princess Leia, pointed to Silverthorne.

He saluted Chewie with Silverthorne. "I made it myself. It's one-of-a-kind."

Chewbacca nodded. "I've got to get me one of those."

Thomas turned back to the two trolls, but though his attention had only been diverted for a moment, they were nowhere in sight. He scanned the street, but he saw no Fae, only trick-or-treaters.

His heart sped. *Too old and too slow,* he berated himself. Lives depended on him and he just lost the trolls. They were his only lead to the fae that would probably try to abduct a child tonight and replace it with a changeling. He could not let that happen.

He forced himself into his classroom persona. Breathe and think, breathe and think. Prioritize. Now that he had lost the two trolls, his next goal must be to find their trail.

He took a deep breath and peered at the spot where the two trolls had been. He hated using this boon from his queen because even though it was immensely powerful and useful, it was like a submarine using active sonar, any fae in the area could now sense him, but he could see the trail of the two fae cutting through a yard and over into the next street. His heart hammered when he worked out where their trails would ultimately lead.

The school. His school.

4. The Vorpal Blade

Thomas crashed through the undergrowth on the traffic island. A long, snaking drive led to the school. The road was bounded by subdivisions on every side. The road, however, had been landscaped to provide a peaceful buffer between the school and the surrounding houses. Hedges, trees, mulch, and pine-needles supplemented the greenery of the traffic island. He heard rustling in the trees, but paid it no mind. A breeze was nice, but he needed to concentrate.

He heard a more substantial rustle above him and frowned. There was no way the trolls could have hidden in the trees, they were too bulky.

Suddenly the creatures burst from the underbrush. Thomas had been right . . . but he'd also been wrong. The trolls had hidden themselves using a glamour, like a chameleon changing colors to match its environment.

Idiot, Thomas raged at himself. *The moment I get the queen's boon of sight, I ignore my other senses.*

"I told you I felt something," one of the trolls said. "Looks like a knight." *Knee-ct* was the way the word tumbled from the troll's misshapen mouth.

The other troll grunted, flexing his huge arms and cracking his knuckles. "A dead knight," he said.

His partner grinned and twisted his neck until it cracked, limbering up like a heavy-weight boxer before a title fight.

Thomas brought Silverthorne into a ready position. His heart pounded, but he did not feel fear—just anger at himself. If he'd listened to his senses, this fight could have been avoided. The queen's boon of sight was joyous, but he would repay her poorly if he got himself killed because of it.

The first troll rushed him.

Thomas slipped to the side and whipped out the silvery white blade of Silverthorne at the troll as he rushed past. *Snicker,* whispered the blade. The troll skidded to a stop and felt his chest where Silverthorne had touched him—there was no injury.

He looked at Thomas and sneered. "This is going to be my easiest kill yet."

He lunged at Thomas who stood his ground and slashed the dark blade of Silverthorne at the troll's chest. *Snackt!* A deep wound opened and the troll screamed. The troll's unnaturally large hand went to its chest and blackish green ichor flowed through its fingers.

Thomas did not smile, but his lip curled. "You know," he quipped, "I was just thinking the same thing."

He had a problem now, though. Both trolls had realized he wasn't going to be easy to kill, so they circled him, like two sharks around a bleeding seal.

Thomas hissed. These two were merely toughs, hired to keep any of the Seelie Court at bay, should they appear. The real menace, their leader, was probably inside the school already.

Spinning Silverthorne like a drum majorette's baton, he slashed, cut, and stabbed at the trolls. They fell back at his furious assault, but one sidestepped a cut and backhanded Thomas. The blow stunned him and he almost dropped the shimmering ivory-ebon blade. The aspirin had worn off and his hands hurt. It took everything he had to keep his grip on the blade.

The creatures closed the distance in moments. They would kill him if he didn't do something. His mind screamed that he was too old to fight them and he should have given up the hunt! Now, because he hadn't, he was going to die.

He closed his eyes. Suddenly, he felt more alive. Sounds, which had been muted with the boon of sight, now seemed sharper, more defined and his sense of smell sharpened as well. He shifted his feet and his demeanor shifted with them.

Thomas heard the air *woosh* as one of the troll's fists surged toward him. Calmly, he spun away from the sound, flicked Silverthorne out and caught the troll in the heart with the ivory blade. With lightning quickness, he reversed his spin and the ebon blade struck in precisely the same spot.

Thomas heard the troll's body break up and fall away like sand through an hourglass.

The other troll ran. He heard the crunching of leaves and pine needles as footfalls moved away. He let it go. He had more important matters to attend.

He opened his eyes and turned toward his school.

5. The Once and Future Knight

The Halloween dance was in full swing. A few of the students were in full costume, but most of them were too self-conscious for that. They wore elf-ears or vampire fangs. Mr. Theron smiled—this was the best thing about the queen's boon. Once every year, he got to see his students. His smile faded though. Somewhere in here was a fae who wanted to harm his kids. He tightened his grip on Silverthorne. He would not allow it to happen.

Mr. Theron threaded his way through the crowded gymnasium.

He saw Lydia dancing with someone in a pumpkin-head costume. He smiled—she was dressed in yellow and black with silvery rounded gossamer wings and glitter-bopper insect headband. She made a fetching bumblebee.

However, as he watched her dance, Thomas realized something was wrong, very wrong. She looked listless—almost lifeless. He looked hard at her dancing partner. The costume—if it was a costume—was first-rate. It consisted of a huge over-sized Halloween pumpkin-head with the traditional black triangles eyes and a rictus of zigzagging black lines that crawled across pumpkin-head's face in place of a mouth. A huge scythe hung over pumpkin-head's shoulder like some massive claymore on an overly muscled barbarian. The rest of the costume was a long black shroud that ended in tatters on the floor.

A samhain—a fae that was rarely seen in the mortal lands that fed on humans' life essences. Like a fly depositing maggots, the samhain also left his spirit inside his victims.

Lydia would slowly withdraw from her schoolwork, her parents, her friends until her spirit finally turned and corrupted and then she would become one of the ban-sidhe, wailing in eternal insanity.

The hand that held Silverthorne trembled. It took all of his willpower not to leap in and cut the samhain's head from its body. Too many kids, too many lives at risk. He had to save Lydia, but he could not put all the other kids in danger. He had to find a way to separate Lydia from the samhain.

He made his way to the dancing couple, knowing that his dark glasses would keep his secret of sight hidden from everyone.

"Hi, Lydia," he said, "glad you could make the party."

"Oh, hi, Mr. T.," she said in a listless and offhand way, "yeah, I guess it's kinda good even if it is a little dorky."

Lydia was usually neither listless or offhand, nor had she ever called him anything other than Mr. Theron. "Who's your friend?"

Pumpkin-head turn toward him. "The name's Sam," he growled.

Mr. Theron's mind raced. "Well, Sam, I hate to do this, but I need to borrow Lydia for a moment. Ms. Shepherd needs to talk to her about the Washington DC trip." He shrugged. "Don't worry, she'll be right back."

Pumpkin-head's hands tightened on Lydia's arms. However, Mr. Theron had chosen the one topic guaranteed to break Lydia out of her trance. No one, and that included the faculty, wanted to miss the DC trip. It was the highlight of every school year. He heard the swish of fabric as Lydia broke free. "I gotta' go see her," she said and her voice had a little more timbre. She moved quickly through the swaying crowd. Mr. Theron, used to listening far more than watching, heard her footfalls gaining confidence the farther away she moved from

Pumpkin-head. He smiled.

He stepped up to the samhain, put his arm companionably around the fae's shoulder, and steered him to the exit. "Let's talk for a couple of minutes until she gets back. I'm curious—I haven't seen you in any of the classes. Are you a new transfer or do you go to another school?"

He could feel the samhain's malice, radiating like waves while it spun lie after lie to his questions. He kept chatting amiably until they were outside the gym.

Once out in the chilly night air, Mr. Theron released the samhain and allowed his voice to take on the same chill that was in the air. "Oh, by the way, Sam, if you ever come to my school again, I'll have to take steps. I don't think you'll much care for them, so I strongly suggest you stay far away from here from now on."

The samhain stiffened.

"Who're you to tell me what I can and can't do?" the fae asked, still playing the role of a surly teen.

Mr. Theron brought up Silverthorne. "I'm a teacher at this school and a knight of the Seelie Court. I do what my principal asks and what my queen commands. My principal asks me to keep these students safe, and I will make sure no one, human or fae, hurts them. My queen bids me to rid the mortal realms of the Unseelie Court, and I will see it done. So I have one suggestion for you: run!"

He knew it wouldn't happen, though. Sure enough, he heard the rustle of clothes as he watched the samhain pull the scythe from its back. Mr. Theron was wearing dark glasses at night, so his vision was diminished, but he wasn't terribly concerned, as he was used to the darkness. He trusted his ears far more than his sight. Of course, "Sam" would have no clue that his hearing was hyper acute. Perhaps he could use that to his advantage.

The scythe whistled as the samhain whirled it through the air. Mr. Theron watched impassively and when he didn't move, the samhain snarled.

Pumpkin-head lunged, but he was prepared for it. Mr. Theron dropped to his knees. They groaned and protested, but he was able to keep his balance and the scythe cut through the air overhead.

If he'd been younger, he might have been able to sweep the samhain's legs, but the throbbing ache in his knees convinced him that would not be an option. He needed to close the distance to bring Silverthorne into play. Gritting his teeth against the pain, he launched himself at the samhain. His shoulder crashed into the fae and they both collapsed in a heap.

He grabbed the samhain, who was on its back, with his free hand and then slashed Silverthorne at its neck. The fae threw him off just as the stroke was coming. Thomas rolled away, but when he heard a sharp whistling sound he stopped and reversed, rolling back towards the samhain. The scythe tore into the pavement, right where he would have been had he continued his original roll. Thomas tried to leap to his feet, but his knees buckled under the exertion.

The samhain roared and lunged.

Thomas watched as the creature seemed to hang in the air. Even through his dark glasses, he could see the deadly glint of the scythe's blade as it tore through the night straight toward his chest. He was going to die. Die.

He felt his heart as it thundered in his chest. A stiff breeze blew across his sweat-stained brow, chilling him. He heard the rustle of leaves as they were torn from the trees by the rising wind. To die in the service of his queen. He was content.

Lydia's face floated in front of him. Not the Lydia he had left in the gymnasium, but an older face contorted in howling madness, locked in some facility somewhere. *No, NO, NO!*

He did the only thing he could and pitched forward, rolling *toward* the samhain. He felt the wind of the scythe's wake as it passed just over him and heard the rip of clothing as it split his coat. Finishing his roll, he gathered himself, prayed that his legs would hold, and thrust his body straight up. His head and back pounded into the chest of the samhain and lifted the fae backwards off its feet. It flailed as it flew backwards and landed hard on its backside.

Gritting his teeth against the arthritic throbbing, Thomas closed the distance. Before the fae could recover, he whipped Silverthorne out with a stroke to its throat and followed it immediately with a reverse stroke. *Snicker-snack.* There was a rolling, bouncing thud as the samhain's pumpkin-head rolled across the white stripes of the parking lot.

The mortal body faded as the fae inhabiting it returned to the Faerie Realms.

Mr. Theron released the Vorpal Blade. Panting, he waited in the night air until he regained his breath and composure.

Mr. Theron smiled—and he knew.

Next year, he would accept his queen's boon again, without question and without fail. As long as his kids needed him, he would be there for them.

~*~

Editor's Note: The thing about this I like best is that the main character has issues. He's tired, he's sore, he'd probably like nothing more than to go soak in a hot bath with two fingers of scotch, but there he is, every year, doing what needs to be done to keep his queen happy and his students safe. At its heart, that is something I think we can all relate to on one level or another. Sadly, we don't all get magical swords with which to fight *our* battles.

~*~

SOLOMON'S FRIEND

Kristina Wojtaszek

Kadie never considered herself a great mom, which made it easy to slide her son's journal out from under his bed and hide it within the curtain of her hair. She made herself comfortable on the plush carpet, lying on her stomach between the two little beds where her boys slept while the moonlight snuck through an opening in the heavy drapes and settled beside her. The boys often found her in this very spot during the day, reading in a pool of sunlight while the oven preheated or the laundry dried; here or in other random places, her laptop propped beside her or yet another book in her lap. She didn't always answer their calls, but they knew the places to look; it was her own little game of hide-and-seek.

Kadie pushed her hair back, the multiplying strands of white gleaming like tinsel in the clean light, and opened the journal's stiff front cover. The pages crinkled beneath her fingers and she glanced up, but Solomon didn't stir; he had always been a deep sleeper. Being only seven, his entries were short and stilted and she smiled over his many misspellings. Though a few sentences were altogether indecipherable, it didn't stop her from scrutinizing every line, prying apart the crudely rendered thoughts and drawings, desperate for a hidden trail into the thicket of his mind.

As night thinned, the moon whittled down from a wide, soft face to a single, brilliant eye. Kadie was just about to close the journal and slide it back under Solly's bed when the moon's gaze fell across the page, setting the dull paper alight with a shock of white. Kadie found her knees, lifting the book to her face at the sight of a flowing, pale script rising from beneath Solly's heavy scrawl. But the moment her shadow touched the page, the foreign writing disappeared. Edging closer to the window, she lowered the book into the well of light once more, and began flipping pages, finding the tight lettering squashed into every bit of white space until it ended abruptly in the middle of the journal; at the very bottom of Solomon's most recent entry.

Kadie gazed at her son as he slept, one arm thrown over his head, his lips thick and slack, revealing the infant still hidden in his elongating features. He was just a little boy; a bit unusual at times, and oddly intelligent, but a child nonetheless. He couldn't be responsible for the lavishly formed letters that burned beneath her fingers. Nor was her husband the type to play odd pranks. It seemed equally ridiculous to suspect his school counselor, the only other person to lay hands on the journal, having asked Solomon to write down his feelings once a week.

Kadie's fingers jittered above the page. The words were oddly formed, each letter twisted like a knot, untangling itself as she stared, allowing meaning despite its strange appearance. She swallowed down her heart as she read.

I knew you'd pick this up one day, and if you're reading these words, it must be by the light of a full moon. Damn. I guess that sounds kind of creepy. And there's no erasing hob blood. Shit, I shouldn't have said that, either! I'm getting too old for this.

Kadie dropped the cover, picturing some deranged old man following her son around. Her gaze flickered to the closet door where she imagined a shift in the shadows before she opened the journal back up.

Let's start over. Thing is, I can't really introduce myself. There are too many rules involved. I'll just say this; remember that day you stopped at that dilapidated old shop out on Highway 49, place called Desert Gems? And your son, the older one, he picked out one of those big rocks that looked like a fossilized piece of shit? A geode, that's what you called it. Well that's where I came from. Guess it was pretty lucky little Solomon picked my rock out of all the rest.

Kadie did remember, vaguely. Solly was probably only five at the time. That meant this creep had been following them around for over two years. She shivered, her breath coming shallow as she wondered how he'd (she'd?) done it, and what it was he wanted. She was half tempted to phone the police right then, but as she slid her cell out of her pocket, the unnatural light obliterated the pale writing. She thought about the moon being full, and wondered how often that happened. Once a month? She glanced up at the moon, a small coin wedged in the top corner of the window, and dove back into the words before they could disappear.

Since I already mucked up and told you I'm a hob, I might as well tell you that's how my kind are born. That hollow stone was my egg. I'd spent half a century gnawing crystal when one day your little Solly picked me up and shook the hell out of me, as though there'd be something to hear rattlin' around inside. I braced myself, but I had a mother of a headache for the rest of the day. In fact, it was the worst damn day of my life, but I owe you big, mamacita, because it could've been my last, too, if it weren't for you. It was a long, bumpy ride home, contemplating my fate, when all of a sudden I heard a crack so loud I thought my skull was gonna split. It happened again, and there I was, my whole world shattered, chokin' on the dust while bits of crystal fell over me like dry rain. I had to shield my eyes from all that light, eclipsed only by the flat, silver wink of death hovering just inches above, clutched in the kid's fist. And then your voice almost knocked me off my enormous feet. It was violently clear, splitting the air like the voice of God, not just grumbles and growls, but real, coherent words:

"That's good, Solly. You can put the hammer down, now."

And in that moment, I realized humans weren't stupid after all. They really could talk, I just hadn't known it because all those years that damn shell of stone muffled everything into Neolithic grunts. Suddenly I was the idiot, because I should've been scramblin' for a place to hide, but I was so stunned by the light and the words that I couldn't have moved if that hammer fell over me like an anvil. It didn't though; the kid listened to his lovely mamacita and set it down on the table top in a burst of thunder. Good boy, I thought, nice kiddie . . .

And there he was, two speckled orbs blinking over me, the deep gray brightening to blue shock as he sucked in a sudden breath, pulling my hair all up on end. Shit, was I in trouble. First day on the job and I'd already blown my cover!

I shivered and sneezed and there it was, my invisibility falling over me with little cold prickles like a first snow, and you know how kids are, they make so much shit up that you just rolled your eyes when he told you there was a fat, hairy little troll in his rock. I rolled my eyes, too. I'm a hob, kid, not a troll, *I wanted to tell him; there's a hell of a difference, especially in size. And hey, I wasn't fat! All right, I was a little pudgy at first, I mean how much exercise can a guy get inside a five inch geode?*

But at least I'd figured out the whole invisibility trick; clap on clap off, and I was out of sight, if not out of mind. The kid was still picking through the broken bits of my former abode, determined to find me, while I took off sliding down the table leg, my eye on a three inch model Harley across the room. It disappeared at my touch, but I don't think the kid ever missed it. Nice little hog, just the right size so I could push off with my big feet on the ground and cruise. Course, carpet's a bitch, but I make do.

After a while, Solly and I came to a sort of understanding, you could say. He keeps quiet about his little friend, and I let him see me on occasion. You know, like whenever I'm in the mood to risk life and limb.

Kadie sat back, half smiling. Someone was playing a trick on her. Someone that knew even more mythology and folklore than she did. A hob? Maybe someone from her writer's group had found Solly's notebook in her bag and swiped it. They'd used some retro disappearing ink and made a great story for her to take home. They'd be waiting for her at the next meeting with a wicked smirk . . .

But Kadie's smile fell. None of those people had known her for two years. And how would any of them have known about that strange little rock shop, or the geode Solly brought home and broke with a hammer, just as he'd described it? She pressed both thumbs into her temples. He. *Who was he?*

Tell you the truth, I didn't feel much of a need to make myself scarce when I saw what I saw in Solomon's eyes. He's a special one, that little guy. Call it a syndrome or part of a spectrum or whatever you will, but there's another facet to his innocence; a kind of clarity of mind you humans don't often have. And it was obvious right away, just in the way he looked at me, like there was nothing in the world to be surprised about, finding a hairy little dude inside his geode. Truth be told, I knew I'd been sent here for a reason, and the moment he split my world open, I was faithfully his.

That being said, I should probably get a few things off my overgrown chest here and now, because you're a wonderful mamacita and all, but you've got some things wrong about your kid. Like when Solly seems to assign life to everyday objects. That's actually my fault (mostly). Remember that time he propped his dirty sock up on the end table and said it was "watching him" play Mario?

I saw that look on your face, your forehead all creased up, and I just want you to know, he didn't actually think the sock was alive. Thing is, I'd kind of made a sleeping bag out of that sock. The little dude knew I was in there, peeking out through the hole where his big toe had worn through, but Solomon is smart enough not to mention the little "troll" living in his sock; he knows the meaning of your looks, too, and he knew how much worse that would sound than the sock was alive.

And come on! If he'd glued a couple of googly eyes to the sock, you wouldn't have thought it was all that crazy, now would you? Kid just wants a friend, is all. Even though you can't see me, and a lot of times (mostly so he doesn't get in deep shit) I stay outta sight, he knows when I'm around. So give the kid a break—it isn't about the sock, ok?

And man is he smart, but you have to take the time to understand his logic. Like just the other day. I was up on his ceiling fan making a regular banquet out of all the dust up there (don't judge, you eat what you like, I'll eat what I like!) when you yelled at him for licking the soap off his hands and sent him to his room. So there I was with a nice five o' clock of sweet, gray fuzz, and I hear Solly down below me start whispering to himself (by the way, he does that when he's figuring something out, so don't mess with that, all right?) So he says, real softly, "I ate it because you said there are germs inside my body, duh!*"*

Duh, mamacita! How else is he supposed to kill those nasty germs that live inside him? Aren't you always harping on him to wash up, and didn't you just read him that Body Book that showed all those little angry-faced germs that sometimes make him sick? So get with the program! He's got his reasons for the things he does.

Another thing, could you maybe keep that side zipper pouch on his backpack cracked open a bit? I know you think he's fiddling around with that zipper and has some obsessive compulsive disorder going on, but really, it's me who asked him to keep it open. It gets awfully damn stuffy in there on the way to school and back, and I'd like a little fresh air, if you don't mind.

You see, he's never really alone when he sits by the door all during recess, waiting right where he knows his teacher will come out so that he doesn't miss her and get left behind on the playground or locked out of school somehow. I know this bothers you, and you really want to see him playing with friends, but the kid's got anxiety, what can you do? At least he's got me to talk to. Those other little shits are just waiting for an opportunity to tease him, anyway. Least he's smart enough to stay out of their way. Besides, a hob makes a hell of a friend, long as you don't insult me. (Not that I'm one to hold a grudge. I forgave you for sucking me up in the vacuum. Twice.)

Now, I know you think you've failed on a lot of levels, and it really isn't any of my business when you turn out the light before leaving his room so he won't see your tears, or you hide on the floor behind the kitchen counter just so you can get a good cry in without him noticing. Look, he might not always notice, but I do. And thing is, I've got a serious case of asthma and I am nasty *allergic to negativity. So get a hold of yourself, mamacita!*

I'm saying this out of my own self interest, I know, and you aren't my human to take care of, but if I'm gonna stay (and that's a big if) it would make it easier on both of us if we could move past all the motherly guilt that really has no place in Solomon's world, and just try to do what we can for the kid. Because like it or not, we're kind of partners in this. Like family, no?

I know, I know . . . I have no concept of what it's like to birth a child (thank you Mother Earth for your great mercies) and I could never love him the way you do, or know what it's like to know that your child will never truly fit in, and will always feel a little alien to you, and to everyone else, for that matter. But I happen to know that some things do exist that you humans don't allow yourselves to see (ahem) *and just because Solomon has a different way of viewing the world doesn't mean his life is going to be eternally shitty. So can we clear out the black aura that hangs out all over the ceiling? Because this emotional pollution is killin' me, and last time I took a lick of Benadryl, that shit knocked me out for a week!*

Look, I just want you to know that I get it. I see how you look at his baby picture propped on your desk (you can thank me for licking the dust off later), and I know how you wonder what connections didn't quite take behind those vivid blue eyes. I've watched your smile fall as you look back at your two kids in the rear view mirror, and the little one greets you with a smile and a wave, while Solomon stares right back without a flicker of emotion.

I get it.

I know how that pains you. Just, keep your eyes on the road, bueno? And quit using that damn wet vac in the car! Don't you know I could live for weeks off that crust of spilled milk and all that glorious mold on the month-old cracker crumbs?

Seriously, though—Solomon loves when you call it a drive-in lunch on those days you're in a rush and have to feed the boys in the car because you don't have time to unbuckle them before heading out again. And when you stay up extra late to tell him stories about when you were a little girl, and all those times you cater to his obsession that every snack and meal be a surprise. It's the little things you do that show him how much you love him. Believe me; I get it. And so does he.

Kadie pressed her fist hard over her mouth, shaking as she fought to keep her sobs silent. She found Solly through her lens of tears, wondering again just how smart he was. But it couldn't be. Nothing made sense. Whoever it was who'd written to her knew them both way too well. And yet, she wasn't so scared anymore. She must be losing it. Had that grape juice they'd had with dinner fermented somehow?

She stared at the heap of dirty clothes in the laundry basket across the room, a little white sock with a large hole in the toe glowing florescent in the moonlight.

I know you won't believe any of this, despite all that crap you read to your kids about Tom Thumb and Peter Pan, and the even shittier stuff you write. You think that because humans are so good at separating themselves from the natural world, beings like us have all disappeared. Or worse, that we never existed outside of primitive misconceptions of the natural world. But far from it. You're always exploring, always bringing little tidbits of nature into your home; a houseplant, a museum store fossil, a blue jay feather, a seashell from a tourist shop, a geode. And we "little folk" come along, too.

We're here, floating in the storms of static that cling to your endless electronics, hovering above your produce and houseplants among the gnats and aphids, even crawling through the mold and rotten crumbs in your forests of carpet. All we require is a home where little ones leave leftovers on their plates and coat the ceiling with dark, sweet dreams, and mamacitas who throw their arms up at last and leave the sugary drips in the fridge, the stains on the carpet and the dust on the fans. Those are your offerings to us. Hell, we live to clean up your messes and lick your plates! The spirits are still here. We never left.

Besides, you and I, doll, we've got a lot in common. If you weren't 1,000 times my size, a century too young, and easily put off by mass amounts of body hair . . . never mind. Besides, me and that dryad in the back yard kinda got a little thing goin' (by the way, if you ever cut that overgrown spruce down, there will be hell to pay!) But I get you, you know.

Sometimes I actually take a snooze alongside you, just to lick up your dreams. I see those peonies from your childhood memories, crushed up against your face while the little ants run out all over your nose, a pink bit of heaven you plucked from the Mexican family's field because they won't miss just one. But then you felt bad and fished out a crumpled bill and left it in the mud, like it grew there. We fairy kind know, and I wouldn't be here if you weren't a Goodie.

And entertaining as hell; the way you dance at the kitchen sink to the music in your head while you scrub the dishes and walk away with your shirt half soaked. How you teach the boys how to walk like crabs and scuttle around the house with them like some kind of oversized, inverted spider. The mountains of laundry you'd rather write poetry about than actually touch, and the green days of your youth that you whisper to your boys about, the oaks and maples and tulip trees that drank straight from the lake, all of them singing crimson and amber in the fall, crushed like candy under foot.

This desert doesn't sing for you, and your dreams feel hollowed out and wind-worn here, crumbling like the slow death of sandstone, but here you are in the cluttered kitchen, dancing again to remember. And when I see you like this, sometimes I wonder. Maybe it isn't the kid I'm here to look after. Maybe it's you who needs a little more magic in your life.

But then again, it's Solly who's got the Second Sight, while all you've got is a vivid imagination. But Solly, well, I would only make more trouble for him as the years go on. You'll be all right, mamacita. Just keep lovin' that boy of yours, it's all he needs to grow, and don't forget to water the cactus a couple times a year (those little sprites get pretty TOed when you forget).

See, thing is, that little set of clothes you've started making for Solly's stuffed monster is actually for me. The kid's got a big heart, like his momma, and I appreciate the gesture, you gotta believe me. But like I said before, there's rules and shit. You just can't offer clothing to a hob; not if you expect him to stick around, anyway. The choice is yours, of course. Finish the clothes and I'll be off. Or don't.

I've already written my goodbyes to Solomon, just in case, so if you see him inspecting the dust on the floor boards or the shape of scars on your Dracaena's leaves or a portrait in the sunlit threads of your balding drapes, he's just reading, is all. I just wanted you to know, you who never bother to dust and leave that burnt skin on your pans to flavor your food; you with your sticky kitchen floor and your smog of worry; you sitting there with your knees up to your chest, hiding behind the kitchen counter, eating loneliness.

You, mamacita, keep a lovely home.

~*~

"Mom?"

Kadie straightened, pressing her back against the cool window as she gauged the expression in Solomon's wide eyes. She didn't bother closing the journal, lit like a sin in her lap. "Hi Baby."

"Is it breakfast time? Do I have school today?"

"No, Sweetie, it's Saturday. You get to sleep in. Why don't you go back to sleep?"

"Okay. Is that my journal?"

Though Kadie had never considered herself a great mom, she prided herself on honesty. She taught them the myth of Saint Nicholas, and labeled their Christmas presents "From Mom and Dad." She never failed to ask what they thought to be true about a fairy tale, and patted their little heads when they said, "That didn't *really* happen." Part of this was a responsibility that evolved from knowing how literally Solomon took things. But last year, when he lost his first tooth, she had surprised herself by playing the role of the Tooth Fairy. She never knew if he suspected.

"Yeah, Baby," she whispered, "I read your journal. Are you mad at me?"

Solly shook his head and yawned, his little silver fillings winking in the moonlight. "Did you see the picture I drew of you? It's on the last page." He sunk back into his pillow, pressing her old stuffed rabbit to his chest as he closed his eyes, not waiting for her answer.

With a trembling hand, Kadie closed the journal and flipped open the back cover. She was surprised he'd chosen to draw her, but there she was, little round glasses circling her dot eyes and a mass of scribbled hair that was actually pretty accurate. Her enormous head floated on a typical stick figure body, and down by her footless left leg was a strange looking plant, ankle high and spiked like a cactus, except . . . No, it wasn't a plant; it had eyes and a crooked little mouth.

Heart thumping, she crawled to the edge of Solly's bed and stroked his soft cheek. "Honey, what's this?"

Solly blinked in the moonlight, not bothering to look at the notebook she held out to him. As he rolled back over, he mumbled sleepily, "My friend Hobby. He writes in there, too, sometimes."

"Can I meet him? Will you show him to me?"

Sollly turned his face to hers, eyes suddenly wide as though he'd let a secret slip. He shook his head solemnly. "No, Mom. You're not s'posed to see him!"

"Why not?"

"Shh, he's sleeping."

Kadie whispered to keep the desperation out of her voice. "Where?"

Solomon rolled over and pointed at the little Kleenex box beside his bed, where he kept the stuffed monster she'd made for him out of fabric scraps. She peered through the slit in the top and spied the soft outline of the monster, and something a little smaller next to it, something darker than shadow. She nudged the box toward the dwindling spot of moonlight on the floor.

"Don't, Mom," Solly whispered, the covers falling from his shoulders as he sat up in alarm.

"I want to see . . ."

"He gets mad if you wake him up. Last time he told me he was gonna go away. Please, Mom. I don't want him to leave!"

Kadie took her hand from the box and stood, finding Solly's eyes. "I won't. It's all right, Solly. Go back to sleep."

He nodded, relieved, and she kissed his forehead. For once, she didn't care if he saw the tears standing in her eyes. She left the little room at last, and made herself a cup of Chai before creeping downstairs. She set the warm mug on her desk, but couldn't sit, couldn't touch the sleeping laptop. Instead, she slipped into the cluttered sewing room and plucked up the tiny shirt and pants she'd been working on. They felt like moth wings in her palm, such little things. She smiled faintly as she reached for her sheers.

When she finished, Kadie brushed the scattering of snippets from her lap and laid the sheers back on the table, where they shone like a silver grin in the moonlight.

~*~

Editor's Note: There are two things I really love about this story. The first is seeing the disparity between how Solomon is perceived by those around him, including his mother, and the reality of what is going on in his world. The second is the hob. The hob, though a gruff smart ass, really does have a good heart. I like to think the whole reason he wrote this note to Kadie is so that she'd do exactly what she did—cut up the clothes and force him to stay.

~*~

A FAIRFOLK PROMISE

Alexis A. Hunter

Cedric writhed and flailed like a wild beast. The Rolfmen gripped his wrists, his arms. They cuffed the back of his neck and drove him forward into the field of corn. Desperation burned within him, fueled his emaciated body. Striking out, he caught one of the Rolfmen square in the jaw and sent him reeling backward.

A guttural cry tore itself from Cedric's bleeding, cracked lips as he twisted down and back. Tearing loose, he darted toward the forest. A surge in his chest—half a heartbeat of freedom, but their hands were as brambles, snagging him. They dragged him to the earth, shouting curses and pummeling his bony sides with their boots.

The wind knocked out of him, he lay immobilized. His lips parted and he sucked in mouthfuls of air as they dragged him forward. The cornstalks whispered around him, their blades slicing little red trails on his exposed arms and chest—nothing compared to the purple-blue bruising marbling his body.

"You hit me again, and I'll strike you dead, *kushna*," growled the Rolfman.

An iron cross stood in the midst of the corn, its vertical pole driven deep into the earth. Cedric forced his weary muscles to move again, to fight. To resist. But he had little hope of victory. They were too many, and they ate hearty meals each night. Slept in beds fluffed by goose-feathers. . Cedric hadn't eaten a scrap of food in the past three days.

They pressed him against the iron cross. The blazing twin-suns above had heated the surface, and it singed his skin. Gritting his teeth, he refused to cry out. Three held him while the fourth and fifth stretched his arms across the horizontal pole. They secured him with thin, sharp wire, laced with barbs. It cut into his skin, drawing blood.

And still he fought.

For Lina and the baby, he fought to be free.

The other workers wouldn't look at him, heating his fury still more. "Why do you stand and watch? Why do you not aid me?" he cried. "We must rise against these oppressors. How can you stand idle while your families starve before your eyes?"

They kept their heads down, fingers moving through the corn and snapping off whole ears. They dumped the fruit of the land into baskets—baskets to be carted away to Lord Rolfere. In truth, he knew why they would not aid him. For the same reason he had never aided the others.

"Shut your filthy mouth," snarled a Rolfman, striking the side of Cedric's head. The blow made his vision dance. A dizzy spell took him and were it not for the cross supporting him, he'd have tumbled to the ground. They continued to roll the snaking coils around his entire body, binding him to the metal.

At last, they stepped back. Their eyes glinted as one tugged a crude, iron crown from his satchel.

"By decree of Lord Rolfere, supreme ruler of these lands, I hereby deem you the Cursed. The Warning—scarer of crows and man." The Rolfman raised his tone, so that all the workers could hear. Cedric knew the words by heart, he'd heard them so many times. They burned him now in a way he'd never felt before. "For your crimes against the lord, for the theft of the ruler's field and crops, you are doomed to stand watch here until the end of your days. May the gods have mercy on your filthy, rotten soul."

They turned their backs and made to retreat.

"May Rolfere burn in the fires of the afterlife," Cedric shouted, thrashing against the wire until blood streamed down his body. "May you face the same fate. You maggots. You are unworthy to tread the land. You are unworthy to even die upon it."

Rolfere's henchmen stalked away, laughing, under the late summer sun.

Cedric tilted his head back against the cross, iron clanging against iron as his crown struck the pole. He turned his bloodshot eyes to the heavens, sides heaving. Each breath made the barbed wires cut deeper into his bare chest and ribcage. Little jolts of pain met every flex of every muscle.

He rolled his gaze across the fields, not lifting his head. A dozen or more iron crosses bore emaciated scarecrows with glazed eyes—some dead, some yet breathing.

Lemuel picked corn nearby, a man Cedric had known since childhood. "Lemuel, set me free. I must go to my wife and babe. They will perish with none to care for them."

The man worked in silence, head down and gaunt features a wall of rock, unyielding.

"Lemuel!" Cedric screamed.

Lemuel moved on to another section, where the scarecrows did not shout and flail.

Cedric could not remain still. The image of Lina and his baby boy drove him on. He thrashed against his bindings, slicing his flesh and drawing ribbons of blood. He cried out to any who wandered near.

At last, he had no more strength for it. His body throbbed as he leaned against the pole.

"You must resign yourself, Cedric."

Cedric looked up at the sound of the cracking voice. A thread of shame wove through him when he realized he didn't remember the speaking scarecrow's name.

"I cannot. The face of my wife drives me on. I must be free. We must rise against our oppressors and take back the land."

The other scarecrow's thin, twisted body sagged against his barbed restraints. Ghostly pale-blue eyes peered back at Cedric. "They will not listen to you. They'll not aid you, no matter how you rail. And can you hate them for it? Did you listen to my cries as they strung me up here? No. We never do. They'll continue on in fear and dread—as we did—until they too are driven to desperation. And in the end, there will be no workers of the land, only a field of scarecrows."

Cedric could find no worthy response. He stilled, eyes closed.

I will not give in. I won't relent.

The warm kiss of the suns lulled him into a kind of half-sleep. A place in his mind that moved back through the years to a time when he dreamed of the fairfolk. A time when they seemed to flit in the shadows and the echoes of their tinkling songs could be heard at night. Before Rolfere and his men. Before tyranny and blood.

~*~

As the twin-suns sank out of the sky, the workers returned to their shacks, filtering out of the fields with the last baskets of the day. Cedric watched them pass, unable to muster strength to scream their names. His dark eyes hunted each one, but they would not meet his gaze.

The scarecrow's words whispered through him. *Did you listen to my cries as they strung me up here?*

No. Of course not. To protect his family, he had plodded onward in silent obedience.

We are a helpless people. There is no savior to rescue us—we cannot even band together.

His thoughts flitted again to older days. Looking down at his torn body, he cursed the iron they laced him with.

"Have you ever called to the fairfolk?" he rasped.

The scarecrow with the pale-eyes twisted his head, slowly as if his neck were a rusted door hinge. His lips opened and closed a few times, jaw working. He licked his lips and then spoke. "It would do no good. They left our lands when Rolfere came. They cannot hear us now."

Cedric shook his head. The action made his coiled muscles groan. "I cannot believe that. They are a stealthy folk. Surely, they remain. I do not think they would abandon the land thus. They are born of it. It is their mother. And who can abandon their mother to a foreign oppressor?"

"You dream, Cedric. And I cannot blame you. You will find many wild thoughts come to you in this place. Even if the fairfolk remained, they would not heed our cries. It is not by chance that we are bound by iron."

Cedric grew still a moment. Deep in the recesses of his memory, he found the words he sought. The tune was rusted in his mind, but after some time, it came back to him. A tune his old grandmother sang. Clearing his throat and licking his chapped lips, he forced his voice to bend to each swelling note.

"Here in times of twilight, while twin-suns kiss the earth—I cry to you, oh fairfolk. I cry to you between the time of moon and sun. Gentle kiss of night, farewell streak of scarlet. I cry—"

"Save your strength, Cedric," said the scarecrow. "It will do nothing. They will not hear you where they have gone."

Cedric tuned the man's words out, pressing his eyes closed. His voice rose, breaking with the passion that lingered still within. Desperation and a flickering hope gave him strength. Lina and the babe. For them. For his people and the land, he sang.

"Here in the coming dark, I cry to you, oh fairfolk. My knees and heart bowed to embrace your earth. Fingers sunk in soil, seeking roots of stone. This soul united with you, by ties of earth and air. Here in the times of twilight . . . while . . ."

His voice sputtered into silence. Nausea swept through his stomach. He sagged against his ties, wincing as they cut into his tender, swollen flesh. Tears slipped across his face as the twin-suns slipped into darkness, plunging the world into the same.

A night breeze stirred the air, brushing against the back of Cedric's neck.

He wept for the hopelessness of it. He wept for Lina.

_*_

The tinkling of distant, tiny bells. Cedric stirred from feverish dreams. Raising his head, he cracked his bloodshot eyes open. Every muscle in his body tensed. He sucked in a quick gasp of air and did not let it out again for a moment.

Fairfolk flitted before his eyes. Tiny figures so perfectly formed. Elegance in their wings and in the curve of their bodies. One hovered close to him, her golden hair glistening in the moonlight. She peered into his face out of dark eyes, her entire form no bigger than his hand.

"I knew you would come," he breathed.

A quick glance through the cornfield told him the other scarecrows slept. He felt the urge to wake them, and yet he did not wish to share these precious beings floating before him. He turned his gaze back to the fairy most near. "Thank you. Thank you for hearing my song."

"You summoned us." She cocked her head. "Desperation was in that song. You are Cedric, steward of the earth."

Tears slipped down his dirty face. "Yes. Or I was. Now I am another nameless scarecrow, a victim of Rolfere."

A tiny sigh escaped the fairy's lips. She turned and spoke in a language he could not understand. A moment passed and the other fairies produced an earthen cup of water. The closest fairy took it. She eased nearer, wincing as if in pain.

"They bind you with iron." A pure voice, soft as the leaves whispering under the kiss of a spring breeze.

"To keep you away."

She pushed forward, quivering, and he gulped down the water as she pressed it to his lips. With a muted cry, she dropped the cup—it was as large as she, but her cry came from nearness to the iron rather than from any strain.

His throat soothed by the cool, sweet water, he spoke with more ease. "Thank you. You are most merciful."

She rubbed her face, her features twisting into shadows. "I am not always so. This mortal—Rolfere—he angers us. By his orders, you scrub the land too rough, not letting her rest as you used to."

Cedric found it difficult to respond. He lost himself in the intricacies of her lithe form, in the realization that all those childhood tales were made manifest before his eyes. Blinking, he pulled himself from under her spell. "Yes, Rolfere must be ended. His reign must be torn down. But . . . I summoned you for a much more selfish need. My wife . . . she is thin and ragged. Our babe is newly born, and sucks the life from her. I stole to give her enough to live by. But the Rolfmen have taken it from her. She will die without aid."

The fairy did not speak. Her companions flitted about behind her, murmuring to each other.

Cedric pried words from his mouth. "I wish only that you would look upon them and . . . and find some way to spare their lives."

The fairy sighed. "I can promise nothing."

He nodded. "You are the fairfolk. You owe me nothing. Even in coming to me, you have blessed me. I knew you did not abandon us. I knew you could not leave your mother."

A fragmented smile—distracted and incomplete—stole over the fairy's violet lips. "You seem to know much of us, Cedric. You honor our mother, and in so doing, honor us. Then before we pass, you will know my name."

She darted forward before he could reply. Hovering next to his ear, she said, "Rhoswen." With another pained cry, she flew back to a safe distance. The tinkling sound of the fairfolks' wings followed them as they darted off into the night.

"Rhoswen," he whispered.

A fairy name—a fairfolk promise.

~*~

Cedric did not tell the other scarecrows about his nighttime visitors. Partly because he wished to hold their memory all to himself, but mostly because he could not find the strength to speak a word. Out of glazed eyes, he watched the workers filter into the fields.

The twin-suns rose with a fury, their scalding heat burning all who worked amongst the corn. Cedric's bronzed skin blistered. The iron cross heated and he attempted to lean away from the poles to find relief from the burning of his back and shoulders. When he tried to stand on his own, his legs gave out and the barbed wire bore into his flesh more cruelly.

His haggard body was more a series of gouges, seeping wounds, blistered skin and crusty edges than the form of a man.

He passed in and out of consciousness through the day, his mind often dwelling in dream worlds where he saw Lina's face again. Her eyes blue like unclouded skies, her smile bright as it had been in the days of their courtship. Often, the fairies rose in his mind, as well. Rhoswen bringing him water and singing melodies of an ancient tongue he could not understand.

At midday the Rolfmen came, bringing scraps of cornbread and tiny clay cups of water. They teased and harassed, poked and prodded Cedric before at last shoving a half slice of bread into his mouth. He chewed quickly, ravenous with hunger, but could not swallow the coarse meal for the dryness of his throat. The Rolfmen laughed and poured the water into and against his lips. Half of it escaped down the front of his chest.

He tried to plead for more, but could not speak around the bits of cornmeal clogging his throat.

They moved on, and he passed out once more.

Twilight came—the earth's only mercy. The twin-suns hid their faces as a slip of a moon took the sky. Cedric tried to keep himself awake, but exhaustion pulled him into murky depths against his will. Only when the tinkling sound returned did he stir into consciousness again.

Rhoswen came alone. He could barely see her features by the paling light of the moon, but he noted that her shoulders drooped a little. She held herself aloft with a few slow beats of her gossamer wings.

"Rhoswen," he rasped.

She flitted closer, but always far enough away to avoid the cruel iron crown. "Cedric. The suns have abused you, and the sons of iron still more."

He tried to smile at her, but the muscles of his face sagged. "I do not know how long I can endure. Some scarecrows last only a week."

"I bear ill news," she said, voice laden with a low pang. "I fear it will be your deathblow."

He grew still. Leaning his head back against the cross, he trembled. ". . .Lina or the child?"

A moment's silence.

"Lina."

A dry sob shook his shoulders. He squelched it by clenching his jaw. Exhaling sharply through his teeth, he tried to fight the burning sensation in his eyes. Tried to keep back the tears.

But Rhoswen wept openly. Her tears were as tiny drops of moisture in a spider's web, glistening in a morning sun.

". . .You . . . mourn my wife?"

"I mourn for the earth and her children. For their torment."

A new thought slipped into Cedric's fuzzy mind. "By the gods . . . what of the child? What will happen to him?"

Rhoswen turned her back, looking out into the corn. Distractedly, he noticed how intricate her wings were—glimmering threads woven into patterns he had only dreamed of. Her voice was but a sigh in the night, almost buried by the scratching of the corn stalks. "They say the Rolfmen will come for him."

Cedric tried to speak, but his words tangled into an unearthly cry. She turned, her own face stricken. There was not enough moisture left in his body for tears, so his gargled cries stood alone for his grief.

She drew closer, bracing herself against the pain. "Do not howl so.

Please. Your anguish is as a tooth broken and throbbing in my mouth."

He strangled his cries, face twisting with the effort. "Will you . . . will you have mercy on my son? Will you rescue him from this fate?"

She hesitated. "How . . . I am not able . . ."

"Please," he begged. "I will give him up to you. You may raise him as one of your own, or do as you see fit. Only let him not fall to the Rolfmen."

She tapped her tiny fingers against her lips, head tilted as she considered him. "You would give him up entirely? Not knowing what will befall him?"

"Anything your folk have to offer will be better than what the Rolfmen are capable of."

She nodded. "A deal we will make then. You will never ask of him?"

"I will never ask of him."

A faint, tired smile flickered on her lips. "Then consider him saved."

⁓*⁓

Two hours of the night passed, but they seemed to stretch into eternity for Cedric. He alternated between dry weeping and indulging himself in imaginations of revenge. Sorrow burned in his stomach, and the hate he added to it threatened to tear him apart. He felt his strength ebbing, but he forced himself to remain awake. To wait and watch in the night.

After a time, a slim form, the size of a middling child, slipped out of the corn. She was larger, hair now a nut brown and eyes shimmering green like a sleeping pool of algae—but still he knew her.

"Rhoswen."

She smiled. The moonlight cast stretching shadows on her face as she lifted a bundle in her arms toward him. Tugging the edge of a worn blanket back, she exposed the sleeping child's face.

"My son," he managed through the thickness in his throat.

"He will be happy where we place him," she said. "I brought him for your goodbyes."

The baby stretched his little fists, tiny fingers curled up. He snuggled into the blanket.

"He did not even have a name," Cedric said, peering into the babe's face. "So young to lose his mother."

"We will name him. We will care for him."

She inched nearer, face paling at the nearness of the iron. Stretching her arms out, she held the child close to his face. He strained against his ties, his numbed body barely feeling the pain anymore. After pressing a kiss to the babe's forehead, he sank back.

Rhoswen's eyes glittered with tears. "Goodbye," she said, slipping back into the corn.

He watched the stalks snap back into place around her. His eyes closed and he breathed slowly. *It is done. My son is saved. He is saved. May the fairfolk protect him from Rolfere's miseries.*

He thought himself broken and weary enough to die. He closed his eyes and waited for the darkness to take him.

But the pit of fire in his stomach would not extinguish. Rage and pain lived on inside his fading flesh. Anger wove into a cord that would not be broken, a tie that kept his spirit tethered to his body.

If I die, I will not die bound. I will not die a slave.

He threw himself forward. Still, the pain only ebbed through the foggy depths of his mind. He leaned back again, pushing into the pole. Then threw himself forward once more. The wires sliced through crusted scabs, deeper into tender flesh. His mind stirred out of the fog. He kept up the movement, rocking back and forth until fresh blood streamed from every line up and down his chest, his ribcage, his thighs. The pain zipped in a steady, rhythmic pattern to his brain.

I will . . . not . . . die bound.

The corn rustled. "Please, stop!"

He froze, looking up into Rhoswen's pleading eyes. She stood now at a woman's height, her form slender and skin pale. Scraps of green covered her, but could not hide her beauty. She had pulled the waves of wheat-blond hair back into a braid. Her wings were gone or invisible.

"Rhoswen, why have you returned?" he managed.

She stepped nearer, tears slipping across her cheeks. "I have spoken with my people and riled them up. We would give a message to Rolfere. A message of fire and blood. I will free you, and you will free the others."

Without another word, she slipped forward. Her fingers reached out, face twisting with pain as she began to unwind the wire from around him.

"Don't," he gasped. "It will kill you."

"The fairfolk . . . would give a message . . ." she spoke between gasps of pain. Her fingers moved quickly, deftly. The skin on her hands and fingers blistered and bubbled an inflamed red. Soon blood bubbled out of the blisters, marbling her moonlit skin, but still she moved.

"Please, stop. Don't do this," he urged as her trembling fingers set him free.

Her face paled still more by the light of the moon. The trembling spread up her arms, as did the burning red blisters. Tears welled, slipped slow down her cheeks. Her breath came in small, painful hiccups, every touch a singeing pain.

But at last, she set him free. She fell back to the earth, and he fell beside her—limbs weak and quivering. She lay still beside him. She grabbed his hand, smearing her fairfolk blood over his hands and fingers, touched his face, leaving a trail of the same earthy brown liquid there too. "I have marked you as our messenger. Keep the fire within you—the earth will revolt with you. The mother needs her children, fairfolk and man, alike. Give him the message, Cedric."

He nodded through his tears. "I will."

"And the message?" she asked, the light fading from her eyes.

"A message of fire and blood."

Her eyes widened a bit. "Now you've seen the love of the fairfolk. Wait . . . watch for the beauty—the wrath of the fairfolk."

She passed. The light extinguished. He wept, for Lina and Rhoswen, for his people and the abused earth. Rhoswen's form shrank as a hollowed out shell of a burned log. Her body crumbled in on itself and faraway he heard a tinkling, mournful song rise from the trees. The fairfolk wept too as Cedric stood. He braced his feet wide, tracing her blood on his face.

The fire inside drove him on—drove him on to deliver the message.

~*~

Editor's Note: I can't lie. One of my favourite parts about this story has nothing to do with fairies at all. I'm talking about the image of iron crosses with scarecrows, living and dead, strung up on them. The world-building in this story is great, and I connected to the main character which made me care what happened, not only to him, but to his son and the fairy who sacrificed herself for him.

~*~

THE FAIRY MIDWIFE

Shannon Phillips

Every birth is different. Any midwife will say that, especially if she's talking to a shiny-eyed mom-to-be. "Your story," Tara would say, "is special and unique and I am honored to be a part of it." And then she would give her best benevolent earth-mother smile.

It wasn't *bullshit*, not exactly. It just wasn't always completely true. After you've delivered a couple hundred babies, it turns out that lots of births are very much alike. First, there's the waiting; second, the earnest attempt to follow the birth plan; and then there's the part right after the birth plan goes out the window, where everything happens in a messy inexorable tide and a new little human enters the world in a wash of blood and pain and wonder.

Which is why Tara didn't really mind when she got a call from the birth center at 4:00 AM. It was only strange because it wasn't her night on call. And because it was the director on the other end of the line.

"This one's a bit unusual, Tara," Madon said. "You've done home births, yes?"

"I—yes," she said, blinking sleep out of her eyes. "In my old practice we did them all the time. But I don't have a kit together anymore."

She'd only been with the Greenbud Birth Center for a few months, and very much wanted to keep the job. They didn't jack her around with the scheduling, they didn't overbook their birthing suites, and they paid twenty percent above her previous salary. Madon, a thirty-something single dude with thick-rimmed glasses and a perpetual scruff of beard, was pretty far from the Wicca-hippie-lesbian-yogini profile she associated with directors of midwifery clinics: but he seemed to keep things running smoothly, and kept the breakroom stocked with really good coffee.

"It's fine," he said. "I'm going to send a taxi to your apartment, loaded with all the gear. We'll bill for time and a half on this one. Thanks for being a team player."

Team player, Tara chanted to herself as she detangled her hair with her fingers and went hunting for a clean pair of jeans. She splashed some water on her face—no time for a shower—and rinsed her mouth with Listerine. The intercom buzzed as she was lacing up her sneakers. *Team player.*

She was too groggy to make small talk with the driver. In retrospect, she might have paid more attention to a few things: like, it wasn't actually a taxi. Just a regular sedan. And the driver was very, very short, with tufts of white hair that stuck up almost like horns. But it was 4:00 AM, she'd only been awake for fifteen minutes, and while she noticed these things they didn't exactly *register*.

The mom and dad were an odd couple too. Tara had a hard time getting a read on them: when the door first opened to her knock she had an initial impression of an old, bent-over man, but as she stepped into their apartment she saw a young hipster type in skinny jeans and plaid. He told her his name and she promptly forgot it. Five minutes later she asked again, and he told her, and she forgot that time too.

The mom was already fully dilated and experiencing intense contractions, so not really interested in chitty-chat. Tara felt for the baby's head, confirmed that it was in the right position, and got the basic details of the woman's medical history. No other children; no prior surgeries, high blood pressure, or other factors that would render the pregnancy high-risk; she said she'd had prenatal care. There was a complicated backstory as to why they'd ended up calling Madon at the last minute. Tara didn't fully understand it, but it wasn't her place to judge. She explained to the mom and dad that Greenbud had a standing arrangement with a local hospital and that they would transfer the mother there if Tara observed any complications developing. But from her initial examination it looked like a perfectly ordinary labor.

Well, it was and it wasn't. The mom bore up in near-silence; the dad faded into the background, startling Tara several times when she'd catch sight of a stranger out of the corner of her eye. Each time she thought it was someone different—a burly man, a long-bearded vagrant, a redheaded little boy. Then she'd look up and it was always the same hipster dad in skinny jeans. Tara started to wonder if her Listerine had gone bad.

She kept the laboring woman mobile for as long as feasible, walking with her slowly around the apartment, pausing to offer counterpressure and massage as the contractions came on. During this time Tara couldn't help but notice that only the front two rooms of the apartment had been furnished. All the others were dusty and bare. When Tara suggested that the mom step into the shower for a bit to let the warm water ease her contractions, neither she nor the dad seemed to know where the bathroom was.

Three hours later there was a baby, a purple-faced and wrinkly little girl. Tara cleaned her carefully and helped the mom position her for nursing. They had some trouble establishing a latch but the baby eventually suckled for a few minutes before falling asleep.

The dad reappeared then, with a little pot of ointment that he carefully smeared over the sleeping newborn's eyes. Erythromycin, Tara presumed—the antibiotic that hospitals would routinely administer to prevent infection—except that the brown ceramic pot didn't look like anything a pharmacy would dispense. "Where did you get that?" she asked curiously.

The dad smiled at her. "From oak and ash and thorn," he said, "and seven grains of wheat laid on a four-leaf clover. Your own father made the same ointment for you, but you have forgotten."

Strangely, Tara only remembered that conversation afterwards, when she was falling back into her own bed in a haze of exhaustion.

And she could not for the life of her remember what she'd said in return.

~*~

"Thanks for handling that special case," Madon said in the breakroom. He'd installed an espresso machine, and offered to make Tara a cappuccino. She watched him as he steamed the milk and brewed the coffee, his hands precise and steady on the controls.

"Every birth is different," Tara said dryly.

"We might be doing more home births," Madon said, folding the milk into the espresso. A deft flick of the wrist at the end left a swirl in the foam, like a heart. "The schedule is unpredictable, but if you're willing to be called up, there'll be a bonus for each one."

"Sure," Tara said.

The cappuccino was the best she'd ever had.

~*~

The next call came in the afternoon, so she didn't have the grogginess of sleep-deprivation or even the Listerine to blame. There was just the same dark sedan, the silent little driver with thistle-white hair, and, at the clients' address, a nondescript apartment that looked like it had been hastily staged for a realtor's tour. It had a couch and a rug and a spray of pussy willows on the coffee table, and at least this time they'd put in a bed. But there were no hangers in the closet, no toothpaste in the bathroom, and the refrigerator light didn't even turn on.

The mom was gorgeous, like she could have been a model, but everything she said sounded exactly like the croaking of a toad. The dad had to give the medical history, and it was, again, some complicated story that didn't quite make any sense. Tara made a noncommittal noise and set about inflating the birthing ball.

The mom croaked louder as contractions intensified. Tara rubbed her back and coached her to breathe: fast-fast-deep, fast-fast-deep. They moved from the ball to the bed to the tub, and ended up delivering on a birthing stool. Tara guided the dad to catch the baby, and found herself getting misty-eyed as the mom gave deep, throaty trills of joy.

The dad tried to pay her in leaves. Oak leaves, brown and crackling, a whole stack of them, and a little bag of acorn caps as well. "No," Tara said gently, "Madon will send you a bill." But he insisted on pressing them into her hands. "So," she said finally, "I guess you guys are fairies?"

"You weren't supposed to know," he said.

"It's okay," Tara told him. "I'm not really freaked out." She didn't know why, but it was true: she was pretty Zen anyway, 'not religious but spiritual.' She had her daily horoscope sent to her email and she kept a rose quartz crystal in her bedroom to pull love into her life. It was not so much of a stretch to believe in fairies. "But I thought," she said, "that you guys couldn't have babies? I mean, aren't there all those stories—about changelings and all?"

As the words left her mouth she realized how offensive they sounded. It was like accusing a gypsy—no, a Roma person—of stealing babies. It was like asking a Jewish person about the blood libel. *Crap,* Tara thought desperately, *I'm racist against fairies.*

But the dad didn't seem offended. "That was the old days," he said. "Things are better now. We don't take infants from cradles. We steal embryos from IVF clinics."

Tara blinked.

"It's like vampires and blood banks," he said.

"What? *Vampires?*"

He gave her a pitying look. "We don't take anything anyone will miss. The embryos we . . . divert . . . are the ones scheduled for destruction. It's a much better system. Now our wives can carry the children themselves."

Tara couldn't seem to keep her mouth from talking. "I guess it's an improvement over the whole stealing-babies racket," she heard herself say, "but that doesn't make it *okay*."

The dad very deliberately removed one of the brown oak leaves from her fistful, tucking it carefully away in his back hip pocket. "Madon never said you were so judgmental," he sniffed.

When she got home Tara dumped the withered leaves and acorn caps into an old coffee tin. Maybe someday it would turn into gold, though on the whole she rather doubted it.

~*~

She thought for a long time about how to phrase things, but when she found Madon in the breakroom (he was loading up the espresso machine with a new single-origin Burundi roast) it just kind of came out. "So your fairy friends are running a kidnap ring," she said. "And I don't want to be part of it anymore."

Madon gave her a funny look. "Is that how you think of it?" he said.

"How do *you* think of it?"

"Fosterage is the old metaphor," he said neutrally. "I grant you, the bio parents haven't consented, and that's . . . ethically problematic. But the embryos we take aren't missed. These babies never would have been born if we hadn't intervened. We give them long and happy lives. Is that so wrong?"

She sighed. "I don't know. I just think, what would the bio mom feel, if she knew she had a kid out there that'd been spirited away by fairies? Pretty shitty, I bet."

Madon flicked a few buttons on the machine, and it began to purr. "You're coming at this from the wrong angle," he said. "You should be asking what happens to the babies. They're still mortal, after all."

"What do you mean? *What* happens to the babies?"

"Well, some grow up and get old and eventually die, while everyone they know stays the same forever. But many get restless at some point. They want to go back to the mortal world. They want an education, a job, a family."

". . .And?"

He shrugged. "We let them go. But we put a charm on their memory, to block their recollection of growing up with the fae. Instead they have a hazy sense of a family somewhere, that for some reason they never have time to see. They don't question it. It helps them settle into the mortal world."

"Creepy," she said. "Look, Madon, I'm giving notice. I'm not going to go to the police or anything . . . but I'm quitting Greenbud."

"Tara," he said. "When's the last time you called your mom?"

The question irritated her, because it was irrelevant and a distraction and she couldn't answer it offhand. Sure, it had been a while, but she talked to her mom enough. She really didn't want to think about it. She opened her mouth to tell Madon to mind his own beeswax, but he kept looking at her in that funny way, and then suddenly she decided to sit down.

"Oh," she said. "*Oh.*"

He took a steaming cup of black espresso from the machine and slid it over to her. "Take the weekend," he said. "If you decide you still want to go, I'll write you a nice reference."

~*~

Tara spent the weekend walking in the park, staring at blowing leaves and splashing fountains. Dimly she was starting to remember things. A man with antlers on his head, throwing her in the air and catching her again. A woman's voice singing a lullaby laced with Irish words. Oddly, she felt no real need to know more, and also no curiosity about her biological parentage. Those questions existed like rocks in the stream of her thoughts, patient, offering no disturbance to the surface currents.

She thought someday the answers might become important to her, but for now they were not.

She noticed babies. She always noticed babies, perhaps like an interior designer notices fabric: she could guess ages and weights with an accuracy that often startled parents. But now she saw a baby and thought of the person it would become, the life it would make: which ones would be *happy*? And which would drift through life with no sense of fulfillment or purpose, ending as the pinched and bitter faces that also passed her as she walked? She noticed which ones were held, which ones were wheeled, which ones had bottles, which ones were nursed. She knew very well the bitter arguments parents waged over these issues. But she found herself doubting that any of it made much difference. It seemed to her that a baby was his own person from the beginning, that he contained his own flowering as the acorn contains the oak.

On Monday she haunted the espresso machine until Madon wandered in. "Make me a latte?" she asked, and he smiled as he opened the mini-fridge for the milk.

"I hope this means you're staying," he said.

She chewed her lip. "I don't, you know, endorse it. But you guys are doing what you're doing, and the babies exist, and I guess it's better for there to be some medical support at the births. What's gonna happen if we need to transfer one of these moms to the hospital?"

"I'll show up," said Madon, gently rocking the milk as it steamed, "and handle the paperwork, which will mysteriously vanish shortly after."

"I was wondering," Tara said, "what your story is. I mean, if you want to tell me. You seem to know more of *my* story than I do."

"Not really," he said. "Not the important things." He glanced up from the machine, and she noticed how soft his brown eyes were behind the glasses.

"Maybe I could take you out to dinner," she said, daring, "and you could explain some things to me. Like where I can sign up for a self-defense class against vampires."

Madon smiled, and poured the foamy milk into the shape of a perfect shamrock. "I'd like that," he said, and offered her the cup.

Cradling the latte in her hands, its warmth spreading into her fingers, Tara thought about how all the old stories warned against accepting food from a fairy. So before she took a sip, she dipped the tip of her pinkie into the foam and drew a line in the shamrock's top-most leaf—turning three leaves into four. "Now it's lucky," she said, and drank to her new life.

~~*

Editor's Note: I wanted urban fairies and Shannon gave them to me. Not only did she give me creatures who are fae or are connected to them, she gave me one who'd forgotten. As much as I love the scene where Tara realises the truth about herself, my favourite part of this story is the awkward father trying to act cool and human, but paying for Tara's services with leaves and acorns. Precious.

~~*

THE PRICE

Kari Castor

The snow was thick, even under the trees. Addie's feet sunk deep into it as she trudged farther and farther from the cottage where her mother and sisters waited for her return. She scanned the undergrowth as she walked, hoping for a glimpse of red berries. The bucket she carried was nearly empty.

There! A crimson flash. She plodded forward to examine the bush that had caught her attention. A few berries, not many. A bird chittered at her from a tree nearby, evidently upset by her intrusion. She peeled one heavy mitten off, tucked it under her arm, and delicately plucked the handful of crimson spheres from the bush.

The bird fell silent.

The berries plunked into the bucket, the sound unexpectedly loud in the stillness.

Addie breathed warmth into her mitten and pulled it back over her fingers. She turned away from the bush and dropped the bucket in surprise.

He was tall and slender, and though he stood just a few feet from her, no footprints marked his passage through the snow.

"I'm sorry," he said. "I did not mean to startle you." His voice was quiet and low.

Addie picked up her bucket again, checking that none of the precious berries had been lost. "What do you want?"

"Only to help." He did not smile. His hair was the color of the ice that formed over the river, dark blue-black, shot through with silver traceries.

Addie shrugged. "Don't need your help." She turned away and began walking.

"No, I suppose you don't," he said. "Still, I could help you fill your bucket faster."

"Don't want your help," she said, and continued deeper into the forest. She found another bush and added another handful of berries to her bucket.

Again, the man was behind her when she turned. "I mean you no harm tonight," he said softly.

"Go 'way," she said, and trudged on.

By the time her bucket was nearly full, the light was beginning to fade. She turned back toward home.

Once more, the man appeared. "Addie," he said.

She stood still. "I'm not afraid of you," she said. "But I know enough not to have truck with strange men in the woods who don't leave footprints."

His smile seemed startled but genuine, though Addie couldn't help but notice that his mouth seemed to have more teeth in it than most mouths do. "All right," he said. "Fair enough." He thought for a moment, then gestured to his left. "Do you see that tree?" It was ancient and gnarled, its limbs twisted painfully.

She looked at it, then back at him, but said nothing.

"Should you ever have need, knock three times at that tree. Understand?"

"When I have need of you," she said, "I'll be pretty desperate indeed."

He turned his palms upward and smiled again, though it didn't reach his eyes this time. "Nevertheless, you need only knock three times if you find yourself in such desperation."

She eyed him suspiciously for a long moment, then nodded once. "I don't suppose your help comes free."

His lips tugged up at the corners again. "Almost never."

She nodded once more and turned away.

_*_

She didn't say a word to her mother or sisters about the man.

_*_

In the morning, a raven was perched on the peak of the little cottage, just above the front door. Its glossy black feathers were threaded through with silver.

"Go 'way," she muttered at it, and threw a snowball. It cawed softly, fluttering out of the way, then landed again. It stayed there all day.

"A bad omen," her mother said.

Addie said nothing.

_*_

She woke, a few nights later, to a sound of splintering, crashing wood. Peering out her window at the rear of the little cottage, she saw a great black bear nosing through the remains of their smokehouse. The moonlight glinted off the silver traceries in its fur.

In the morning, she went outside with her mother to see what was salvageable. They picked through the ruins but found little. She saw smoke begin to trickle out of the chimney as one of her sisters kindled the fire inside.

Her mother began sorting the timbers. "We'll burn the ones that are ruined," she said. "The bear has chopped our firewood for us."

"And the rest?" Addie said.

"We rebuild." Her mother was already heaving the wood into two piles. After a few moments, she pulled her sweater off, hung it over an evergreen nearby, and went back to work, her sinewy arms bare in the winter sun.

Addie watched her for a moment, then retrieved the axe from where it lay, half-buried in the snow, near the shrinking woodpile.

~*~

A blizzard howled round the cabin that night. Addie looked out her window to see the silvery snow streaming through the darkness.

~*~

Their food dwindled. Scraps of smoked meat and dried berries rattled emptily in their stomachs.

~*~

Her youngest sister fell ill. The girl groaned with fever, and sweat ran in silvery rivulets over her skin. Her mother rubbed her body with handfuls of snow, but the fever would not break.

Addie set snares for rabbits and winter birds, and dug for the hardy roots that hid under the snow. She made weak stews, adding some of the precious medicinal herbs her mother kept, and spooned them into the girl's mouth. Still she burned.

Several days after the fever set in, Addie found her mother sitting still and silent by the fire. "Say your goodbyes, Addie," she said.

Addie glanced fearfully to the cot where her sister lay.

"Not yet," her mother said. "But soon."

Addie knelt by the cot. The girl's breath was shallow, barely discernable. Addie stroked her hair and squeezed her hand, but could find no words to say.

Finally, she stood. Silently, she pulled on her furs and walked out the door. Her mother watched her go, but said nothing.

When she found the tree, she banged savagely on it. Three times, then three times more. She was lifting her fist again when she heard his voice behind her.

"Desperate, are you?" he asked.

She whirled angrily and flung herself at him.

He stopped her easily, gripping her wrists. "Peace, Addie, peace."

She sagged in his grip, then wrenched away. "You did this."

He said nothing, but his eyes glittered icily.

"What do you want?" she said.

"What do *you* want?" he said.

She cursed at him. "My sister."

He waited.

"Make her well."

He waited.

She shivered. "I'll do whatever you want if you make her well."

He waited.

"Damn you, what do you want?" she yelled.

He smiled that cold, strange smile again, and held out his hand. "Plant this," he said. "When it blooms, boil one petal for tea and give it to your sister."

She sank into the snow. "She doesn't have time to wait for plants to bloom," she said.

"She has time," he said. "I swear it."

She tilted her head back, trying to keep the tears in her eyes from spilling out.

"I am many things, Addie," he said, "but I am not a liar."

"And what then?" she said. "After I make the tea, what then?"

"Then your sister will be well."

"And what do you want from me? What's the price?"

He spread his hands wide. "You," he said. "You are the price."

She stared at him.

"Plant the seed," he said. "I will come to you when it blooms."

_*_

Addie tried to explain what she had done to her mother, but she wasn't interested. "This is not the time for fairy stories, Addie," she said.

Addie dug a chunk of soil up and put it in a bowl. She carefully buried the seed and dripped a bit of water onto it.

In the morning, a tall sprout had sprung up through the dirt. Her sister still breathed.

The next morning, the stalk had grown taller still, and a flower bud, furled and tight, clung to it. "Tomorrow," she told her mother. "Tomorrow it ends," she murmured. Her mother gathered her into her arms and hummed an old lullaby to her.

~*~

The flower bloomed, silvery white petals with delicate black veins. Addie carefully plucked a single petal from it, boiled the tea, and dripped it down her sister's throat.

An hour later, the fever broke.

~*~

Looking out her window that night, she saw him waiting for her. She padded softly outdoors in her bare feet and short sleeves.

"Are you afraid?" he said.

She nodded. The snow gleamed in the moonlight. He took her hand and she saw that her veins showed blue-black through her pale skin.

"Are you ready?" he said.

She turned to look at the cottage behind her. The bare tree branches all around stood starkly against the moonlit sky.

"Will you give yourself to me?"

She turned back to face him and saw him staring intently at her. He held out his hand.

She nodded, closed her eyes, and took it.

The darkness was endless.

~*~

Editor's Note: Part of me is sad to be writing this note, because I'd really like to leave the reader with the feeling evoked by the end of this story rather than my thoughts on it. *The darkness was endless.*

It's the perfect ending for a wonderful, old-fashioned fairy story.

The darkness was endless.

Yes.

_*_

CONTRIBUTORS

Sidney Blaylock, Jr. is a Science Fiction and Fantasy writer as well as a Sixth Grade Language Arts Teacher. He has worked previously as Adjunct Instructor of English, a Library Assistant, and a Bookseller. He holds two Master's Degrees, one in English and one in Education.

In addition to *Faerie Knight,* appearing in *Fae*, Sidney has another story, *Knight of the Wylde West* appearing in the upcoming anthology, *Book of Sylvari: An Anthology of the Elves* (Nov. 2014). Sidney's other publications includes a fantasy short-story entitled, *Dragonhawk*, in the Winter 2013 issue of Tales of the Talisman (Kindle and print editions are available from amazon.com). Previous publications include *Sister-Knight* in the May 2012 Sorcerous Signals, *The Ghost and the Shadow* in the 1996-1997 issue of G.W.N. Litmag, and an article, "The Art of the Rough Draft," in the Sept.-Oct. 2005 issue of the Writer's Journal.

You can find Sidney's Blog at sidneyblaylockjr.wordpress.com.

~*~

Amanda Block is a writer and ghostwriter based in Edinburgh, UK. A graduate of the Creative Writing Masters at the University of Edinburgh, she is often inspired by myths and fairy tales, frequently using them as a starting point to tell other stories.

Amanda's work has been featured in anthologies such as *Modern Grimmoire: Fairy Tales, Fables and Folklore* and *Stories for Homes,* as well as magazines including *Vintage Script* and *Bookanista.* She has been shortlisted for the Bridport Prize and the Chapter One Promotions

Short Story Competition.

Amanda is currently working on a collection of short stories, and thinking about getting back to her half-finished novel.

~*~

Kari Castor is a writer and educator. Her fiction and poetry has appeared in a variety of magazines and anthologies, including most recently In *Gilded Frame, Spark: A Creative Anthology Vol. 3*, and *Serial Killers Tres Tria*. She is co-writer of the monthly comic series *Shahrazad* and, in addition, serves as line editor for Big Dog Ink comics. She lives in the Chicago area with her husband, two dogs, and a cat named after a space princess. Find her online at karicastor.com.

~*~

Beth Cato's debut steampunk novel THE CLOCKWORK DAGGER will be released by HarperCollins Voyager in September 2014. She's originally from Hanford, California, but now resides in Arizona with her husband and son. Her short fiction, poetry, and tasty cookie recipes can be found at bethcato.com.

~*~

Liz Colter lives in a rural area of the Rocky Mountains and spends her free time with her husband, dogs, horses and writing. Over the years she has followed her heart through a variety of careers, including working as a paramedic, an Outward Bound instructor, an athletic trainer, a draft-horse farmer and a dispatcher for concrete trucks. Her true passion, though, is her writing. She has been reading speculative fiction for a lifetime and creating her own speculative worlds for more than a decade. Her short stories have appeared *Emerald Sky*, *Andromeda Spaceways Inflight Magazine*, and *Enchanted Conversation*, among others, and she is a winner of this year's Writers of the Future competition. In longer works, she has two completed fantasy novels and is working on a third. Her website can be found at lizcolter.weebly.com.

~*~

Rhonda Eikamp is originally from Texas and lives in Germany. She wrote for the small press up to 2001, with two honourable mentions in Datlow's Year's Best Fantasy and Horror. More recently, her fiction can be found in Daily Science Fiction, The Colored Lens, Lady Churchill's Rosebud Wristlet and Birkensnake. A story of hers will soon help annihilate SF in the upcoming Lightspeed special issue "Women Destroy Science Fiction". Her past lives have included working at the UN in Vienna and picking grapes in Mainz. She currently translates for a German law firm.

~*~

Lor Graham is a fidget. A proper fidget, so she splits her time between reading, writing, knitting, crocheting, baking, playing all manner of brass instruments or studying guitar, doing really badly at video games and feeding her twitter addiction. Most of her time is spent with pen in hand, however.

She knows more than is likely healthy about Pirates, despite being one of those dirty hippies that never wears shoes, is a Japanese graduate currently learning Italian and talks entirely too much. She is also entirely Scottish.

(Her first published short story, Islands to Auld Reekie, was published in the Pandemonium Press collection *1853*.)

~*~

Since she was a child of nine years old, **Alexis A. Hunter** has reveled in the endless possibilities of speculative fiction. Short stories are her true passion, despite a few curious forays into the world of novels. Over forty of her short stories have been published, appearing recently in Spark: A Creative Anthology, Read Short Fiction, Scigentasy and more. To learn more about Alexis visit idreamagain.wordpress.com.

~*~

L.S. Johnson lives in Northern California. Her work has appeared or is forthcoming in such venues as *Corvus, Interzone,* and *Long Hidden: Speculative Fiction from the Margins of History.* Currently she is working on a novel set in 18th century Europe. She can be found online at traversingz.com

~*~

Jon Arthur Kitson recently came back to writing after a 23 year hiatus. During the interim he spent time as a photographer in the United States Navy, a portrait photographer for a large company and, for the last twelve years, as an employ of the State of Michigan. Fortunately, a stint as Dungeon Master for a D&D game reminded him just how much he loved writing 'back in the day'. Since retaking up the pen (computer, really) Jon's short stories have appeared in *Mad Scientist Journal, Fiction Vortex, Perihelion SF, Lakeside Circus* and *Geek Force Five.*

~*~

Adria Laycraft is a grateful member of IFWA and a proud survivor of the Odyssey Writers Workshop. She co-edited *Urban Green Man,* which launched in August of 2013. Look for her stories in Tesseracts 16, Neo-opsis, On-Spec, James Gunn's Ad Astra, Hypersonic Tales,

DKA Magazine, and In Places Between. Author of *Be a Freelance Writer Now*, Adria lives in Calgary with her husband and son.

_*_

Lauren Liebowitz lives in Austin, Texas, which (if you listen to city marketing) is simultaneously the "live music capital of the world" and "a city within a park"—the perfect home for humans and fae creatures alike. She works as a copywriter at a small local university, but in her free time, she writes fiction, bakes too much banana bread, and leads a video game cover band in which she sings and plays flute.

_*_

Christine Morgan works the overnight shift in a psychiatric facility and divides her writing time among many genres, though her true calling seems to be tending toward historical horror and dark fantasy (especially Viking-themed stories). A lifelong reader, she also writes, reviews, beta-reads, occasionally edits and dabbles in self-publishing. She has several novels in print, with more due out soon. Her stories have appeared in more than three dozen anthologies, 'zines and e-chapbooks. She's been nominated for the Origins Award and made Honorable Mention in two volumes of Year's Best Fantasy and Horror. She's also a wife, mom, and possible future crazy-cat-lady whose other interests include gaming, history, superheroes, crafts, and cheesy disaster movies.

_*_

Shannon Phillips lives in Oakland, where she keeps chickens, a dog, three boys, and a husband. Her first novel, *The Millennial Sword*, tells the story of the modern-day Lady of the Lake.

_~*~_

Sara Puls spends most of her time lawyering, researching, writing, and editing. Her dreams frequently involve strange mash-ups of typography, fairy creatures, courtrooms, and blood. Or maybe those are nightmares. Her fiction has appeared in Daily Science Fiction, The Colored Lens, The Future Fire, Plasma Frequency Magazine, and elsewhere. She's also the Co-Editor of the speculative fiction magazine *Scigentasy: Gender Stories in Science Fiction & Fantasy*, which you can visit at scigentasy.com.

_~*~_

Laura VanArendonk Baugh was born at a very early age and never looked back. She overcame childhood deficiencies of having been born without teeth or developed motor skills, and by the time she matured into a recognizable adult she had become a behavior analyst, an internationally-recognized and award-winning animal trainer, a popular costumer/cosplayer, a chocolate addict, and of course a writer. Now she has letters after her name and writes best-selling non-fiction as well as fiction in various flavors of historical and fantasy. Find her at www.LauraVanArendonkBaugh.com or on Twitter at @Laura_VAB.

_~*~_

Kristina Wojtaszek grew up as a woodland sprite and mermaid, playing around the shores of Lake Michigan. She earned a bachelor's degree in Wildlife Management as an excuse to spend her days lost in the woods with a book in hand. She currently resides in the high desert country of Wyoming with her husband and two small children. She is fascinated by fairy tales and fantasy and her favorite haunts are libraries and cemeteries.

Her fairy tale retellings, short fiction and poetry have been published by World Weaver Press including the novella *Opal* and its forthcoming sequel *Obsidian*, *Far Off Places* and *Sucker Literary Magazine*. Follow her @KristinaWojtasz or on her blog, Twice Upon a Time (authorkw.wordpress.com).

~*~

Sara Cleto and **Brittany Warman** are PhD students in English and Folklore at The Ohio State University. They both specialize in the intersection of folklore and literature and are particularly fascinated by fairy tales and fairylore. Sara is currently exploring the implications of disability in fairy tales, while Brittany is working on fairy tales, fairylore, and the Gothic aesthetic. Creative writers as well, their co-written poems have appeared in *Niteblade* and *Ideomancer*. Separately, they have also published in *Mythic Delirium*, *Cabinet des Fees*, *Stone Telling*, *Mirror Dance*, and others.

~*~

ABOUT THE ANTHOLOGIST

Rhonda Parrish is driven by a desire to do All The Things. She has been the publisher and editor-in-chief of *Niteblade Magazine* for over five years now (which is like 25 years in internet time) and is the editor of the benefit anthology, *Metastasis*.

In addition, Rhonda is a writer whose work has been included or is forthcoming in dozens of publications including *Tesseracts 17: Speculating Canada from Coast to Coast* and *Imaginarium: The Best Canadian Speculative Writing*.

Her website, updated weekly, is at rhondaparrish.com.

FORTHCOMING ANTHOLOGIES
EDITED BY RHONDA PARRISH

Starting July 1, 2014, **Rhonda Parrish** will be reading for **Corvidae** and **Scarecrow,** two new anthologies in the same series as *Fae*. Like *Fae,* each of these new anthologies will focus on a single construct treated in many varied and enthralling ways by new speculative fiction short stories.

The twin anthologies also present a unique opportunity: to create a conversation between the two volumes, between the crows and the straw-men, between the bird tales of Corvidae and the totem tales of Scarecrow.

Anthologies to be published in 2015. More information at WorldWeaverPress.com.

ALSO BY FAE CONTRIBUTORS

*White as snow, stained with blood,
her talons black as ebony . . .*

OPAL
a novella by
Kristina Wojtaszek

"A fairy tale within a fairy tale
within a fairy tale—the narratives fit together
like interlocking pieces of a puzzle,
beautifully told."
—Zachary Petit, Editor *Writer's Digest*

In this retwisting of the classic Snow White tale, the daughter of an owl is forced into human shape by a wizard who's come to guide her from her wintry tundra home down to the colorful world of men and Fae, and the father she's never known. She struggles with her human shape and grieves for her dead mother—a mother whose past she must unravel if men and Fae are to live peacefully together.

"Twists and turns and surprises that kept me up well into the night. Fantasy and fairy tale lovers will eat this up and be left wanting more!"
—Kate Wolford, Editor, *Enchanted Conversation Magazine*

Available now in ebook and trade paperback.

MORE GREAT SHORT FICTION

Far Orbit: Speculative Space Adventures
Science fiction in the Grand Tradition—Anthology
Edited by Bascomb James

The King of Ash and Bones
Breathtaking four-story collection
Rebecca Roland

He Sees You When You're Sleeping
A Christmas Krampus anthology
Coming Holiday 2014
Edited by Kate Wolford

Wolves and Witches
A Fairy Tale Collection
*Witches have stories too. So do mermaids, millers' daughters, princes
(charming or otherwise), even big bad wolves.*
Amanda C. Davis and Megan Engelhardt

Cursed: Wickedly Fun Stories
Collection
*"Quirky, clever, and just a little savage." —Lane Robins, critically
acclaimed author of MALEDICTE and KINGS AND ASSASSINS*
Susan Abel Sullivan

BEYOND THE GLASS SLIPPER
TEN NEGLECTED FAIRY TALES TO FALL IN LOVE WITH

Introduction and Annotations by Kate Wolford

Some fairy tales everyone knows—these aren't those tales. These are tales of kings who get deposed and pigs who get married. These are ten tales, much neglected. Editor of *Enchanted Conversation: A Fairy Tale Magazine*, Kate Wolford, introduces and annotates each tale in a manner that won't leave novices of fairy tale studies lost in the woods to grandmother's house, yet with a depth of research and a delight in posing intriguing puzzles that will cause folklorists and savvy readers to find this collection a delicious new delicacy.

Beyond the Glass Slipper is about more than just reading fairy tales—it's about connecting to them. It's about thinking of the fairy tale as a precursor to *Saturday Night Live* as much as it is to any princess-movie franchise: the tales within these pages abound with outrageous spectacle and absurdist vignettes, ripe with humor that pokes fun at ourselves and our society.

Never stuffy or pedantic, Kate Wolford proves she's the college professor you always wish you had: smart, nurturing, and plugged into pop culture. Wolford invites us into a discussion of how these tales fit into our modern cinematic lives and connect the larger body of fairy tales, then asks—no, *insists*—that we create our own theories and connections. A thinking man's first step into an ocean of little known folklore.

Available now in ebook and trade paperback.

SHARDS OF HISTORY

a fantasy novel by
Rebecca Roland

"A must for any fantasy reader."
—*Plasma Frequency Magazine*

Malia fears the fierce, winged creatures known as Jeguduns who live in the cliffs surrounding her valley. But when she discovers an injured Jegudun, Malia's very existence—her status as clan mother in training, her marriage, her very life in the Taakwa village—is threatened by her choice to befriend the intelligent creature. But will anyone believe her when she learns the truth: the threat to her people is much bigger and much more malicious than the Jeguduns. Lurking on the edge of the valley is an Outsider army seeking to plunder and destroy her people, and it's only a matter of time before the Outsiders find a way through the magic shield that protects the valley—a magic that can only be created by Taakwa and Jeguduns working together.

"Fast-paced, high-stakes drama in a fresh fantasy world. Rebecca Roland is a newcomer to watch!"
—James Maxey, author of *Greatshadow: The Dragon Apocalypse.*

"One of the most beautifully written novels I have ever read. Suspenseful, entrapping, and simply . . . well, let's just say that *Shards of History* reminds us of why we love books in the first place. *Five out of five stars!*"
—Good Choice Reading

Available now in ebook and trade paperback

FAR ORBIT

Speculative Space Adventures—Anthology
Edited by Bascomb James

*Modern space adventures crafted by a new generation
of Grand Tradition science fiction writers.*

Smart and engaging stories that take us back to a time when science fiction was fun and informative, pithy and piquant—when speculative fiction transported us from the everyday grind and left us wondrously satisfied. Showcasing the breadth of Grand Tradition stories, from 1940s-style pulp to realistic hard SF, from noir and horror SF to spaceships, alien uplift, and action-adventure motifs, Far Orbit's diversity of Grand Tradition stories makes it easy for every SF fan to find a favorite.

Featuring an open letter to SF by Elizabeth Bear and stories from Gregory Benford, Tracy Canfield, Eric Choi, Barbara Davies, Jakob Drud, Julie Frost, David Wesley Hill, K. G. Jewell, Sam Kepfield, Kat Otis, Jonathan Shipley, Wendy Sparrow, and Peter Wood

"Daring adventure, protagonists who think on their feet, and out of this world excitement! Welcome to FAR ORBIT, a fine collection of stories in the best SF tradition. Strap in and enjoy!"
—Julie E. Czerneda, author of SPECIES IMPERATIVE

"Successfully captures the kinds of stories that were the gateway drugs for many of us who have been reading science fiction for a long time. Well done!"
—Tangent

Available now in ebook and trade paperback.

The Devil in Midwinter

Paranormal romance (NA)
Elise Forier Edie

*A handsome stranger, a terrifying monster,
a boy who burns and burns . . .*

Mattawa, Washington, is usually a sleepy orchard town come December, until a murder, sightings of a fantastic beast, and the arrival of a handsome new vintner in town kindle twenty-year-old reporter Esme Ulloa's curiosity—and maybe her passion as well. But the more she untangles the mystery, the more the world Esme knows unspools, until she finds herself navigating a place she thought existed only in storybooks, where dreams come alive, monsters walk the earth and magic is real. When tragedy strikes close to home, Esme finds she must strike back, matching wits with an ancient demon in a deadly game, where everything she values stands to be lost, including the love of her life.

Night Owl Reviews top pick!

Available now in ebook and trade paperback.

ALSO FROM WORLD WEAVER PRESS

Far Orbit: Speculative Space Adventures
Science ficttion in the Grand Traditon—Anthology
Edited by Bascomb James

The Haunted Housewives of Allister, Alabama
Cleo Tidwell Paranormal Mystery, Book One
Who knew one gaudy Velvet Elvis
could lead to such a heap of haunted trouble?
Susan Abel Sullivan

The Weredog Whisperer
Cleo Tidwell Paranormal Mystery, Book Two
The Tidwells are supposed to be on spring break on the Florida Gulf Coast,
not up to their eyeballs in paranormal hijinks . . . again.
Susan Abel Sullivan

Heir to the Lamp
Genie Chronicles, Book One (YA)
A family secret, a mysterious lamp, a dangerous Order with the mad desire
to possess both.
Michelle Lowery combs

Legally Undead
Vampirachy, Book One—*Coming May 2014*
A reluctant vampire hunter, stalking New York City
as only a scorned bride can.
Margo Bond Collins

Glamour
Stealing the life she's always wanted is as easy as casting a spell. (YA)
Andrea Janes

Forged by Fate
Fate of the Gods, Book One
After Adam Fell, God made Eve to Protect the World.
Amalia Dillin

Fate Forgotten
Fate of the Gods, Book Two
To win the world, Adam will defy the gods, but his fate rests in Eve's hands
Amalia Dillin

Beyond Fate
Fate of the Gods, Book Three
The stunning conclusion, coming September 2014
Amalia Dillin

Tempting Fate
Fate of the Gods Novella, #1.5
Mia's lived in her sister's shadow long enough
Amalia Dillin

A Winter's Enchantment
Three novellas of winter magic and loves lost and regained.
Experience the magic of the season.
Elise Forier Edie, Amalia Dillin, Kristina Wojatszek

Cursed: Wickedly Fun Stories
Collection
"Quirky, clever, and just a little savage." —Lane Robins, critically acclaimed author of MALEDICTE and KINGS AND ASSASSINS
Susan Abel Sullivan

Blood Chimera
Blood Chimera, Book One—*Coming August 2014*
Some ransoms aren't meant to be paid.
Jenn Lyons

Virgin
Paranormal/Urban Fantasy (YA)
Coming Fall 2014
Jenna Nelson

Specter Spectacular: 13 Ghostly Tales
Anthology
Once you cross the grave into this world of fantasy and fright, you may find there's no way back.
Edited by Eileen Wiedbrauk

For more on these and other titles visit
WorldWeaverPress.com.